Stolen Blessing
(Fr. Tom Series #3)

A Novel
by
Jim Sano

Full Quiver Publishing,
Pakenham, ON

Stolen Blessing
copyright 2021
by James G. Sano

Published by Full Quiver Publishing
PO Box 244
Pakenham, Ontario K0A 2X0

ISBN Number: 978-1-987970-27-2

Printed and bound in the USA

Photos courtesy: iStock (credit OSTILL) and Alamy (credit Brian Jannsen)
Cover design: James Hrkach and Jim Sano

NATIONAL LIBRARY OF CANADA
CATALOGUING IN PUBLICATION
ALL RIGHTS RESERVED

I would like to dedicate this book to three women:

The Blessed Mother, whom I've come to spend more time appreciating and asking to pray for my family and these stories. Without her courage, complete trust in God's plan, and her consequential "Yes," our gift of truly being beloved sons and daughters of our Father would not have been possible. Each book has been released in her honor.

My mother, Rita Marie Doherty, who embraced Mary's example to "let go and let God," as she would always tell me. Despite being bedridden with multiple sclerosis for the last twenty-five years of her life, she was never without a smile, a look of love in those Irish eyes, and her rock of faith, trusting that she just had a new role to play in God's plan.

Finally, my wife, Joanne, who took a chance, taking a journey of friendship and love with this boy from Lynn in 1986. I am eternally grateful for her love, her grace, her adventurous and fun spirit, her ever-growing faith, and her support, as she has had the painstaking chore of the first pass editing of these stories. Sharing life with her has been a blessing I look forward to thanking God for every day. She loves mysteries, so I wrote this one for her.

Chapter 1

Woodhaven Queens, NY 1993

The coach held out his stopwatch as the short blasts from his whistle blew, "Fweet! Fweet! Fweet!"

Ten sweat-soaked boys labored to sprint from baseline to baseline, up and back again as the shrill sound of the whistle sounded each time they reached the line, commanding them to turn and sprint back.

Just when they thought they had been pushed past their limit, they heard, "All right, boys! That's enough for today. We need to save some energy for tomorrow's big game."

The boys stood, grabbing the hem of their shorts as they hunched over, trying to catch their breaths, sweat dripping onto the old wooden floor of the high school basketball court. Being an unusually warm day in March, the gym had grown hot, and the practice had been intense and grueling.

Erick glanced up at his brother, Jack, and winked before mumbling, "What energy?"

The coach shook his head. "Mr. Comghan wants to know if we have any energy left. Let's find out if he has ten more in him."

The other boys watched as Erick reluctantly pushed himself to run ten more wind sprints before collapsing into Jack's arms, gasping out, "Why does he always push me so hard?"

Jack quipped, "Why do you always test him so much?"

The coach walked the boys out through the gym doors and into the foyer, where a glass case held a handful of trophies and a 1957 championship basketball signed by the winning team. "Boys, tomorrow is our time. Someday, young men like you will be staring into this case and see your names on the State Championship trophy, but only if you give it everything you've got and play like champions. Go shower up and get some rest tonight."

As the boys filed out of the foyer, Erick remained with his arm around his twin brother's sweaty neck. "Erick and Jack Comghan. New York State Champions. I can see it now. Norwich is a tough team, but no one's going to beat the lads from Woodhaven this year!"

Jack laughed. "Wouldn't that be nice? But in the meantime, let's get showered and have some fun. The girls are waiting for us, and how often do we get a sixty-five-degree day in March?"

Within ten minutes, they were showered, dressed, and out the gym door to a glorious day that had that first-day-of-spring feel to it. The sight of Addie Kerrins leaning against her mint-green convertible with the top down brought instant smiles to their faces. Addie was a cheerleader for the basketball team and had caught the boys' attention from day one.

"So, what are the two handsomest boys in Woodhaven up for on a day like this?" asked Addie with a smile and raised eyebrows.

"I vote for a cruise along Rockaway!" exclaimed Rachel, Addie's younger sister, who sat in the back seat of the open convertible. Rachel seemed disappointed when Erick and Jack slid into the front seats, and Addie joined her in the back, but it didn't last long when Erick put in a CD of the Ramones singing "Rockaway Beach."

Erick drove along the parkway as Jack laughingly sang along with Addie and Rachel, "Rock, Rock, Rock, Rockaway Beach!" They drove slowly along the shore and breathed in the fresh salt air. Erick smiled as he caught Addie in the rearview mirror perched on the edge of her seat, with her sunglasses on, a smile on her face tilted to catch the sun, and the breeze playing with her long hair. He was smitten, as was Jack.

They stopped at The Clam Bar and then walked along the boardwalk, eating their clam rolls, drinking shakes, and reminiscing about the fun they had in high school and how much they were looking forward to summer. Addie stopped in front of a new apartment building. "Remember when the old Playland was here? I miss it."

Jack jumped behind Addie and pulled her headband over her sunglasses. "I remember you with your hands over your eyes when you got to the top of that old wooden rollercoaster for the first and last time!"

Not to be left out, Rachel grabbed Jack's arm. "What was that thing called?"

Erick smiled as his eyes widened. "The Atom Smasher! I can't believe that rickety thing stayed up. What were we that last time we rode it—twelve?"

Rachel pouted a bit when Addie said, "Yeah, but Rach was only ten."

The next afternoon, Erick and Jack were dressed and ready for the State Championship game at the Glen Falls Civic Center. The arena and crowd were bigger than anything they had experienced in all their years of playing basketball together.

"I'm feeling some butterflies today," Erick whispered to Jack.

Jack rubbed Erick's hair. "You always say that and then go out and play better than anyone else. Maybe that's because you are better than anyone else?"

Erick glanced up at Jack, taken back by how easily his identical twin seemed to be okay with that reality and how much Jack admired him. He loved his brother. He loved spending time with him, whether they were playing ball, working hard on their grandfather's farm, or just hanging out. As he glanced over to see Addie leading a cheer and Rachel screaming from the stands, he smiled at how much fun they always had together and how much he didn't want this ride to end. The only thing that could make his high school senior year better would be to win this State Championship, and he was more determined than anyone to make that happen.

Maybe then, Coach will think I'm good enough?

Chapter 2

South End, Boston, 2006

Father Tom Fitzpatrick stood at the sacristy doorway inside of St. Francis Church. He never tired of gazing up at the beauty of the high arched ceilings and the light streaming through the rose window over the front entrance at the back of the church. He smiled as he noticed his parishioner and friend, a new dad, standing by the baptismal font, playfully holding his baby girl.

Tom approached him. "Erick, you're early. I like your enthusiasm, but I like hers even better," he said as he gently placed his hand on the side of the baby's head, gazed into her eyes, and was rewarded with Elizabeth's return smile. "She is such a beautiful baby. It's the luck of the Irish that she's got her mother's looks."

Reaching out his free hand, he said, "You must be Father Tom. I'm actually Erick's brother, Jack, and the proud godfather. It's good to meet you."

Tom stared at him more closely, wide-eyed with surprise. "Oh—Jack. I'm so sorry. It's good to meet you, too. I can't believe it. I've known Erick for five or six years now and never knew he had a brother, never mind a twin. You look so alike—you're not possibly pulling my leg, are you?"

Jack shook his head and laughed as he held Elizabeth closely. "I'm not completely surprised he hasn't mentioned having a brother. I was living in Britain for six years and moved back to Connecticut about a year ago." The thirty-one-year-old Jack Comghan stood slightly taller than Tom's six-foot-one frame. Like his twin brother, Jack was handsome, with an athletic build, auburn-colored hair, and an infectious smile. His smile broadened as Elizabeth's mother, Addie, appeared at the entrance door and returned the obvious fondness.

Tom approached her. "Addie—or are you her identical twin?"

Addie smirked. "No, no. Luckily there's only one of me. Uhm, Erick is running a quick errand, and he should be here shortly."

Tom greeted all the family and friends as they entered the church and left them to socialize until Erick finally arrived, shaking hands and apologizing for keeping everyone waiting. Tom stood to one side and studied Erick and his twin side by side, noticing a few slight differences. Erick seemed a bit stronger physically and in personality than Jack. He'd done well financially with a chain of specialty grocery stores in New England, which were focused on quality and locally sourced produce. He and Addie moved to Boston six years ago when they began attending St. Francis.

Erick excused himself and walked over to his brother, Jack, and gave him an unusually formal handshake as he reached to take baby Elizabeth from him for the baptismal service.

Tom was ready to begin the service. He smiled as he waved everyone around the baptismal font. "Feel free to come closer. This is a very special day for Elizabeth, and for her mother, Addie, her father, Erick, and godparents, Jack and Rachel, and for everyone that will be a part of her life as she joins this believing community. We're all human and share a weakness for sin, but through the strength of God's grace, we are transformed in the living waters of baptism as adopted sons and daughters of God and with it the inheritance of eternal life with Him. With His love and grace, she won't need to look to others, to things, or to accomplishments for acceptance or her self-worth and identity, but to the only place it exists, which is in God Himself. So, baptism is a great gift of grace for Elizabeth and each of us."

After Tom asked Erick and Addie and then Jack and Rachel if they accepted the responsibility to teach her the faith Christ gave us, and if they would do everything in their power to help get her to heaven, he anointed the baby with the oil, to which she made a loud cooing sound, and everyone laughed. Tom explained the meaning behind the sacrament and smiled as Elizabeth made a face when he poured the water over her forehead. "Elizabeth," he said, "I baptize you in the name of the Father, the Son, and the Holy Spirit."

Tom wasn't normally one to be distracted during a service, but some things seemed curiously odd. He knew Erick and Addie fairly well and enjoyed them as a couple. They seemed happy together and were generous with their time and resources to the parish. Tom often played basketball with Erick, and the only marital frustration Erick had ever expressed was the inability to conceive a child and start the family of which he had always dreamed, but then they were blessed with Elizabeth. Anticipating Elizabeth's birth often brought spontaneous smiles to Erick's face, but something seemed different today. Erick was tense and distant as he held onto his daughter for the entire ceremony. As a couple, they weren't showing their normal level of affection for each other, and Erick seemed almost cold to his twin brother, someone he'd never even mentioned in all the time Tom had known him.

Addie was still holding the baptismal candle as Tom smiled at her. "Congratulations, Addie. That's a beautiful and precious girl you have."

Addie sighed, "I know. She is at that."

"Is everything okay?"

Addie nodded slightly as she pulled herself out of some deep thought and glanced up at him with a weak smile. "Sorry. Yes. Everything's fine, really. I was just thinking about everything being ready at the house for the party. Are you sure you can't drop by at all?"

"Addie, you know I love you guys and wouldn't miss a free meal for anything, but I have a wedding this afternoon and then Mass. I feel bad about the conflict. It's a blessing and a hazard of the job."

"I understand, but we'll have you over sometime soon," replied Addie as she turned and then placed her free hand on Tom's shoulder. "Can you excuse me for a second?"

"No problem," replied Tom as he took a few steps towards Erick. "Erick. Big day for the Comghan family! Congratulations."

Erick gave half a smile. "Couldn't do it without you."

"Hey, I told Addie that I couldn't make it to the house. I'm sorry, but Saturday weddings are ramping up this time of year."

"I'll save you a piece of cake," said Erick as his attention drifted towards the back corner of the church where Addie was conversing with his brother. It seemed to consume Erick for the moment.

"I'll be looking forward to it," responded Tom as he grinned at Elizabeth kicking her legs back and forth, then stared more closely at her skin. "Is Elizabeth okay?"

"What? Oh, sure, she's fine. Why do you ask?"

"She seems very happy, but I just noticed several red dots on her heel and leg."

Erick followed his gaze and looked at Elizabeth's feet. She had kicked off one of her pink booties. Tom reached down to retrieve it for Erick, who covered her foot again. "Yeah, she's good. I had the doctor check those, and it looks like bug bites. I need to get the screens in her window. Hey, since you can't come over today, would you have any time tomorrow? I wanted to talk to you about something. Would three-o'clock work?"

Tom shook Erick's hand and smiled. "Sure, that works fine. See the three of you for my cake then."

"Addie has a business trip, so it will just be me and Liz."

Tom continued to be taken with Elizabeth's playfulness and glanced up at Erick. "The way you hold her—I can see why Addie trusts you to take good care of her. I'll drop by at three."

Chapter 3

Tom stood in the garden helping Angelo, the church custodian and his close friend, fix one of the rose trellises in the garden. "I don't know what we'd ever do without you, Angelo, but you should take it easy sometimes. Sunday is a day of rest, you know."

Angelo was Italian, short in stature, with coarse hands and years of character that showed in his face. He was also strong and very energetic for someone well into his seventies and who had spent thirty years in prison. "I love to work and look who's talking. You had a baptism, wedding, and four Masses to say this weekend, and here you are working in the garden with me on a Sunday afternoon."

Tom quickly glanced down at his watch and saw that it was already two-thirty. "Sorry to leave you hanging here, but I promised to be somewhere at three."

Angelo smirked. "Day of rest, huh?"

Tom patted Angelo on the back, went inside and washed up, then headed over to Erick's apartment on Commonwealth Avenue in the Back Bay. The light May breeze played with the pink and white flowering dogwoods and budding maples as he strolled down the sidewalk, admiring the old revival architecture of the brownstone buildings with the impressive marble front steps and doorways. Erick and Addie Comghan's spacious first-floor apartment also had a small backyard entrance and private parking area. As Tom approached the front door, he noticed it was standing slightly ajar. He assumed Erick had left it open on purpose since he knew that Tom, who had been to their home many times, was on his way over.

Tom pushed open the door and shouted, "You know, Erick, any old priest could wander in when you leave the door open like that."

No one replied.

He guessed that Erick might be putting Elizabeth down for a nap, so he stepped slowly down the hallway. He glanced at his watch—3:05. Erick had said 3:00. Surely, he was home and expecting him.

The stark silence in the apartment felt unsettling.

Tom continued down the hallway past the living room, calling in a hushed tone, "Erick?" No response and not a sound.

The door to the study was open. Tom peered in, and his heart jumped, pounding against his chest. Next to the desk, Erick's body lay face down on the carpet. Tom dashed to him and placed his hand on Erick's back. He was still breathing! But there was blood on the back of Erick's skull.

Adrenaline raced through Tom's body as he quickly got to his feet and scanned the room. There was no sign of Elizabeth in the bassinet behind the desk or anywhere in the room. He ran down the hall, darting from room to room to see if she was there, but each room was empty and undisturbed. Frantically, he tried to remember their conversation after the baptism: "So, it will just be me and Liz." He was sure Erick said that Elizabeth would be with him while Addie was away.

Quickly, Tom made his way back to the study and back onto his knees next to Erick's still body. He was breathing but unconscious. He got to his feet and took out his handkerchief to pick up the receiver of the phone on the desk and dialed the police.

"9-1-1, where is your emergency?"

"Um. I'm at Erick Comghan's apartment on Comm Ave.," Tom replied, feeling panicked.

"Who am I talking with today?"

"I'm Father Tom Fitzpatrick."

"Okay, Father. Can you tell me what the address and emergency is?"

"Yes. I'm at 165 Commonwealth Avenue, Erick Comghan's apartment. He is unconscious and bleeding!"

"We will have an ambulance dispatched immediately," replied the dispatcher in a reassuring voice.

Tom could hear the call to the dispatcher while he held the line. "Thank you. I was expecting Erick's baby daughter, Elizabeth, to be here as well."

"Can you look for the baby?"

Frantically, Tom replied, "I've searched in each room, and she's not here! There's no sign of her in the apartment."

"Okay, Father Fitzpatrick. The ambulance and officers should be there momentarily."

Just as she finished, Tom could hear the sirens outside the apartment. He dropped the phone and approached the door, opening it with his handkerchief-covered hand, noticing bloodstains on the inside of the door stile. Two uniformed officers stood on the top stoop. "Thank you for coming so quickly. There's a wounded man, Erick Comghan, on the floor, and I think he needs some immediate attention."

"I'm Officer Jackson. Where's the victim?"

Tom waved them to the study, and the other officer dropped to the floor to check on Erick. Tom felt dazed as he stared down at Erick's motionless body with a head wound that didn't appear to be from a fall. Officer Johnson was talking, but Tom was blanking out, peering around the study to see all the things he hadn't noticed minutes earlier. On the desk was an opened package sitting on top of a receipt, but he couldn't make out what it might have contained. There were small remnants of gravel, mostly gray and some red, on the rug near Erick's feet, but his soles were flat and clean.

As the officer exclaimed, "He's still breathing!" Tom noticed some blood on Erick's right arm above the elbow.

Finally, Tom could hear Johnson. "Can you tell me your name and what happened?"

"I don't know. Is there an ambulance coming?"

"It's on its way. Can you tell me what you do know? What's your name?"

"Father Thomas Fitzpatrick—"

The officer glanced up and tipped the brim of his hat up with his pen. "From St. Francis?"

"Yes. I had an appointment with Erick—"

"You said Comghan, right?"

"Yes, with an 'h' after the 'g.' I had an appointment at three-o'clock, and ahh—I came in and found Erick unconscious in the study."

"How did you get into the apartment?"

"Oh, the door—" Pointing, he said, "This door was open, so when I didn't get an answer, I stepped in and called out, but got no response."

The ambulance sirens got louder as it made its way down the street until the flashing lights were in front of the Comghans' front door. Before EMTs were out of their vehicle, Tom noticed two other people on the stoop examining the front entrance door.

The man in the well-worn jacket and tie nodded. "Jackson."

"Detective Brooks," replied the officer.

"Who is this?"

"This is Father Fitzpatrick. He found the body and made the call."

The detective eyed Tom up and down, while Tom did the same to him. Brooks was in his late thirties, with olive-colored skin, dark brown hair, and stood about five-foot-ten. He reached into his jacket for a pen and notepad. "Father Fitz, huh. My name is Detective Tony Brooks, and this is my partner, Detective Jan Mullen. What are we looking at?"

Officer Jackson pointed to the second door on the left side of the hallway. "An unconscious man is bleeding from a blow to the back of his head. We don't know anything else at this point."

Detective Jan Mullen, an attractive woman in her early thirties, her blond hair pulled back in a ponytail, appeared as if she had plenty of Boston street smarts. She pointed to the blood marks on the door.

After taking in their surroundings, the two detectives proceeded to the study where Officer Towns was attending to Erick.

Towns stood up. "He's out cold but still breathing. Looks like two blows with some blunt instrument, maybe a bat."

"Thanks, Towns. Get the EMTs in here," commanded Brooks, raising his open-palmed hand toward the front door as he looked around the study. "Father, what do you like to be called?"

"Tom is fine."

"I'll go with Father Tom. Tell me exactly what you did when you came into this room."

As Tom talked, Brooks squatted down to study Erick's wounds and the position of his body. Detective Mullen took samples of the blood from the back of Erick's skull, his arm, and the rug. She also pushed some of the gravel on the rug into other plastic bags. Finally, Detective Brooks waved the EMTs in, and with their shoes wrapped with sanitary hospital foot covers, they gently lifted Erick's body onto a stretcher and off to one of the many local hospitals.

"So who is Erick Comghan to you?" inquired Brooks.

"He's a parishioner of mine, and he asked me to come over. What I'm worried about is the baby."

Jan Mullen immediately lifted her head and stared at Tom. "What baby?"

Tom replied, "I told the dispatcher. The Comghans had a baby girl a month ago. Elizabeth. She was baptized yesterday at St. Francis, and Erick asked me to stop by this afternoon to talk about something. He said his wife, Addie, would be out of town on a business trip, but I'm fairly sure I remember him saying Elizabeth would be here with him."

Brooks barked at the officers, "Check every room!" then turned back to Tom. "Where did you say the mother was?"

"I don't know. I think a lot of her business is in New York. Erick's brother and Addie's sister were here for the baptism service along with other family and friends, and then they were having a party here at the house. I'm just hoping Elizabeth is with one of them."

Brooks and Mullen exchanged concerned glances as they inspected the blood on the front door before closing it and stepping under the yellow police tape that had been wrapped around the scene. "Father Tom, thanks for your help. What I don't know is what this case is yet. A robbery? A kidnapping? An attempted murder? I'm sure we'll need to ask you more questions, so I'd appreciate your being available when we do."

"I will, and, in the meantime, I'll be praying."

Brooks glanced up at the blue sky. "Sure. I just hope it's all a miscommunication, and we don't need them."

Chapter 4

Tom walked home in a daze, praying that Elizabeth was safe and trying to figure out what could have happened. When he got back to the rectory, he called Boston Medical Center, what was once the old Boston City Hospital, to see if Erick had been transported there since it was closest to the apartment. They were able to confirm he had been admitted but provided no other information, so Tom decided to make his way over to check on him.

Angelo stepped out from the area where he was working. "Father Tom, you're bleeding! Are you okay?"

"What? I'm fine, but Erick Comghan was attacked, and he's in the hospital. I'm going over to see how he's doing."

"Let's wash that arm, and then I can walk with you."

Despite being almost twice Tom's age and a good eight inches shorter, Angelo had no trouble keeping pace with the athletic priest.

"I don't know what happened. When I knocked on the door, it was ajar, and I found the house completely quiet."

"Was he expecting you?"

"Yes. That was the appointment I mentioned to you. We were supposed to meet at three. I found him on the floor unconscious with blood on the back of his scalp."

"Any signs of a break-in?"

"Not that I could tell. Nothing in the apartment was really disturbed either, but there was a wound on his head and blood on the side of his arm."

When they reached the hospital and found the room where Erick was staying, the nurses told them he was still unconscious but in stable condition. Since Tom was Erick's priest, they allowed them to sit with Erick as he rested, breathing slowly. There was a large bruise on his upper arm and a thick bandage around his head. Tom made the Sign of the Cross on Erick's forehead and said a short prayer before sitting down with Angelo.

"Break-ins during the daytime on the weekend aren't common. You said there was no sign of any mess in the house? What about the room you found him in?" asked Angelo.

"Not much of a mess there either. He was face down on the floor and no signs of a struggle that I could see."

"What else?"

Tom let out a deep breath and replied, "Let's see. I mentioned the blood on his head and his arm. Um—" Tom closed his eyes, trying to visualize the room while shaking his head. "Oh, on the desk was a package that had been opened, but I didn't see anything in the box. The bassinet was behind the area where Erick was lying." Tom ran his hand through his hair. "I can't think of anything else, except for the blood on the front door."

Tom could tell that the wheels were turning in Angelo's head. Angelo had grown up without a father and in tough conditions, becoming a thief as a child and then a professional one for many years before finally being caught and sentenced to thirty years in prison. Over those thirty years, he was fortunate enough to share a cell with a man that changed his life and saved his soul. After being released, Angelo had come to St. Francis to help do the same for the son of his cellmate. Those years of breaking into buildings and houses, however, had left him with instincts that never left him. "Very curious."

"I was thinking the same thing. There was no sign of the baby, and I don't know how to get in touch with Addie or his brother, Jack."

"I didn't know he had a brother. As a matter of fact, I don't remember Erick even mentioning his parents. That bruise on his arm is curious too," remarked Angelo.

"Why is that?"

"Do you see any cuts?"

Tom got up and moved closer to inspect Erick's arm. "No, just a large welt. So, he must have taken the hit on his arm after the blow to the head to leave the blood?"

"Maybe. Why would you hit him there after you knocked him out?"

"Why would you hit anyone anywhere?"

Angelo nodded. "A good thief wouldn't have been there while someone was home, and a murderer would have hit him more than once on the skull. Did the police think it could be a kidnapping?"

"Angelo, I really hope not."

They sat together quietly for quite some time until two familiar figures stood at the doorway. Tom turned and queried, "Detective Brooks. Detective Mullen. Did you find out anything?"

Detective Brooks grunted, "A little. If you're here to give Mr. Comghan his last rites, I think he's going to be okay. Who's your accomplice?"

"Sorry. This is Angelo Salvato. He works with me at St. Francis."

"He looks more like a thief than a priest," Brooks replied with a smirk.

Angelo nodded at his perception. "And you don't sound like a Brooks. What's your family's real name? Italian?"

Brooks appeared impressed and seemed to hesitate to give Angelo the satisfaction before confessing. "It's Brucato. My grandfather changed it because when the migrants from Italy were being discriminated against and he couldn't get work. Look, I can't really discuss the case with you two."

Tom responded, "I understand, but do you know what the case is yet?"

"I don't know."

Angelo eyed Brooks. "Were there blood samples from two people or one?"

Brooks shot a piercing glare at Angelo, while Mullen was visibly surprised by the question. "How did you know to ask that?" inquired Mullen before Brooks quickly grabbed her arm.

"We don't have lab tests back yet. By the way, I'll need an accounting of your whereabouts today with witnesses," grumbled Brooks as he made a motion for them to leave the room.

On the way back to St. Francis Church, Tom and Angelo tried to figure out possible scenarios. A robbery gone bad? Kidnapping? Failed murder attempt?

Tom stared ahead as they walked the several blocks home. "I hope Brooks can locate Addie, and she can bring some good news about Elizabeth being at a relative's or a friend's house."

Angelo made no response.

"Angelo, you asked about blood from two people. You're not thinking that Elizabeth is one of the people, are you?"

Angelo remained silent for the rest of the walk.

Chapter 5

That Sunday night, Tom lay in bed, but his eyes never closed. He was feeling too restless to sleep with all the possibilities racing through his mind. He pictured Elizabeth in Erick's arms, her face so sweet. He couldn't fathom any harm coming to an infant so vulnerable and precious. As he sat up and his feet touched the cool wooden floor, he decided to go for a walk. The neighborhood streets were quiet and the air chilly as he headed toward the police station on Harrison Avenue. Tom was in good physical shape and could take care of himself, but the sudden sound of the footsteps directly behind him put him on guard. The steps came closer, and Tom turned to look—a man wearing a long coat and black hat.

Tom breathed a sigh of relief. "Angelo, what are you doing walking the streets in the middle of the night?"

Angelo joined Tom, now side by side with him. "Just looking after a friend of mine. Plus, I think I know where you're headed."

The station was only a mile from the church, so they were at the front desk in short order.

The desk sergeant peered above wire-rimmed glasses that perched on the end of his nose. "What can I help you boys with?"

Tom asked, "Sorry to bother you, but has there been any news on the Comghan girl?"

"Do you have information on the case?" grumbled the sergeant in a gravelly voice.

"Would we be asking you if—"

Tom pressed Angelo's shoulder. "I know the family and was the one who found Erick Comghan. We just wanted to know if there has been any news—" He glanced at the name tag. "Sergeant Doherty."

The sergeant didn't answer but picked up the phone and pressed one of the buttons. "Detective Brooks, we have some curious citizens here to see you."

Tony Brooks came out seconds later, shaking his head and appearing tired. "What are you two doing here in the middle of the night?"

"Like you, not sleeping. I didn't want to bother you, but I wondered if we found out anything about Elizabeth?"

Brooks waved them into the detectives' room and asked if they wanted any coffee. Brooks sat for more than half a minute, pressing his lips together before saying anything. "I don't know. The blood on Mr. Comghan's sleeve was not his, and I'm very sorry to say, it looks like it could be from the baby. The fact that she was taken tells me the assailant either came for her or was concerned about—um, about a murder rap. I just don't know at this point. I'm sorry; I can't tell you more."

Brooks picked up a pen and stared at them expectantly. "It would help to know everything and anything about Mr. Comghan – his wife, his family, friends, or enemies. Also, anything going on recently, especially on Saturday."

Tom sighed before beginning. "Let's see. Erick and Addie moved to Boston about six years ago as newlyweds. They seemed happy, close, and genuinely committed to their marriage. They came to church most weeks and got involved with volunteer work. I play basketball with Erick fairly often and think I got to know them well as a couple. They wanted a family pretty badly but didn't get pregnant for some time."

"How did that affect them?"

"Uh, it seemed to bother Erick a lot more than Addie, but I spent more time with Erick, so I'm not sure. He was really happy when Addie did finally become pregnant with Elizabeth, really looking forward to being a dad."

"Are you saying that she didn't want any kids?"

"I'm not sure. She was building her career, which meant a great deal to her and would travel often for it, so it may have been a tough adjustment for her to deal with."

"That's funny. Usually, it's the guys hesitating to take on the change in responsibilities and lifestyle, but I'm probably living in the past. How did the family feel about it?"

Tom hesitated. "That is one of the odd things. Erick seemed to be so looking forward to building a family, but he never talked about his own family. Hardly mentioned his parents, whom I believe live in New York. In fact, he never even mentioned to me that he had a brother—never mind an identical twin named Jack." Brooks was writing frantically as Tom continued. "I did meet Addie's sister, Rachel, for the first time on Saturday, too." Tom shook his head.

"What is it?" inquired Brooks.

"I don't want to throw out things I don't know for sure."

"Just give me your gut."

"Do you have any siblings?" asked Tom.

"Two brothers and two sisters."

A smile of fondness emerged on Angelo's face as Tom said, "I have a brother nineteen years younger than me, but we are still close and talk all the time."

"And?"

"It just seemed as if neither Erick nor Addie were close at all with their siblings, almost cold—yet they were all very charming individually. Just an odd feeling I had watching them at the baptism. I'm probably thinking too much about it since they did pick them to be Elizabeth's godparents."

"Anything else? Anyone acting oddly in recent months or days?"

"I don't know. I saw Erick a lot less over the recent months. Addie did come to see me about something, but that was confidential."

"Confidential, how? Like confession confidential?"

"Not exactly, but I know she talked to me in confidence."

"Well, if it can help that baby, it may be a confidence you want to reconsider," said Brooks, putting his pencil down and taking off his glasses to look directly at Tom.

As Tom pondered the request, the detective pulled out a cigarette from his top pocket, fiddled with it, then stuck it back in again. Tom responded, "I will take that into consideration."

"Anything else you can tell me?"

Tom shook his head and checked with Angelo to see if he could offer anything.

Angelo frowned in concentration. "It's an odd time for a robbery, Detective Brucato."

"It's Brooks," snapped the detective.

Angelo smiled and nodded. "Father Tom did say there was an empty package on the desk. Without a scuffle, the direction, and angle of the blows, it looks like it was a surprise attack by a shorter right-handed man—or woman. I'm sadly guessing it was a kidnapping job, and they took the opportunity to grab what was in the package."

Brooks smirked. "I'll let you know when we're hiring. The package had a receipt printout underneath it. Thirty-thousand in fifty one-ounce gold coins. No trace of them anywhere. The blood on the door didn't match Erick's, so, for now, we're going to have to assume it was the baby's. None of this goes anywhere, and I'm only telling you because your alibis and timeline check out—and I may need you to stay in touch. Can I trust your confidence?"

Tom nodded and shook Brooks' hand as they left the office and waved at the front desk sergeant on their way out. "Have a good night, Sergeant Doherty."

Out in the brisk air, Tom quickened his pace. "I feel numb, Angelo, and I don't mean because it's cold out. None of this sounds good. I feel just sick thinking about it."

"Let's just not think beyond what we know for sure."

Chapter 6

Tom stopped in his tracks once he got an idea of what Angelo was thinking, but Angelo continued to proceed past the street for St. Francis. He caught up to Angelo as he turned down the back alley behind the Commonwealth Avenue apartments. They stopped behind the Comghans' apartment building. "No, Angelo. We can't go into a crime scene."

"Sure we can, but we need to be careful not to touch or rub up against anything." Angelo took out his handkerchief and waved it for Tom to do the same. He pulled out a small leather pouch, selected a metal pick, gently turned it until he heard a click, and then opened the back door with his covered hand.

"Angelo, aren't you retired? Why do you need to carry a lockpick?"

Angelo shrugged. "You never know." They didn't turn on the lights and instead used a small light from his pouch.

Tom smiled nervously at Angelo. "I know. You never know." They checked the bottoms of their shoes to make sure they were clean and then quietly walked down the hallway. "One thing I do know is that criminals return to the scene of the crime, so this isn't going to look good if we get caught."

Angelo methodically moved from room to room. The back entrance, kitchen, and bedrooms were clean and undisturbed. Tom felt the same eerie silence as the day before. It unnerved him a bit, as if they might find another tragic surprise. When they reached the doorway to the study, Tom whispered, "This is where I found Erick on the floor."

Angelo waved the flashlight around the room with a surgical methodology. The empty package that was on the desk was now gone, and red tape outlined the exact position of the body on the carpet as if Erick had died on that spot. Angelo moved the light along the floor, noting the pieces of gravel that must have come from someone's shoes. Angelo held the light on the taped outline of the body. "Was this reddish material here before? I mean, right where I'm holding the light?"

Tom tried to think back, picturing the EMTs lifting Erick's unconscious body onto the stretcher. "I'm not sure—no, wait a minute. I did see it and thought it was odd. I forgot to mention it to the detectives because I was focused on Erick and Elizabeth."

Angelo slowly moved to the other side of the desk and pulled on the top drawer with his handkerchief-covered hand. The heavy wooden drawers were locked tight but opened within seconds once Angelo applied his magic. He tried not to touch anything as he opened each drawer, inspecting for any clues. The second drawer had ledgers and a wedding picture of Erick and Addie that was face down. In the third drawer, under some ledger books, they spotted a metal case. Angelo gently slipped it out and noted the small lock on the side. As he inserted the right pick for the job, he whispered, "You never know." Opening the lid, they could see papers inside.

"These are private, Angelo."

"I know, but we both know that a baby's life is at risk."

"True. Is there anything here that will help?" Tom lifted a folded sheet and opened it up. "This looks like a travel itinerary. Adelyn Comghan. August 13-16, 2005. Port Jefferson, NY." Angelo was writing as Tom read. "Adelyn Comghan, November 3-5, 2005. Sag Harbor, NY. Reservation, July 14-16, 2006 Sag Harbor, NY. Hotel Baron's Cove. Someone underlined the name of the Hotel with a heavy stroke."

Angelo picked up another paper that appeared to have been visibly crumpled and then smoothed out. He moved the flashlight across the sheet to read what appeared to be a list of numbers in two separate columns.

"Angelo, what is it?"

"Huh."

"Huh, what?"

Angelo handed it to Tom.

He could see from the top that it was a paternity test from Boston GenTech BioLabs. DNA Testing. Child and Alleged Father showed only number IDs, but the test results read, Probability of Paternity 99.9998% positive. The cover letter was addressed to Erick Comghan, stating the positive results and signed by Dr. Stan Levin, Pediatrics. The rest of the papers looked like legal documents for Erick's business and one other odd item—a small butterfly needle. Angelo closed the metal box, locked it, and placed it back in its original position before locking the desk drawer, making sure no prints were left.

Tom nudged him, nervous that they were spending too much time, testing their luck.

As they turned to leave, they saw the empty bassinet with a light pink blanket on one side and felt more determined to find Elizabeth, who was hopefully still alive. Leaving everything as they found it, they stepped into the hallway entrance, and Angelo moved his light along the floor, seeing bits of the gravel, and then along the door frame where he noticed the blood marks. He opened the door to inspect the side and front before closing it back. "I don't think they went out by this door."

"With those blood marks?"

"There isn't a speck of blood on the side or outside knob—and it would be too dangerous to go out the front door with a baby in broad daylight and be spotted by someone. I would've used that back entrance."

"But there's no blood anywhere in the back."

"I know. Lots of things don't add up with this one."

On the short walk back to St. Francis, Tom said, "That was my first."

"First?"

"First break-in."

"Let's make it your last—and you are absolved for good intentions."

"The road to hell is paved with good intentions," replied Tom.

Angelo chuckled, "I would have thought that was the last thing it was paved with! You'll be okay."

Tom peered up at the early morning starlit sky. "I'd just take a healthy little baby girl."

Angelo didn't respond. They both knew the odds of finding Elizabeth, if she was kidnapped and alive, were very slim, at best.

Chapter 7

The nameplate on the counter read Maggie Pappas. "Next," called the older woman, peering over her reading glasses.

Jimi Johnson rubbed the scruff of his beard and stepped up to the counter. "I need to rent a car for four days."

"Will this be a one-way?"

"What? One-way?"

"Will you be dropping the car off at your destination or bringing it back here?"

"Oh. I'll have a one-way."

Maggie smiled. "One-way it is. And where are we headed?"

"I don't know."

"Well, unless you bring it back here, I'll need to know where you are planning to drop the car off."

"Oh. Tijuana."

"Well, you can't drive our rental into Mexico, but we have a drop-off location just across the border in San Diego."

"Okay, I'll take San Diego."

"You'll need a car seat for the baby."

"Okay.

"And how would we like to pay today?"

"I wanna pay in cash."

"That's fine. I just need to see your license, fill in these forms, and I'll get you on your way."

Chapter 8

Despite his mind racing from one thought to another, exhaustion finally allowed Tom to get a few hours of sleep before getting up to say morning Mass. Even the perennially late altar boy, Tony Cappolla, was in the sacristy getting ready before Tom arrived to put on his vestments, for which Tony seemed relieved.

As they readied to proceed down the aisle, Tom leaned over to Tony, "This doesn't make us even on the 'being late score' by a long-shot," and then gave him a wink. Tom was impressed by the number of people that would take the time before work or the day's plans to attend Mass at 7:00 am. He always tried to give them a good homily and say the Mass with the reverence it deserved. Today he made a personal petition. "As some of you may know, Elizabeth Comghan has gone missing. I want to ask each of you to say a prayer for Elizabeth and for any information that could help to locate her."

After Mass, Sister Helen approached Tom. She was maybe five-feet tall but no pushover; she ran the St. Francis school with the right combination of high expectations and loving encouragement. Despite her no-nonsense exterior, her Irish brogue always exposed her playful side, something she was not in the mood for that morning. "I can't believe people would do such a thing to a precious soul or her parents. Have you heard any news this morning, Father?"

Tom admired and looked up to Sister Helen in many ways but had to glance down to respond. "Very little. We have to keep praying."

Sister Helen shook her head and started to walk away, saying, "Praying is good, but I'm thinking the good Lord uses his hands on Earth to help answer some of those prayers."

Tom stood there, nodding at her constant wisdom.

After a quick breakfast, Tom made his way back to the hospital to check up on Erick. When he arrived at the door, a doctor was holding a clipboard, and a nurse was disconnecting the intravenous tubes from Erick's arm. They all turned to see Tom's hopeful expression. "Are you family?" asked the doctor.

"He is," said Erick, who lifted his head from the raised bed pillow with a noticeable grimace.

The doctor said, "Okay. Well, despite the nasty bump and swelling, it looks like Mr. Comghan will be with us for the foreseeable future." He turned to Erick. "However, we need to monitor you and get that swelling down, so it will be several days of bed rest before you can go home." The doctor tilted his head, peered at Erick over his glasses and said, "Take it easy, Mr. Comghan."

Tom stepped out of the doorway with the doctor while the nurse completed her work. "I'm Father Tom Fitzpatrick. How's he really doing, Doctor?"

He shook Tom's hand. "Pleased to meet you. I'm Dr. Sabado. I think he should be fine. That was a nasty gash, and head traumas are always dangerous, but I think the angle of the blows helped to minimize any concussive damage to the brain. There's still considerable swelling that, hopefully, should come down in a few days with care."

"Thanks, and I hope you're right. Erick's a good guy, and we don't want to lose any of those."

Dr. Sabado smiled. "No, we don't. He hasn't been conscious for very long, but I suspect things will start coming back to him slowly. I want to make sure the realization of what happened and the stress of the situation don't make him do anything that would jeopardize his health."

"I understand. I won't stay long."

"Good. I'll be checking back frequently, Father."

As Dr. Sabado turned to check on his next patient, Tom reached out his hand. "Doctor, quick question. You said 'blows.' I assume you meant the one to the arm and one to his skull?"

"He was struck with a light blow and then a harder one on the skull, and also the one on the arm you mentioned. It was the second blow to the head that caused the damage and opened up the scalp. The initial one was much more tentative. The arm was struck at a straight angle, but there was no blood or breaking of the skin."

Tom thanked the doctor and returned to Erick's room, where he was lying at a slight angle. "How're we doing, Erick?"

"Hey, Father Tom. I don't know. My head aches, and I feel disoriented—fuzzy."

"You just take it easy and do what the doctor says."

Erick closed his eyes and inhaled with a shudder. Tom noticed his face tighten, and then tears started rolling down the sides of his face. His breaths started to get shorter and more pronounced. "Oh, my gosh." He looked at Tom with horror filling his eyes. "Elizabeth! Where is she? Where is she?"

Tom froze for a moment and gripped Erick's shoulder. "Erick, do you know what happened to you?"

Erick's eyes darted around the room, and then he jerked. "I don't know. I was holding Liz. I was holding her, and I felt something hard. I didn't know what it was." Erick tried to lift himself, but his face tightened with pain, and more tears started streaming from his eyes. "I—I, tried to protect her with my body, but—I don't know. Tell me what happened! Where is she?" Erick's panicked voice brought the nurse back in.

She gently put her hands on his shoulders to calm him. "Mr. Comghan, breathe, breathe slowly."

Another nurse entered with a needle that she applied to his upper arm. Erick slowly relaxed and then closed his eyes. The first nurse turned to Tom. "It's really important that he doesn't get overly stressed or excited while that fluid build-up on his skull is coming down. He'll rest for a while with the medication."

"I understand," Tom replied. "I don't want to do anything to harm his recovery. I think he just remembered things." He cocked his head, thinking over this different side of Erick, panic, tears, unlike his usual staid personality.

Tom glanced down at the light pink sweater, with an attractive lace embroidery across the front, draped over the arm of the visiting chair next to the bed. He remembered seeing Addie wearing that sweater in church sometimes. He assumed she must have been sitting with Erick in the early morning hours. "Was Addie—Mrs. Comghan here this morning?"

"Yes, she was sitting here most of the night. I think she took a walk to the café in the lobby to get some coffee. He woke for the first time a short while after she left."

Tom headed down to the first floor and searched for Addie in the café but saw no sign of her, so he continued to the front of the main entrance where a large open green offered benches under huge shade trees. There, he found Addie sitting on one of the benches with her head in her hands. As he approached her, she gazed up at him with eyes and cheeks red from crying. Tom sat beside her and put his arm around her as sobs continued to rock her body. He shoved aside the platitudes that rose to mind and waited for her to speak first.

"I don't understand what's happening. Why would God let this happen to someone so small—so precious? Why?"

Seeing that Addie was shivering, Tom took off his jacket and placed it over her shoulders. "Addie, I can't give you a good answer. I wish I could, but I have to trust."

"Trust? This is what trust looks like!"

"We're going to do everything possible to find her. Everything. I was just with Erick, and he was conscious and awake."

Addie jumped to her feet. "I have to see him. I was there most of the night, but he was out. I can't lose everyone."

"Wait! He started to remember the attack and panicked, so they gave him something to rest. I don't think they want to take any chances with the fluid on his brain, so he's probably still sleeping."

Addie dropped back onto the bench, rubbing the sides of her face with the palms of her hands. "I don't know what to do. I need to do something."

Tom put his arm around Addie again as Detectives Brooks and Mullen approached them.

"Mrs. Comghan?"

Tom nodded.

"My name is Sgt. Detective Brooks, and this is Detective Mullen. We're working to find your daughter and your husband's assailant."

Addie lifted her head but didn't respond.

"I'm sorry to ask you this, but would you be able to talk to us—maybe inside?"

Addie nodded. "Okay."

Inside they found an empty visitors' room. Brooks motioned for Addie to sit on the couch. Despite her red eyes and her mussed-up, honey-blond hair, one could not help but notice how attractive Addie was. Her facial features were striking, the type that caught one's attention, and her slim figure was accentuated by her classically tailored white blouse and taupe-colored skirt.

Officer Mullen placed the Kleenex box between them as she sat on the couch with Addie. "Mrs. Comghan—"

"Please, call me Addie. Can someone tell me what's happening?"

Detective Brooks sat on the edge of his chair, scratching his head. "We don't have a lot to tell you at this point, but we're working around the clock to solve this. I can promise you that. The doctor believes your husband will recover, so all of our focus is on finding your baby daughter and getting her back safely."

Addie gulped deep breaths as the reality seemed to sink in even more. Tears welled in her eyes. "Do you think this is a kidnapping?"

Brooks hesitated before replying, "We have to treat it that way, and we need to act fast. That's why anything – and I mean anything you can tell us – will be important. I can ask Father Tom to leave if you'd prefer."

Addie shook her head, "No, no. What do you want to know?"

"Was anything different in the last few days? Anything suspicious or unusual?"

Addie sighed. "No. I don't know."

Mullen said, "Just take your time and think back."

"How can you be looking for Elizabeth if we're here asking questions?"

"We need clues. Something to go on. It doesn't matter how small or common a thing it may be. Did anyone come to the house—deliveries, handyman, cleaning—anyone?"

"No. No deliveries or anything. We had some caterers drop off food Saturday morning."

"Anything unusual? Do you have their name?"

"Nothing unusual. It was from Maggiano's. Oh, and we've been finishing off Elizab—" Addie's voice cracked, and it took her several moments to collect herself as Mullen put a comforting hand on her shoulder. "Elizabeth's room, so Erick had someone over to check out the room to do the wallpapering."

"Do you normally hire out for wallpapering?"

"Actually, no, but with everything going on, Erick thought it would be easier."

"Makes sense. Do you know who that contractor was?"

Addie rubbed her fingers on her forehead. "I'll have to look for a card. I think he said he worked alone. He was average or less than average height, slim, black, um—I can't think of anything unusual, except he wasn't really dressed for wallpapering if he had any jobs that day."

"Was he dressed in expensive clothes?"

Addie shook her head. "No, they were pretty rag-tag. He took dimensions of the room, and then Erick talked with him in the study. I was in the bedroom feeding Elizabeth, and he was gone before I came back out."

"Thanks, Addie. Anything else unusual? How has your husband been lately?"

"He's great. He's busy with his business, and I've been busy building my practice."

"Law?"

"Yes—mostly small business law."

"Good for you. I went to Suffolk nights but never finished. It's a grind. So, no change in behavior lately?" queried Brooks.

Addie stared up at the light on the ceiling and hesitated with her answer, pressing her lips together. "Nothing too much lately. It's been a stressful year. Maybe it's just the transition of having a baby and changing how we are going to live—I don't know."

Brooks sat on the edge of his seat. "Okay, thanks. I'm sorry to ask you this, but we have to ask everyone, including Father Tom here. It's procedure. Can you let us know your whereabouts over the weekend?"

Addie leaned back in the chair and shook her head. "Why do you need to ask anyone who isn't a suspect? I don't understand."

"Like I said, I'm sorry to have to ask, but we have to be thorough in ruling everyone out."

"I hope we aren't spending all of our time doing that while the kidnapper is running loose out there!" Addie squeezed her eyes tight. "Sorry. Just very emotional at the moment. I was getting the house ready on Friday, getting flowers and cleaning mostly. Saturday morning, um—let's see, just showering, dressing, and getting the food in from the caterer. Jack came by and helped me do that while Erick was running an errand."

Mullen was taking notes. "That's Jack, your brother? When did he come to the house?"

"Jack is Erick's brother. He came just after Erick went out, I guess. Yeah, they didn't talk until he got to the church. Jack and I walked with Elizabeth to the church. We had the baptism and then the party at the house afterward."

"How many people came?"

"Um, we had tw—twenty. No, nineteen, since Bill couldn't make it."

"Would you have a list of the names you could provide?"

"Yes. I can write them down for you. After the party, we cleaned up together, had leftovers for dinner, went to bed, and I got up for an early train to New York."

"Why the trip?"

"For work. I had to meet a client on Sunday afternoon to prep for a company board meeting on Monday. I came home late last night when I got your call and went straight to the hospital." Addie's face tensed as she closed her eyes to collect herself again.

"Thank you, Mrs. Comghan—Addie. I know this isn't what you want to be doing right now. If you can write down that list of people, the train you took, where you stayed, and the name of the person you met with, that would be great."

She scrawled down the names and information and handed the paper to Mullen without comment, then rose and left.

Mullen stared at the paper. "She didn't include where she stayed or the name of the person she met."

Chapter 9

Detective Brooks stood on the sidewalk in front of the hospital, letting the sun warm his face. Father Tom stood beside him, wearing his black jacket again, which now smelled faintly of perfume. "I really hate asking parents of missing children questions like that. It's like talking with the grieving spouse of someone who's just been murdered and treating them like a suspect—it's insulting. But so many times, the culprit is someone who knows the victim."

"Is that what you think in this case?"

"My gut says no. Over the past year, there have been several cases of infants abducted in Boston, most likely sold into the Black Market. They generally work to attract young pregnant girls with cash, food, shelter, and medical expenses. There are networks of unscrupulous adoption facilitators, doctors, midwives, and attorneys—baby brokers hiding under the cover of 'legitimate' professionals. They either pay girls to get pregnant or advertise to help them, only intending to broker their baby to a couple anxious to have a family. The problem is that the process is quicker and the expenses lower if you steal a baby, get some young girl to claim it's hers for the birth certificate, and then pay her to sign it over for adoption. The adoptive parents think they're doing a good thing for the baby and the mother, so they are more than happy to pay the high fee to adopt. It's hard to catch these cases through all the layers of deception."

"That doesn't sound good or promising."

Brooks shook his head. "It's not." He sighed and closed his eyes a moment before looking Tom in the eyes. "Do you have time to show me your church?"

Tom pointed ahead. "Sure, it's just a short walk from here."

"I do go to Mass sometimes."

"Me too," said Tom, which brought a smirk to Brooks' face.

"You'll have to tell me why you became a priest someday."

"And you can tell me why you became a cop."

When they reached St. Francis Church, Tom opened the large wooden door, letting in a stream of light that landed on the tiles inside the entrance space. In front of them was an attractively sculptured baptismal font full of holy water. A light trickling sound softened the large space.

"Tell me again what happened the morning of the baptism."

Tom pointed to the front. "I walked out from the sacristy and mistakenly thought I saw Erick standing over here holding Elizabeth, but it turned out to be his identical twin, Jack. I think I mentioned that in all the years I've known Erick, he never mentioned even having a brother. Erick was running an errand, and we started the service when he arrived. Things that were unusual? Well, Erick's greeting of his brother seemed very formal and almost unfriendly as he took the baby from him and held her for the entire service. After the service, Addie excused herself, and I later saw her having a private conversation with Jack over there in the corner. It seemed to get Erick's attention as well. Other than that, I really can't think of anything else that stood out."

"I need to talk to this brother, Jack, and to Erick when he comes around."

Father Tom turned to Brooks. "He was conscious this morning. I spoke to him for a bit."

Brooks peered up at the arched ceilings and shook his head. "Glad someone told me. Could he talk?"

"He was in a lot of pain but very awake. When he recalled what happened, he started to panic about Elizabeth. He remembered the whack on the arm and hunching his body to protect her, and then he couldn't remember anything. The doctor said that Erick was lucky with the angle of the hit to his head. Bending down might explain it—or the assailant could have been shorter."

"Huh. I guess that makes sense if I'm swinging across, and it might also explain the height of the first blow to the arm."

Tom rubbed his upper lip. "Dr. Sabado also said that there were two blows to the head."

"Two?" asked Brooks.

"Yeah, one much lighter and then a harder blow."

"But Erick doesn't remember a lighter blow to the head, right?"

"Not as far as he could recall, but it might not be fair to expect a total recall at first. If he went down, I can't see how the angle of the second harder blow would make sense—it would have been downward instead of across." Tom peered down at the tiled floor in deep thought.

Brooks glanced at Tom. "What else?"

"I think we'll have to talk to Erick more about what he remembers happening."

"You're not getting off that easy. Let's have it."

"From what Erick told me, he didn't know anyone was behind him, and he never saw the attacker, most likely dropping to the ground with the blow to the head. There were fragments of dried mud and gravel in the hall and the study."

Brooks nodded. "Yes, we have those in the lab."

"Did you notice that there was some under Erick's body too? If he dropped to the ground after a surprise attacker's blow, how would those fragments get under the body?"

Brooks rolled his eyes. "You're supposed to be making this easier, not more complicated. I'd better get over to the hospital to see if our main witness is up from his nap. Just to let you know, we've got everyone out asking neighbors if they saw anything suspicious on Sunday and trying to sweep through all the adoption agencies, reputable and not-so-reputable, to see if we can get a lead. Since this is a potential kidnapping, we had to bring the suits in."

Tom wrinkled his eyebrows with confusion.

"The FBI. They have jurisdiction over interstate kidnappings. I hate working with them. We do that work; they come in, steal the case, and hold a press conference," quipped Brooks, shaking his head as he turned to leave.

As Brooks headed down the sidewalk, Tom shouted out, "Have them focus on the backdoor entrance."

Brooks stopped in his tracks and turned back. "And why do you say that?"

"Just a hunch from Angelo. Blood marks on the inside of the front door would make it look like that was the exit path, but there were no signs of blood on the side or front of the door. Plus, it'd be too risky to walk out the front entrance with a bleeding baby."

"Angelo? He didn't go with you when you visited Erick, did he?"

"Ahhh, no."

"Remember, I'm a police officer, and I've read his rap sheet. I better not find out you two have been breaking into houses and trespassing on a crime scene."

As Tom stood still watching Brooks disappear down the sidewalk, he felt the presence of someone beside him.

"He's gonna need some help," said Angelo.

"I'm not sure how much we're helping," sighed Tom.

"Well, I talked with some old pen friends in town about the underground baby market. If it's one of the organized broker groups, kidnapped babies are moved out so quickly that it's almost impossible to trace them."

Tom frowned, distressed. "Angelo, don't tell me this."

"I know. They told me there are a few smaller operations and freelancers that work more locally and may not move as quickly. They may be holding the baby until they can process a birth certificate from a young girl posing as the new mother willing to put her baby up for adoption instead of aborting. They funnel them through agencies looking to promote better options to abortion."

"What are the odds of this being a freelancer?"

"I really don't know, but the kidnapping didn't look professional to me. Too many odd and risky details that bother me on this one."

As they started to turn down the driveway, a black car pulled up to the curb. For an instant, Tom started at the sight of Erick driving the car until he realized that it had to be Jack.

Jack parked and stepped from the car. "Father Tom, do you have a moment to talk?"

"Sure," he replied with a wave of his arm, "we can talk in the rectory. This is Angelo. Angelo, Jack Comghan."

"Good to meet you, Angelo. I hope you don't mind my stealing Father Tom for a bit?"

"Not at all. Father Fitzpatrick, I'll see if I can make some progress on that project."

"Thanks, Angelo. Jack, let's go in. Can I get you anything?"

"No. No. I'm good. Well, none of us are good at all right now, are we?" As they stepped into the kitchen, Tom made another offer of a cold drink, and Jack took him up on it as he talked. "I haven't been over to see my brother. Not that I don't want to, but I don't want to upset him if he's still in recovery. I can't believe someone would do something like this to him, or Addie, or an innocent baby like that. It's making me sick to my stomach just thinking about it."

"I feel the same way. It just keeps turning over and over in my mind, and I feel as if the clock is ticking if we're going to have any chance of finding her." Tom joined Jack at the kitchen table. "Sorry, but that's my fear." He paused for a moment. "I hope you don't mind my asking. I saw you and Addie talking after the baptism. Was everything okay?"

"Oh, yeah. Everything was fine. We were just catching up."

"I guess if you've been away and haven't seen too much of your brother since you've been back, you wouldn't have seen much of Addie either."

34

"A little bit more. My veterinary business in Bridgeport has some important business owners as clients, and I've helped Addie make connections for her practice. She's been doing really well growing her customer base in New York."

Tom poured Jack's glass of ginger ale and ice and set it down. "Let me know if I'm getting into sensitive territory, but how is your relationship with Erick?"

Jack stared down at the kitchen table while swirling his drink. It took him almost a full minute to respond. "Not great. Not what I would've ever guessed when we were growing up. We were really close, even for twins. We enjoyed each other's company, playing together, working on our games in sports, but always cheering each other on. I really loved and looked up to my brother." Jack made a crooked smile. "He's a few minutes older than me."

Jack wrung his hands together as he drifted back in time. "Erick was always bailing me out of trouble. He was more serious, a harder worker, and driven—much more than I. It's odd we could share so much in common: a womb, physical traits, family, sports, schools, and friends, but be so different in so many ways. It's not that I wasn't highly competitive, but I guess I didn't need it as much as he did. When he was in a good place, we had so much fun together. Something happened in high school, and then he seemed more obsessed with recognition, especially if I was involved in any way. He needed it from teachers, coaches, but most of all from our father."

"What were your parents like?"

"They were old school, first-generation Irish." Jack smiled. "Isaac and Becca were high school sweethearts. They were great to us. Maybe because they had problems having children? My mother lost two to miscarriages and one as a stillborn. I think it devasted her, and they were resigned to a life without children until we surprised them—twice over. They were in their early forties when we were born, so they may have spoiled us a bit along the way. My father was a hard driver, though, especially as a coach."

"Your dad coached?"

"Yeah. High school basketball, and he was determined to coach the two of us to a State Championship.

Tom smiled, "Ah, so that's why Erick has been such a tough one to beat at basketball. Where did you grow up?"

"Woodhaven in Queens. My grandparents came over in the twenties, and my dad was born in the thirties. I heard a lot of stories about the hard times, the discrimination they faced, and how hard they worked to create a local grocery business, but I rarely heard them complain. My grandfather grew up farming in Ireland, and, over time, he had saved up enough to buy land on Long Island that they turned into a farm. Erick and I worked most summers on that farm and watched a great dream grow into something special. My brother gravitated to farming work, but I liked working with the sheep, goats, and chickens more than digging dirt. Those long summer days and nights were something," said Jack with eyes glowing.

"The fruits of hard work. That sounds like a great life. What part of Ireland was your grandfather from?"

"Killeshin. It's a small town southwest of Dublin."

Tom said, with a slight Irish brogue, "Ah, me folks are from Donegal. So, life was good for your family?"

"It was great."

"But, then, something happened?"

"I guess." Jack ran his fingers through his short wavy hair and stared at the ice cubes in his drink before changing the subject. "Do you know if they've found any leads on Elizabeth?"

Tom was now standing at the kitchen sink, staring out the window at two budding lilac trees. "Nothing yet." He turned and asked, "Jack, can you think of anything? Anything with friends or family or whatever?"

His gaze down, Jack shook his head. "No. Nothing."

"You said that you came over to talk about something?"

"I did? Yeah, it was something about Addie, but it's nothing, really. I talked with that Detective Mullen earlier today and told her everything I knew, which wasn't much. Some guys from the FBI even talked to me. They've got Erick's phone line routed to the station in case there is a ransom call. I just hope they can find Elizabeth—and she's safe with whoever she's with."

"I'm praying that's the case. Have you been staying in Boston since the baptism?"

"Funny, Mullen asked the same question. Maybe you missed your calling, Father Tom. I stayed Saturday night but went home early Sunday and then came back today when I got the call from Addie."

Tom asked, "Do you need a place for tonight?"

"No, thanks. I have my stuff at the hotel."

"Well, you're welcome to dinner."

Jack got up and handed Tom his empty glass. "Thanks for the drink and your ear." As Tom opened the door for him, Jack turned. "Father Tom, you know that confidentiality thing priests have?"

Tom nodded.

"Is it just for confession? And would it be the same for anyone who knew something because that person told them?"

"Boy, that really depends on the expectations that other person has. Are you conflicted about something someone told you in confidence?"

With an anxious expression, Jack replied, "Hey, I'm always conflicted about things these days. Thanks again for the drink."

Tom watched Jack drive off, wondering what the conversation he just had was all about.

Chapter 10

That afternoon, Tom decided to take advantage of an opening in his schedule to check up on Erick. Addie was sitting quietly next to the bed. Erick was awake, but no words were being exchanged. With a rap on the door, Addie turned, and Erick glanced over with a nod. Tom said, "I don't want to intrude. I just wanted to see how the recovery was going."

Addie stood up. "He's still in a lot of pain, and they're continuing to work on reducing the swelling on the brain."

Erick grumbled, "I don't know what good it's doing to lie here while Liz is out there in danger. I can't just sit by when she's—"

Addie peered at Tom. "Father Tom, can you talk some sense into him? The doctors said it would be very risky to move around too much. The police will find her—" A tear rolled from the corner of her eye. The small amount of makeup she wore was smudged where she wiped it off. "Tell me they're going to find her!"

Tom approached and put one hand on Addie's shoulder as she sat on the edge of the bed and the other on Erick. "I can't imagine the emotions you are both feeling right now. I haven't slept well since Saturday, myself. There are a lot of experts, including the FBI, doing everything possible to find her. And I can tell you, God will take care of her, no matter what—no matter what."

Erick used his arms to push himself up a bit, wincing with pain. "I want to believe you. I just feel so frustrated and helpless sitting here when she should be safely in my arms. Why doesn't God bring her back to us?"

Tom took his hand and Addie's. "Why don't we offer a prayer for her? Our Father, in heaven, please protect Elizabeth from all harm. Bring her home safely to the parents you have entrusted her with and guide the police to solve this quickly. In your name, we pray. Father, Son, and Holy Spirit. Amen."

"Thank you," said Addie as she opened her eyes.

"Erick, I don't want to upset you again, so let me know if you don't want to answer any questions."

"No. I'll do anything to get Liz back."

"Do you remember anything else from that day? From Sunday?"

"Detectives Brooks and Mullen were here asking. I told them it was a quiet morning. I fed Elizabeth early and rocked her while I sang to her." A slight smile came to Addie's face as she held his hand. "She napped from about noon to two. I was working in the study while she was in the bassinet behind me. There were no sounds, nothing suspicious that I can recall. She was cooing, so I let her play until she started to fidget, and then I went into the kitchen to warm a bottle for her. I remember going back into the hallway and unlocking the door because you would be coming over and then went into the study to get Liz." Erick smiled. "She looked so sweet and grinned when she saw my face. I picked her up and rocked her in my arms while backing up a few steps, and then—" Erick closed his eyes with a painful grimace. "And then I felt this sudden sharp pain on my right arm, a blow. I don't know if it hit Liz, but my reflex was to hunch over to protect her. I never saw or heard anything else, then I woke up here this morning. I don't know if, when I fell, I held onto her. I just don't know. I should have protected her, and I failed her. I'm so sorry."

Addie pulled Erick close to her, and she held his head gently against her chest. "No one could have known. You can't blame yourself."

Father Tom nodded. "Addie's right, Erick. You can't blame yourself."

"I will always blame myself if—" He took a deep breath. "No ifs."

Tom asked, "Where were you standing when the first blow came?"

Erick thought for a second. "Um, I was maybe a step in front and to the right of the desk. Where did they find me?"

"Right where you said."

"Why did you ask?"

"No reason. Just curious. Hey, I saw your brother, Jack, this morning."

Erick and Addie both appeared surprised by that news. "Jack? Where did you see him?"

"He dropped by the church."

Erick asked, "To see you about something?"

"I think he did, but he never got to it. We talked a little bit about your childhood in New York, your summers on your grandfather's farm. It sounded very special."

"For a while. It was never the same after my grandfather died."

"How old were you when that happened?"

"Tenth grade, so fifteen, almost sixteen. I hadn't experienced death and loss before—not with anyone that close. I felt devastated, and I still remember my heart actually aching. I was pretty angry with God for some time."

"He can take it. It sounds like you had a special relationship with your grandfather. What did you call him?"

Erick laughed a little. "The Irish name for grandfather is Athair Crionna. I could never say it correctly as a kid, so I called him 'Creena.' It means 'great father' or 'father of the heart.' That's what he was to me."

"That's a special gift few kids get these days."

Erick yawned, his eyes closing.

Tom said, "I'm going down to the café to get a coffee. Can I get either of you anything?"

Addie turned to Erick. "I think you should close your eyes for a bit." She stood. "I'll come down with you, Father Tom."

Down in the café, Tom sat across from Addie, who was holding a large cup of hot coffee. As he watched the steam rise from his coffee, he asked Addie, "How are you holding together?"

"I'm not. I'm really not." Tears welled in her eyes. "I don't know how to do this. I should never have gone on a trip when she was so little. I don't know what to do or feel. I'm empty inside."

"Addie, neither of you can blame yourselves for this. I think we need to focus on any information we can provide to the detectives."

Addie bit her lip and nodded, staring down into her coffee.

"You and Erick knew each other when you were young, right?"

"Yeah. We both grew up in Queens—Woodhaven. I met Jack and Erick in school when we were young. In high school, they both played on the basketball team, and I was a cheerleader, so we started hanging out together even more."

"What were they like?"

"They were close. I never knew siblings that enjoyed each other that much. It was so much fun to be with them. They were handsome, smart, and the stars of the basketball team." Addie playfully flicked back her hair. "What else could a girl ask for?"

"How about their mom and dad? What were they like?"

"They were great to me. I liked them a lot. They had the boys late in life, so they were very loving parents, and I loved them. I do think that Erick's mom was a bit over-protective of Jack growing up, probably because Erick was first and a stronger individual in many ways. Jack was always more fun and took more time to appreciate the little things in life, less intense, and maybe a little less responsible at times. He wasn't preoccupied with what people thought about him. Maybe that was because his mother preferred him?"

"What about their dad? Did he prefer Erick?"

"He was harder on Erick. Pushed him more because I think he saw more in him or something. It was hard for Erick to deal with at times. He felt like he could never satisfy his father's wishes or live up to his expectations. Erick's grandfather adored Erick, so I think that Erick's need for approval fell on Dad once Grandpa died. Erick talked about it sometimes when he was down."

"Jack mentioned that their father coached basketball," said Tom.

"Yeah. He was a tough coach. Driven to win the State Championship, and Erick and Jack were his stars. You could tell how much he loved the game, though, teaching the boys from the time they could walk, from what I hear. They knew each other so well that they played like two athletes of one mind. Jack just knew where Erick was going to be, and Erick knew what move Jack was going to make. The boys were really competitive but learned to enjoy and appreciate the game itself. They had fun, and the road to the State Championship our senior year was such a great ride. I remember that last game being so intense; I thought my heart was going to burst when they were down by one point with four seconds to play. Dad called the play in the huddle, and I could see Erick arguing with his father about the play. I think he wanted to take the last shot, but he was inbounding the pass to Jack, who was supposed to drive hard to the basket and try to win the game."

Tom blurted, "Don't leave me hanging! What happened?"

"Well, the Brooklyn team was making it hard for Erick to inbound the ball, and he called a timeout before the five-second rule, or whatever it is, expired. When we went out to cheer, I could see how upset Erick was with his father because he was calling the same play. Erick was inbounding again and this time made a good pass to Jack, who faked left and then drove hard right. With two seconds left, he stopped and jumped, but instead of shooting, he made a bullet pass to Erick, who made an incredible shot at the buzzer. I could see the clock go to zero as the ball floated in the air and then through the hoop for a one-point win. I was so happy, and the players were all jumping up and down, hugging and cheering."

Tom smiled. "So Erick was the hero."

"You would have thought. When the local paper interviewed Coach Comghan after the amazing win, he focused on the pass Jack made. 'Unselfish team play is what got us to this game and what won us the Championship!' The headlines read THE CHAMPIONSHIP PASS. Erick was devastated. Barely a word about his game-winning shot or his play during the game. Jack was getting all the praise from his father. Erick believed that nothing he did was good enough, and things were never the same afterward."

"Sounds like that approval and acknowledgment meant a lot to Erick."

"I think it meant everything. I think it changed his relationship with Jack too. Everything was relative to Jack for Erick. Jack just wanted his brother. I wonder sometimes if Erick picked me because—" Addie hesitated but didn't finish the thought.

"Did Jack love you?"

Addie remained silent and then stood up. "I'm sorry. I should be getting home. My folks and sister are coming this afternoon. We're going to stay at the Eliot."

"Your sister, Rachel?"

"Yes. Rachel, Elizabeth's godmother. She's two years younger than me. She was very quiet at the baptism, and I didn't really get much of a chance to talk to her at the party before she left. Part of me thinks the only reason she came to my wedding and the baptism was because Jack would be there."

"Did Rachel date Jack?"

"No, but she has always wanted to."

"Oh. Are you two close?"

"Growing up, we were, but not for some time now." Addie fiddled with her wedding band.

"Sorry to hear that. Please, don't let me keep you."

Tom sat for a while after Addie left. He thought about all the hidden areas of people's lives and feelings you never know about, even when you think you know them so well. The lack of sleep had finally caught up with him when he got back to the rectory, and he nodded off for a few hours before being woken by a sudden tapping sound at the side door. Outside the kitchen door, he could see Detective Brooks waiting impatiently. Tom ran his hands through his hair, smoothing it down, and opened the door. "Detective, come in. What can I do for you?"

"I heard you were at the hospital talking with Mr. Comghan again?"

"Yes. He was with Addie, and I wanted to see how he was doing."

"And how is he doing? Since you seem to be the only one talking to him." Brooks started reaching for the cigarettes in his front shirt pocket. "Do you mind? We can talk out here if that's okay with you?"

"No problem," said Tom as he stepped outside. "Erick seemed quite lucid and upset about Elizabeth, blaming himself for not protecting her. I think he feels frustrated about not being able to be out of the hospital to help find her, which I can totally understand. I want to go door to door myself to find her."

Brooks' eyes squinted as he lit the cigarette pressed between his lips. "Well, that's exactly what we've been doing. Asking everyone in the area if they saw or heard anything."

As Brooks blew the smoke upwards, Angelo appeared from around the corner and motioned Tom over to tell him something. Tom quickly glanced at Brooks. "Have you had a chance to have anything to eat today, Brooks?"

"Haven't had the time."

"How about if it's a working lunch? I'll pay."

Dempsey's Pub was just a few blocks from the church. As they entered, Dempsey himself glanced up with his usual smile lighting up his round face and pink cheeks. "Let me see if I can't find you boys a table." It was an old Irish pub with a welcoming feel and normally full of patrons engaged in debates and friendly conversation, but things were quiet and empty on a late Monday afternoon, except for the few men chatting with Dempsey at the bar.

Tom laughed as he grabbed his favorite booth, and the three of them sat, Tom and Angelo across from Brooks. "How about some of Dempsey's famous burgers and a Guinness for everyone?"

Angelo and Brooks nodded as Dempsey took the order.

Tom asked Brooks, "So, you were talking about going door to door in the neighborhood for witnesses?"

Dempsey put down their beers, and Brooks took a refreshing sip before responding. "We have, but nothing yet. We've hit all the adoption agencies and the questionable adoption operators we know of. The FBI is checking the larger multi-state operations. Nothing to match." He turned toward Angelo. "Somehow, I don't think you came to the rectory for a gardening talk. Anything related to Elizabeth that prompted this working lunch?"

Angelo glanced at Tom and back at Brooks. "Maybe something. I have some old friends that live in town."

"I know your past," said Brooks. "Are these guys clean?"

Angelo didn't answer the question. "They have connections. None of the major operations know anything about this one. If they did, she'd be long gone by now. They don't take any chances trying to keep a baby for long or near the hit. This is the next tier down, or a loner job, or even something personal. That creates some hope since they're usually slower to process things." Angelo took a long sip of his Guinness. "If she's dead, you have time to find the killer, but if she's alive and being sold for adoption, then we may have a very small window to work with."

Brooks rolled his eyes. "Tell me something I don't know already."

Angelo didn't seem to take it personally. "I think it was one person inside and a driver out in the back alley. Speed is the critical item on an operation like this."

Brooks shook his head. "Why would he leave careless blood markings on the front door if he or she escaped out the back?"

"I don't think there was much that was careless about this. Maybe the mud and gravel on the rug that was under the body, maybe leaving the packaging on the desk."

Brooks peered at Tom. "He sounds like he was the one in the apartment instead of you?"

"I would focus on the back exit for witnesses. I'd widen the net for where they might have gone to process the adoption—" Angelo hesitated before finishing. "And I would check any personal connections for motives for doing something like this or paying someone to do it. Who have you ruled out so far?"

Dempsey approached the booth with three steaming plates of burgers, steak fries, and pickles. "You boys don't look like you're talking about the Sox. I heard about that Comghan case. How could anyone do a thing like that to a baby?"

When Dempsey was back at the bar, Brooks leaned forward. "I haven't ruled out anyone yet, and that includes the two of you—" He took a large bite of his burger and finished, "Which is why I shouldn't even be talking with you about what I've ruled out!"

"I thought you confirmed our alibis," said Tom in surprise.

"You two have vouched for each other, but who says you didn't pull this off together? Salvato here says it was a two-man job. I have a hunch you two may have even returned to the scene of the crime. How about that for remaining on my list?"

Tom responded, "I think you need to get some sleep. Angelo might inflict some harm on whoever did this, but he would never harm a baby."

"Who said this was done to harm the baby? Maybe the kidnappers thought they were saving her?" quipped Brooks.

"But you said that some of the blood matched Elizabeth's?"

"I know. I don't know. The time crunch to find something, anything, is just getting to me. Having the Feds breathing down our necks hasn't been helping either. Sorry if I'm talking nonsense. I can't eliminate any possibility," grumbled Brooks as he dipped one of his fries into a generous mound of ketchup.

After Brooks had finished his late lunch and left, Tom and Angelo stayed behind at Dempsey's. Angelo said, "He seems wound up kinda tight."

"I feel the same way, and the pressure is on him to solve this quickly."

Angelo nodded. "I know. I took a piece of that gravel left in the study and hallway and walked the area to see if there was anything to match. Demolition sites have that mix of gravel. Nothing yet. The public alley in the back is pretty narrow, so any vehicle they used wouldn't have been a wide truck or anything like that. I don't figure this for a random thing, so the kidnapper would've been watching and planning this for some time. It's still odd that they would have picked that weekend when Mrs. Comghan was out of town. All that family in town just adds to the list of potentials. I wonder if they know which ones went home after the party and who stayed in town?"

Chapter 11

Tom stopped at the bar to pay the tab and say goodbye to Dempsey, who stood with his usual bar towel over his shoulder. Dempsey slid his change across the counter and leaned in. "Was that the detective working on the Comghan case? I saw his picture on the news flash while you were talking. He was asking for people to come forward if they had any information."

"Yup. That's Detective Brooks."

"Funny, he don't look like a 'Brooks.' What was he doing talking to you and Angelo?"

"Just comparing notes."

Dempsey smiled. "Well, I'd put my money on you. I hope they find that little girl."

"Me, too, Demps. Me too."

Outside the pub, Angelo said, "I'm going to do some more digging, but I think I need to see the inside of the apartment again."

"Angelo, I don't think that's a good idea. Jack said something about the FBI setting up shop at the apartment. We took a big risk last time, and you're still on parole, you know."

Angelo quipped, "He said they normally would, but, with Erick and Addie not at the apartment, the calls are being routed to the station."

Angelo didn't seem as if he was in the mood to change his mind. Tom said, "You're still going, aren't you? All right, I'll meet you there at 8:30. It should be dark by then."

Instead of going directly home, Tom turned down Mass Avenue and headed to the Eliot Hotel, where Addie was meeting her family. He could see the hotel up ahead, but as he approached, he spotted Rachel coming toward him on the busy sidewalk. He remembered the darker hair and blue scarf from the baptism. Before she noticed him, she stepped into a restaurant. Tom approached slowly and saw her smiling as she sat down at a small table with a man already having a drink. Jack Comghan. *Huh,* thought Tom. He knew he would be spotted if he stood outside the window for long, so he slipped into the restaurant and walked directly to the bar where he could watch from a stool that was out of sight from their table.

Addie had mentioned something about Rachel only coming to the baptism because Jack would be there. Addie hadn't answered his question about Rachel ever dating Jack, so he didn't know if they'd had a relationship or not. Tom ordered a water with lemon as he tried to get a read on their conversation. There was a lot of back and forth in the discussion that seemed more agitated than romantic. He couldn't see much of Jack's face, but Rachel was no longer smiling, maybe frustrated or discouraged by Jack's words. Jack's hands moved up and down as he spoke, and then, at one point, Jack stood up. He appeared more serious than angry as he gave her some parting words before leaving money on the table and walking out the front entrance.

Rachel remained seated, shaking her head.

Tom went over to her. "Rachel?"

With tears in her blue eyes, she looked up. "Father Fitzpatrick? What are you doing here?"

"I was passing by and thought I recognized you through the window."

"Oh. You have a good memory."

"I was supposed to meet someone, but they can't make it now. Are you having dinner with Addie and your folks?"

"No. I dropped my folks off and checked in on Addie. I'm not meeting anyone."

"Well, since neither of us has a date, can I buy you a drink or something?"

"What? Oh, um, sure. I could use the company, but do you mind if we go elsewhere?" They strolled a few blocks and found a small café to sit inside, out of the chilly, late evening air. They ordered two coffees. "Are you sure you don't want anything else, Rachel?"

"No, no, thank you. I don't think I could eat right now. Please order something for yourself."

"I'm fine with just the coffee for now, but let me know if you change your mind," responded Tom as he studied her. She was a few years younger than her sister, Addie, probably twenty-eight or twenty-nine. In some ways, she seemed more sophisticated and older, but in other ways, much less mature. Her hair was dark brown and full-bodied, and her face was strikingly attractive, especially when her unique smile appeared. She seemed much more athletic than Addie, and Tom wouldn't have guessed that they were sisters.

"I didn't know priests wandered the streets." He paused. "By the way, I really liked the things you said at the service on Saturday. It seemed like you believed them."

"What in particular stood out for you?"

"I think it was something about being transformed. Becoming a new person." Rachel took a cautious sip of her hot coffee. "I think that is what I need to do. Disappear and become someone new."

Tom smiled. "Actually, I think the idea is to become the person God made you to be, versus the one we try to create ourselves to be. Be free to be our true selves."

"Huh. Seems like everyone I know feels free to do what they want and not what God tells them to—but I guess not too many of them seem all that happy."

Tom replied, "Our idea of freedom can often become an unsatisfying prison—and what we often think is not freedom, letting go and trusting totally in the one who made us, turns out to be our source of real freedom and happiness."

"Like I said, you sound like you believe it. I guess it's the letting-go part that seems scary."

Tom smiled. "It can feel that way. So, did you drive back with your folks today?"

Rachel hesitated. "No, they drove back up from Woodhaven. I met them here, and Addie was already at the hotel."

"Oh, okay. I thought Addie said you were all coming up today. I must have misheard her. So, you are all staying at the Eliot?"

"No, I'm at the hotel I've been staying at—I mean the one that I've stayed at before."

"So you must have known Erick and Jack growing up too?"

A small grin made its way to Rachel's face as she stirred another half sugar into her coffee. "I was a few years behind them, but I went to watch all their games. Sometimes they would come over to the house. At first, it was weird trying to tell them apart, but then it got easy. Jack has a small speck in his left eye and a different smile. I've always loved that smile." Rachel seemed to drift back to those first days when she must have become infatuated with Jack, a feeling that had obviously grown stronger with time.

"So, you liked Jack back in high school?"

Rachel nodded.

"And did Addie date Erick back then?"

Rachel's expression changed dramatically as she rubbed her hand across her mouth. "Addie. Everything was about Addie. Always about Addie. She had everything, and everyone loved her. I was never anything but Addie's kid sister, then and now." She closed her eyes, stopping the tear that

48

threatened to fall. "I'm sorry. I just feel a little emotional right now."

Tom clasped her hand. "I'm the one who's sorry. I didn't mean to overstep my bounds. I was just interested."

"Jealousy's a sin, isn't it?" asked Rachel, keeping her gaze down.

"It can be. If someone has something good that you would like to have, you might feel jealous, and you might want to have it too. That can be okay. It really depends on how deep that feeling goes and, more importantly, how it affects your sense of self and how it impacts your ability to love that other person."

"Love. How can you love someone you're jealous of?"

"Think of love as more than a feeling, but actively willing the good for another. You want the best for them but not in comparison to you or for what they may do for you. If they have something good, you are happy for them—even if you would like to have that something good too. Now, it's envy that is really the deadly sin. Envy brings sorrow, sadness, or even anger at what the other person has that you don't. You see what they have as making you less—and you want to either possess what they have or destroy it. We can come to resent or even hate that other person for having what we do not. It's deadly because it acts like an insidious cancer that lurks in your soul, sometimes building an obsession to destroy that other person's happiness."

Rachel exhaled a long breath. "That sounds like a sin."

"It's sad when it goes deep. It's deadly because it leads to other sins, but it's important to realize that the source is often from fear or hurt. A person who feels envy is afraid of something, insecure, and vulnerable. People aren't generally bad; they need love, acceptance, and understanding. They long for the happiness that they don't have, instead of the loneliness and self-loathing they often live with."

Rachel finished the last of her coffee and stood up, appearing more stunned than enlightened. "I think I need to walk a little—alone. Thanks for the coffee and talking with me.".

"I don't think I let you talk very much. I'm sorry about that. Are you going to be all right?"

"Tonight? Probably. Long-term? I really don't know." She started toward the door and then turned. "What's the antidote?"

Tom asked, "Antidote?"

"For envy. What's the cure in your priest's bag of tricks?"

"Oh. Virtues are always the best medicine. For envy, humility, and especially kindness can conquer even the worst cases."

Rachel's brow furrowed. Instead of disagreeing, she nodded, waved goodbye and strolled towards town.

Chapter 12

The evening darkness had fallen gently over the city, and most of the commuters from the suburbs had gone home. Tom made his way down a darkened public alley, which was just wide enough for the tenants' cars to squeeze through. He tried to find the back of Erick and Addie's place in this long row of three-storied bricked apartments when he suddenly heard a sound from the darkened corner.

"Psssst."

"Angelo," he said softly. "Is that you?"

He saw a figure step out so that the moonlight highlighted his short, distinctive silhouette. "You'd better hope so." He glanced in both directions and then quietly opened the wooden gate to the back entrance and picked the lock. Angelo stepped inside without a sound while Tom's initial step over the threshold emitted a loud creak in the wooden floorboard. Angelo turned and gave Tom a look that said he'd better feel out each step to move silently down the hallway. Angelo's flashlight illuminated the way with a low glow as he searched for any missed clues. When they reached the dark study, a sudden movement erupted from the corner, followed by a loud whack. The flashlight fell as Angelo dropped to the ground, and Tom couldn't make out anything in the pitch black of the study until he heard the front door open and the first few fleeing steps of the assailant. Tom rushed to the entrance and onto the front stoop, but he saw no one on the sidewalk, only the lights of a cab driving away, partially obstructed by the parked cars along the street.

Tom turned on the lights and saw Angelo crouching on the floor, holding his head. "Angelo, are you okay? Don't get up too fast."

"I'm all right. We need to shut that light and close the door."

Before he could reach the switch, Tom noticed the flashing blue lights moving down the street and stopping in front of the Comghans' front entrance. "Too late."

Instead of dashing towards the back door for an escape exit, Angelo got up and made his way to the other side of the desk and saw the drawer opened that had contained the thin metal box they'd searched during their previous visit. He closed the drawer with his knee as the officers entered the front door with their guns drawn. Tom and Angelo slowly raised their arms and were immediately escorted to the holding area at the station on

Harrison Avenue. Before long, Detectives Brooks and Mullen stood at the waiting room window, shaking their heads as they watched the two amateur sleuths. Brooks opened the door and motioned with his head for them to get up and follow him.

As they walked down the hall, Brooks eyed Angelo. "You look like you need some ice for that bump. Do you want to tell me how you got it?"

Angelo smirked. "I don't remember."

"And I just won the lottery, or you just broke your parole."

Jan Mullen handed Angelo an ice pack as they sat in the mostly empty detectives' room. The lighting was poor, the paint on the ceiling peeling, and the old wooden desks covered with files. Brooks put the clipboard he was holding down on his desk. "You know that I haven't ruled out anyone as a possible suspect—and returning to the scene of the crime is usually a sign of a guilty party." He took a sip of his coffee and, glancing up, added, "Especially twice in two nights."

Tom and Angelo glanced at each other, probably looking more guilty than when the police showed up at the "break-in." Brooks stood up and sat on the edge of the desk with his arms folded and his lips pursed. "So, what were you two doing there tonight—and last night?"

Neither Tom nor Angelo answered. Brooks rolled his eyes. "Can you at least tell me if you found what you were looking for?"

Tom turned toward Angelo, who slowly nodded. This caught Tom by surprise as he noted the large whiteboard behind Brooks' desk. The whiteboard was plastered with pictures, names, and lines making connections between some of them.

Brooks caught Tom eying the whiteboard and walked over to it. "I think we all know that time is against us. There's no sense in you two playing detective unless you have something to add to this puzzle."

Angelo winced as he stood up. "What do you have so far?"

Brooks stared at the floor and rubbed the sole of his right shoe across the uneven wooden floorboards. "Isn't that what I'm asking you?"

Angelo remained silent as he studied the whiteboard.

Brooks shook his head. "All right. At the center, we obviously have Erick and Elizabeth. We still don't know for a fact if this was a robbery that resulted in an assault and taking the baby as an unexpected opportunity, or an intended kidnapping with an unexpected opportunity to steal thirty-thousand in gold coins, or an attack intended to hurt or even kill Erick Comghan. We don't have enough evidence to know what criminal intent we are dealing with. We do know Erick was assaulted, his money was stolen, and most importantly, we have a missing baby girl that is either dead, sold on the black market, or is being held somewhere.

"Possible suspects would be professional black market baby sellers, freelancers or a first-time kidnapper, or," he paused a moment, taking in the expressions on both men's faces, "possibly even friends or family. Addie, Jack and Rachel are all family members without an alibi for Sunday. We've checked all the other people that attended the baptism, and we have confirmation on where they were. The other obvious answer is that someone could've paid someone else to do the dirty work."

Tom pointed to the picture of Addie. "Do you really think Addie could do this to her baby and husband? And Jack or Rachel—what motive would they have?"

Brooks stared at Tom. "I need to be objective. Most murders are done by someone who knows the victim. Most kidnappings are committed by an estranged parent, but a parent, nonetheless. I cannot rule anyone out yet—anyone. Sometimes crimes are committed for what the perps think is a good reason, and things backfire. Right now, the trail for professional black market operations being involved is stone cold. I need to know what you know."

Tom continued to stare at the board. "Just tidbits here and there. Nothing to solve the case. When I spoke to Erick, he said he was holding Elizabeth in the study. He said that when he was hit on his right arm, he hunched over to protect her and never saw the assailant before he was hit."

"We know this."

"When I spoke to Dr. Sabado, he said that Erick was hit three times. First to the arm and then twice to the back of the skull, the first a lighter hit and then the stronger blow that opened the wound and shook his brain."

"Okay."

"Also, if he was surprised and dropped to the ground, how could some of those remnants of gravel be under the body? Unless he was moved? His shoes were clean. Angelo believes that the intruder may have entered through the front but would have left by the back entrance."

Brooks said, "We talked about that, and we've tried to talk to anyone who might use that public alley to see if they saw anyone leaving at that time with a baby. Nothing so far. I see no evidence that Erick was dragged or even carried to that spot. The position and bloodstains were too consistent with a sudden drop."

"I spoke with Addie," Tom continued. "She seemed to indicate that there have been tensions in the marriage over the past year. It could simply be the adjustment to the pregnancy, but Erick seemed to be increasingly suspicious."

Brooks' head moved slightly. "Suspicious of what? Of whom?"

Tom eyed Angelo as he thought about the confidential nature of conversations he had and also about revealing information they shouldn't have seen. Angelo exchanged the glance and then pointed to Addie. "We found some of Erick's papers indicating that he was tracking her itinerary or at least specific trips to towns in New York, including an upcoming reservation at Sag Harbor. We also found a paternity test, possibly for Elizabeth."

Brooks stood from his perch on the desk. "Where did you find these papers? Where are they?"

Angelo patted the fresh bump on his head. "Ask whoever gave me this. It was in a metal box in Erick's desk drawer—and a pretty effective weapon."

"What? Someone broke in to only steal that box with those papers in it? I don't believe in coincidences. Did you get any type of look at this guy?"

Tom said, "It was pitch black and unexpected. When I ran to the front door, I couldn't see anyone running, only a cab pulling away."

"What kind of cab?"

"I couldn't make it out in the dark and with all the lights."

"We'll check for prints. What was on the paternity test papers that you can remember?"

"There were only number IDs for the child and the father, but it was addressed to Erick Comghan. The test was over 99.9% positive of the father tested. Dr. Stan Levin was the pediatrician on the form, and I just happened to drop by his office earlier today."

Brooks' eyes rolled toward Tom. "And?"

"He said that Erick had asked him if he could do the test, and by his expression, I'm gathering he wanted it to be confidential. He provided a swab of his saliva, and they took a sample from Elizabeth. The test was done by some DNA testing lab in Boston."

"GenTech BioLabs," interjected Angelo.

Brooks asked, "That was it? The doctor said that Erick wanted to make sure he was the father, and the test was positive. I'm not sure if any of this gets us closer or not, but you two do put in the legwork for part-time sleuths."

Tom said, "There's a little more. When I spoke with Addie again, we talked about Erick and Jack's childhood. It seemed as if they were very close, but something changed in high school. There seems to be some resentment between the brothers and even between Erick and his parents. Earlier today, Jack dropped by the rectory to talk. He seemed to want to tell me something and then decided not to. There's definitely something there, but I don't know if it has anything to do with the case. Finally, I also spoke to Rachel earlier today. She appeared to have a lot of bottled-up emotions when it came to talking about her sister, Addie. We ended up talking about how jealousy and envy poison relationships. There are a lot of dynamics going on with the four of them, but as I said—it might have nothing to do with anything. It would be interesting to talk with Erick and Jack's parents at some time to shed some light on family dynamics."

Brooks sat down at this desk and scratched the side of his head. "Sounds more like a soap opera than evidence. I'm going to let you two go after the EMT takes a look at that bump." Brooks grinned. "He does kind of look better with it, though." After a moment, he stood and scowled at them. "All right. That's it. Now, I don't want to catch you breaking into any more houses, never mind crime scenes. I don't know if you knew this or not, Mr. Salvato, but breaking into houses is illegal in all fifty states."

Angelo handed Brooks the ice pack and muttered, "I heard something about that."

As Mullen escorted Tom and Angelo out of the office, Tom turned and said, "Now that I think about it, I think that cab had an ad on the back bumper. Something about diaper changing services. Um—Boston Bottoms was the name. Not sure if that helps?"

Brooks laughed. "Who knows. By the way, thanks for passing on what you know."

Chapter 13

After eleven hours of driving, Jimi Johnson pulled into the Roadside Motel and Inn just outside of Columbus, Ohio. He was tired and feeling sleepy, but the baby was awake and in need of food and a change. He had made quick stops along the way for feeding and diaper changes, but this was the first extended stop where they could get out of their seats. He booked a room for one night and prepaid in cash, only asking where there was a local grocery store that might open early.

The desk clerk and owner, Betts Hardy, was not fazed by the cash transaction, the baby, or the lack of friendly conversation. She had seen all types come through and stay at their inexpensive rooms just off the highway. The tip of the cigarette in the corner of her mouth glowed as she drew the smoke into her lungs and exhaled to the side before glancing up from the register at the baby he was cradling in his left arm. In a gravelly voice, she remarked, "Very sweet, Mr. Atkins. It's a girl, right?"

Jimi's eyes were fixed on the baby as he nodded. "She is. You have a microwave in the room to warm the formula, right?"

"We do. Let me know if you need anything else for her—or yourself. I was going to recommend some things to do if you were going to be around town tomorrow, but she's a little young to be taking in attractions."

"Yeah. Thanks. I think I'm set then."

"You coming from Boston? I have a sister that moved up there, and she's starting to pick up that accent."

Jimi lowered his eyes as he took his keys from the desk. "I think we'll be headin' to the room. Thanks." He held the baby against his chest and opened the door to a slightly musty-smelling-but-clean room. After changing and feeding her, he picked up food and supplies at a small grocery before a restless attempt to sleep amidst the sound of passing trucks and the lights of the nearby highway. He thought about his life. Poverty didn't keep him from having fond memories as a young boy, but reality set in too quickly. With no father to guide him and friends who found crime to be the only opportunity to survive, Jimi had chosen a path that only led him to emptiness and even prison for a time. But despite the life of deception and dead ends, Jimi was never one to go back on his word. He could be trusted, and now, for the first time, he had someone to trust him.

That was one trait that attracted Mariana to Jimi almost a year ago. She was in her early thirties, pregnant, and had been living on the street when Jimi met her. Despite the physical and emotional scars of abuse as a child, she was a strong-willed and determined woman. Jimi offered a friendship to Mariana that was sincere, protective, and without judgment. Mariana was the first woman in his challenging forty years of life that actually believed in him. He would do anything for her, and she'd sacrifice no less for him, even though her losing bout with cancer might leave her little time to show it.

Chapter 14

After saying Mass on Tuesday morning, Tom picked up a few breakfast sandwiches and large coffees to-go from the Eastside Café where he and Erick met some mornings for breakfast. When he entered the bright hospital room, he found Erick awake and sitting up. "I thought these might be a good change from the gourmet hospital food you have been spoiled with," said Tom with a smile. "How're we doing today?"

Erick grinned. "Eastside?"

"Eastside. Linda says hello and hopes you're better."

Erick laughed. "Linda said something nice? This is Linda, the waitress from the Eastside, we're talking about, right?"

"The same one, and I think she meant it. She doesn't want to harass sickly customers."

Erick's face lost its smile.

Elizabeth was still missing.

"Father Tom, I want to think that prayers will work, but I'm starting to lose hope. I can't stop thinking about what I could've done to save her—and didn't. I'm supposed to protect her."

"It's understandable you could feel that way, but you can't blame yourself for things you couldn't control. I don't feel like we can lose hope either."

Erick gazed out the window at the wispy clouds against the early morning blue sky. "I want to believe that. I want to believe it. When I asked the detectives what the chances were of finding her, I could see the truth on their faces." A tear rolled from the corner of Erick's eye and down his cheek. "If something has happened to her, I don't think I'll ever forgive myself. I don't even know if I could live with it. I really don't."

Tom walked around to the other side of the bed to stare directly at Erick. "We're not giving up on Elizabeth, and don't you think Addie needs you even more now?"

"I don't know if Addie ever needed me. I can't imagine she could ever want me after all this."

"Erick. This isn't healthy. Of course, Addie loves you. That's been something I have always seen in her. Hey, how did they say that skull of yours is doing?"

Erick exhaled and tried to shift gears. "They said the swelling has begun to come down. I guess I was lucky—well, that's a bad choice of words."

Tom took a sip of his coffee and let the quiet of the moment sit for a bit before talking again. "I was thinking about your brother dropping by yesterday. I told you that, right?"

"Yup. Still, don't know why he would go see you. He doesn't even really know you."

"I think he just wanted to know where things were with Elizabeth, and I think he might be missing the relationship he had with you."

"He has an interesting way of showing it."

"Do you mind if I ask what happened? Jack said you were pretty close growing up."

Erick's thoughts appeared to drift back, and Tom could see a little glimmer of a positive memory in his eye—just for a second, and then it was gone. "Yeah, we were close. Very close, but kids grow up, I guess."

"Sounds like you guys knew Addie and Rachel back in high school?"

"Yeah, Rachel was a few years younger, but we got to know her when we stopped by Addie's house or went out after the games. She took a liking to Jack right away, but everyone did."

"I heard you guys won the States your senior year. I figured you'd still be bragging about that. Your dad was the coach?"

"Yup, he really pushed us. I still can't figure out what pleases him. Jack did, but I never have."

"Sometimes, a parent's intent gets lost in translation for a kid."

"Or you're just not good enough for them," snapped Erick.

"From my years of experience, that's rarely the case. Sometimes we push the ones we love and think are stronger a little harder because of it."

"You haven't met my dad, have you?"

"Not yet, but I'd like to, sometime. I can ask him why he never coached you up enough to take on an old man like me on the court."

Erick's eyes shifted toward Tom. "I've done my share of beating you—plus, I wouldn't want to take advantage of an old man."

"Let's get you healthy and test that out again."

"After we find Elizabeth," said Erick, frowning.

"After we find Elizabeth," nodded Tom in agreement as he put the lid back on his coffee and said goodbye to Erick. "You take care of that head, and we'll do everything possible."

Outside of the hospital, Tom could feel the sun warming the cool morning air and drying the dew on the lush green grass. Without hesitating, Tom walked purposefully toward the police station. The desk sergeant didn't wait to see what he wanted and picked up the phone to let

Detective Brooks know Tom was there. Brooks poked his head out of the door and waved Tom in. "Thank you, Sergeant Doherty," said Tom as he walked past the desk.

"Anytime," grumbled Doherty under his breath.

Brooks said, "Good morning, Father Brown. Any more illegally obtained evidence we have to share this morning?"

Tom responded, "Not today, Detective. I did stop by to see Erick Comghan this morning. He seemed to be on the path to recovering physically but putting a lot of blame on himself. I was hoping you might have a break to share."

"I don't know. I'm bringing Jack Comghan in for questioning."

Tom raised his eyebrows. "You don't suspect him of being connected to this, do you?"

"In the absence of any other leads, his explanations look very suspicious. There seems to be tension and resentment between those two—and I don't know if something is going on between Erick's wife and Jack. He claimed to have stayed only Saturday night at the hotel and left early Sunday morning, but the hotel records had him booked for Sunday night too. I can't get anyone to corroborate his whereabouts on Sunday afternoon or much of that evening. Plenty of time to be up to no good. I have the same issue with Rachel's alibi, and Addie's, for that matter. I don't know what Jack's hiding, but it's something."

"Are you charging him?"

"I don't have enough for that, but I need to smoke this one out of his hole. We need some answers."

"I told you that I'm not a trained detective, didn't I?" said Tom.

"I think we're both very aware of that."

Tom paced a few steps. "It just doesn't seem like enough to suspect Jack of doing anything criminal."

"Yeah, well, he's gotta come up with some cleaner answers than he has so far."

"I'm sure there's a good explanation for any inconsistencies. Does he have an alibi for last night when Angelo was attacked?"

"It's on my list."

Tom left the station and made his way to the Eliot Hotel. He thought that Addie should know that they were questioning Jack. When he got to the hotel desk, the woman pointed to the pub area, where breakfast was being served. Weaving around the tables, Tom searched for signs of Addie but didn't see her. As he was ready to return to the desk, he noticed two people he recalled seeing at the baptism and approached the table. "You wouldn't be Addie's parents, would you?"

"Yes, we are. You're Father Fitzgerald, right?"

"It's Fitzpatrick, but I've been called worse. I'm very pleased to meet you. Sorry we didn't get to talk after the baptism, and deeply sorry for this terrible—I don't even know what to call it. I can't imagine what you're going through as grandparents."

"Thank you for your concern, Father. This is Addie's mother, Ann, and I'm Shaun Kerrins."

"Please to meet you, Mrs. Kerrins, Mr. Kerrins. I did talk with Rachel yesterday evening."

Shaun glanced at Ann. "I'm glad someone has seen her. We haven't seen her since Saturday."

"Huh. It was just a few doors down from the hotel here. Well, you have two very lovely daughters, and I pray we'll have Elizabeth back soon."

Ann shook her head. "This is like a nightmare. I keep trying to pray, but how often are these babies found? I don't know how Addie's even functioning. She's always been so strong, though. I've always told Rachel she should be more like her sister and good things would come her way, but she's never been a listener. Instead of being so jealous and angry all the time, enjoy your sister and figure out why life's going better for her."

Shaun put his hand on his wife's shoulder. "Now, don't get yourself all worked up again. She's got to be herself, and there are more important things going on right now."

"Oh, I know. I just can't think about it; I can't," said Ann as she began to cry on her husband's jacket-clad shoulder.

Tom noticed Addie approaching the table and stood up to hug her. He whispered into her ear, "Do you have a second?"

Addie nodded to her parents. "Could you excuse us for a second?" They walked to the lobby area and sat on one of the couches.

"What is it? Did they find out anything?" asked Addie.

Tom shook his head, and Addie's shoulders dropped. "No. But they are talking to someone."

"Talking to whom?"

"Jack."

"What?! Why would they be talking to Jack?"

"It's something they have to do to officially rule out everyone in the family."

"Are they going to bring in my parents? Me? Why would they waste precious time like this?" Addie exclaimed in frustration, "They should be out there finding her!"

"I don't fault you for your feelings, but I think the faster they get clean alibis they can verify, the faster they can focus the investigation," responded Tom.

"What investigation? It's already been days, and they have nothing!" cried Addie. Then she lowered her voice as people in the lobby turned their heads. "This can't be good. She could be living in someone else's house right now—or worse. What would Jack be doing kidnapping a baby, stealing, or trying to kill his brother?"

"Addie, they'll ask him to tell them where he was and what he was doing, and then let him go."

"They have to let him go!"

"They will. I did have something else to tell you."

Addie drummed her fingers against her knee. "What else is there? Isn't everything that's happening already enough?"

"Look, um—Angelo and I were in your apartment last night."

Addie's brow tightened as she gave him her full attention.

"We wanted to find some evidence. Well, it was dark when we entered, and there was someone already there."

"What?!" exclaimed Addie.

"Whoever it was hit Angelo over the head in the study and took something—a file box."

"Oh, my gosh. This is never going to end. What did they take? What file box?"

Tom didn't answer but simply shrugged his shoulders. "Look, if Jack has an alibi for last night, then it will show he's very likely not a suspect. I mean, can you think of any reason Jack could even possibly be a suspect?"

Addie paused for more than several seconds before saying strongly, "No! I can't."

"I'll push my luck a little more. Please don't be insulted, but what about your sister, Rachel?"

"What?"

"Can you think of any reason she would do something like this?"

"Father Tom! She's my sister! My parents' daughter."

"I know, but the police will ask both of you. They have to think objectively and not personally."

Addie exhaled through pursed lips. She closed her eyes and rubbed her neck as though it were sore. "If I were the police, I guess you're right. They have to think of everyone. She's pretty agile and strong, so she could do it physically. She seems to have become angrier and more resentful towards me as we have gotten older, but I don't think she would ever sink to something like this." Addie opened her eyes and spoke convincingly, "No! I don't think she could do this. Plus, she told me she was heading home right after the baptism, so she wouldn't even have been in Massachusetts on Sunday."

Tom ran his hand across the back of his head. "She just needs to convince the police. Right now, they said they don't have a clean alibi from Rachel or Jack, or—" He stopped himself short and stood up. "Addie, I'm sorry, but I forgot I had an appointment. I'm really sorry for all of this. Keep praying. Tell your folks that I enjoyed meeting them and apologize for stealing you away."

Instead of standing up, Addie leaned back on the couch to sit and think. She reached up to Tom. "I will. I appreciate your coming over to tell me the news, even if it isn't pleasant news."

"I know. I did see Erick this morning. The swelling seems to be coming down some. I hope he's out soon. Do you know if his parents have come to see him?"

"I very much doubt it."

"Where do they live?"

"They moved full-time to Erick's grandfather's farm in Southbury several years ago. Mr. Comghan, Isaac, has an eye issue and doesn't drive anymore, so they're there most of the time."

"Does Erick visit them often? I know he loved that farm."

"Not for a long time."

"That's sad to hear. Okay, you take care."

"I will. Tell Angelo, I hope that bump isn't too bad."

Father Tom smiled. "He's got a hard head, but I will let him know.

Chapter 15

What Tom enjoyed most about this job was his interactions with people, from joyful moments to the most difficult trials. In them were the stuff of life and the opportunities for people to grow in their relationship with God, with themselves, and with others. Even hitting bottom could be a life-transforming moment, but, so far, he wasn't feeling anything hopeful about the Comghan's or Kerrins' family dynamics. The more he heard, the more toxic and negative it felt, but he was an optimist and believed that no one faced their path alone. He kept thinking that God used others to walk along the way, and he tried to listen for a sign of his role—even if it were simply to pray, which is what he did the rest of the way home.

When Tom reached the rectory, he walked around to the converted shed where Angelo insisted on living, which was small and simple, but much more comfortable than the cell where he had been imprisoned for thirty years of this life. What it did lack was the company of his dearest friend and cellmate, Gianni Fidele. Tom thought of him for a moment and raised a prayer to heaven for him. Gianni had saved Angelo's soul. He knew Angelo often thought of Gianni and missed him dearly.

As Tom tapped on the door, Angelo glanced up with a distant smile. "Father Tom, I wanted to see you. How are you this morning?"

"I've been better. What's on your mind?"

"Remember when we went back to Comghan's apartment last night?"

"I remember, but I didn't get a bump on my head."

Angelo took something out of his jacket pocket and held it out.

"What's that? Is that some of the gravel on the floor?"

Angelo nodded. "Something was bothering me, and that's why I wanted to go back. Most of the gravel was mixed with dried mud, but there were a few pieces of reddish stone, some under where the body was. I found this larger piece nearer to the back entrance."

"What's that telling you?"

"Don't know for sure, but this looked like a fragment of old red brick, maybe from a building demolition site. What caught my eye was the yellow spot on the side here. I could only think of those ads printed on the side of those old brick buildings built a hundred years ago."

Tom held up the fragment to peer at the flecks of yellow. "I think you're right. Should we show this to Brooks?"

"Do you have time for a short walk?"

They passed several blocks before entering some of the poorer and tougher neighborhoods of Boston. Where low-income apartment buildings hadn't yet been constructed, many of the older buildings and homes from Boston's past remained, generally worn down and in need of attention. There were lines you could draw around Boston marking neighborhoods according to the color of residents' skin. Tom and Angelo were now overwhelmingly in the minority and catching the attention of young and old residents congregating on stoops and benches.

When they approached a group of younger men on the sidewalk, one of them asked, "You crackas lost?"

Tom and Angelo stopped as a group of twelve young black men blocked the sidewalk. "How are you guys doing?" said Tom.

The leader was wearing a doo-rag, baggy jeans, and a Paul Pierce basketball jersey over his T-shirt. "Doin' all right." He glanced Tom up and down. Tom was taller, but the boy was broader and more muscular. "Do you need help gettin' back home?"

Angelo pointed down the street to a vacant lot. "Do you know when they took down that building?"

"That old thing? It would have fallen down anyway. They took the ball to that a few weeks ago. One next to it is goin' soon."

"Anyone living there?"

"Not officially."

Angelo smiled. "Thanks. Oh, do you remember if there was anything painted on the building they tore down?"

The young man's face winced with confusion. "What? Wait a minute, yeah, there was a big old, faded ad on the side. Yellow paint. Um—" He turned to his crew. "What was that old picture of?"

Another answered, "It was a woman looking back and holding a cigarette."

A third jumped in. "Cigarette? It was some kind of perfume. It was faded pretty good—but it was definitely perfume that chick was sellin'."

The leader stepped up closer, running his hand across his lips. "Whatcha asking all these questions for? You like Sherlock and what's his name?"

"Watson," one of the others shouted and then laughed.

"Yeah, Yeah. Shylock and Whitson. What's the gig?"

Angelo reached over and zipped down Tom's jacket zipper. When the leader saw Tom's black shirt and white collar, he smiled. "You got me there, man." He extended his hand like Moses with his staff and opened up the path for them to proceed. As Tom and Angelo thanked them and started to walk on, the leader yelled out, "I always wondered why you guys wear those black clothes and white collar."

Tom stopped and turned. "I'm guessing you wouldn't believe that it's just a fashion statement, would you?"

The leader shook his head and waited. Tom said, "Well, black is for mourning and death and symbolizes the death of self for others, and the white collar is just made to be uncomfortable to remind us of that vocation." He chuckled. "Actually, it really means that we are no longer our own but belong to God."

"Huh. We fought all those years not to belong to someone else, and you sign up for it! Sounds crazy, Sherlock." The rest of the crew laughed as Tom and Angelo made their way to the vacant lot.

Tom peered down at the empty lot where a five- or six-story brick building most likely stood. Now it was as if it never existed. The wrecking ball had done its work, and the bulldozers cleaned up the pieces. There was a chain-link fence around the perimeter with one opening cut for someone to squeeze in and out of, which it appeared someone did regularly by the signs of a path leading to the vacant building next door. Tom reached down and picked up some of the remaining crushed brick and cement pieces. He held it up to the sample Angelo had taken from the crime scene. "Yellow flecks, just like the piece you have. How did you find this?"

Angelo shook his head. "I've been walking these streets for the last few days now. I needed to go back and get a piece of the brick to be certain it was the same type. I haven't found any other sites in the area with this match either."

Tom half-smiled and nodded. "Why don't you call me Watson? And how about if we let the real detectives in on this?"

Angelo squeezed through the small opening in the fence. Tom rolled his eyes, bent down, and did the same. They walked the worn path created by earlier footsteps and reached an old wooden door with green peeling paint as the likely entrance to the vacant building. "Angelo, what are we doing?"

"If the person who took Elizabeth came from here, we should find out if they're still hiding here."

"Well, that person also almost killed Erick and then you," chided Tom in a hushed voice.

Angelo quietly opened the door, and they peered into the bottom floor. Despite the sunlight trying to make its way through the layers of dirt and grime that had built up on the windows, it was dark, dingy, and vacant inside. It appeared as if no one had been there for years outside of some possible homeless men sleeping off a bottle of Captain Jack. Tom could feel eyes staring at him and stepped back when he watched a rat on the top of the foundation sill scurry off into a hazy dark corner. He grabbed the fold in Angelo's jacket. "There's no one here."

Angelo silently pointed to the staircase, where each rising step was made a little brighter by the sunlight from above.

The stairs were sure to creak as they ascended, so Angelo felt out the best spot to place his weight on each step. Tom followed the path he marked. By the time they reached the top step, it was clear that this floor was not deserted, with sunlight coming from the southeastern side brightly illuminating a swept wooden floor. There was an eclectic assortment of furniture pieces creating a sitting area, a kitchen-type table with two chairs, and a mattress with pillows and blankets on the floor. To someone living on the street, this must have felt like a homey alternative. The living space was as quiet and deserted as the first floor, except there were no signs of rats. Suddenly there was a loud whistle as steam rose from the counter behind the table. A kettle of water was boiling on a hot plate, and a quick look around showed no signs of anyone there. Tom turned the heat off and moved the kettle. "We should go."

Angelo stepped gingerly over to the far side to peer down another set of stairs that were cleverly padded to allow for a quiet getaway. "Someone was here when we came in. It looks like they can get a good view of that opening in the fence from here. Smart. I just want a quick peek around."

"Okay, but not too long. This place is someone's home—at least for now."

Although it likely took a man to heft some of the furnishings, the décor had elements of a woman's touch here and there, and they could see cast-off clothes of both sexes. As Angelo moved over to the mattress, he turned to Tom and pointed down toward the floor next to it. Tom could see blankets shaped into a crib and some bottles and containers of dry formula beside it.

"I wonder if they've been keeping Elizabeth here? I hope we didn't lose her again," said Angelo.

Unnerved at the thought, Tom spoke up, "Why did we come in on our own? I think we need to get out of here and over to the station."

Angelo agreed, and they made their way to Harrison Avenue. The officer at the desk shook his head at the sight of them coming in the glassed doors. "Good morning, Sergeant Doherty, can we—"

"I already called, and Detective Mullen is coming out."

Jan Mullen entered the hallway and waved Tom and Angelo to come in. "We just finished interviewing Jack Comghan."

Tom tipped his head. "Did he clear everything up for you?"

Mullen opened the door to the detectives' room and let them in. "Not really. He wasn't all that cooperative with certain questions. I don't know if having the FBI agents in there really helped either."

As they sat down, Brooks came in through the door, appearing more agitated than ever.

Angelo asked, "No sleep again last night?"

Brooks gave him a sharp stare. "No, and not a lot of answers or progress either."

Tom asked, "You had Jack in?"

Brooks reached for his cigarettes before stopping himself. "Yeah, he was here. He was okay in the beginning but got a little testy when we asked to corroborate his whereabouts on Sunday and Monday or talk about his relationships with Erick and Addie."

"Are you holding him?"

"Part of me would like to, but I have no solid evidence. Why's everyone in this family so damn sensitive? When I asked him about his side conversation with Addie at the baptism, he said they were simply catching up. You buy that?"

Tom didn't respond.

"I asked him why he said he drove home Sunday morning, yet paid for that night at the hotel. He just said that he didn't realize he booked for two nights. Then I ask him why no one in his neighborhood remembers seeing him or his car at his house in Connecticut. He said there was a lot of traffic, and he got back late, put the car in the garage on a nice night in a safe neighborhood, and went right to bed without turning on the lights." Brooks smirked. "You buy all that?"

Angelo ran his hand across the top of his bald head.

Brooks continued, "So, I asked him where he was last night at eight-thirty. He said he was thinking about Elizabeth and just walked around town for five hours but has no witnesses, no credit card expenses—and no alibi. Now, do you want to ask me how I'm doing? I need a smoke."

They all followed him outside, where he tapped the bottom of the pack before pulling out a cigarette to light.

Tom waited until the detective had taken a long drag before speaking. "Detective Brooks, we might have something for you."

Brooks let the smoke filter out of his nostrils and mouth as he asked, "What do you have now? Is this another break-in for the parolee here?"

Tom smirked. "Only sort of."

Brooks shot him an impatient glance.

"The reason we went back to the apartment—well, Angelo, you tell him."

Angelo flicked off the ashes that had fallen on Brooks' shoulder. "I wanted to go back to take another look at the fragments of gravel and mud left at the apartment. Most of it was gray-colored gravel, but here and there were some fragments of red—seemed like crushed old red brick material. It was in different places than the grayish gravel and dried mud pieces. There was one fragment under where the body was marked, one next to the body, and one by the back entrance. There was no gray gravel by the back door."

"Okay, we noted all this."

"One piece of brick had flecks of yellow on it, like old paint. I walked up and down all the streets around here for hours, checking for a demoed building with old red brick that possibly had a painted ad or something on it with this type of paint. I found a vacant lot with a recently demolished brick building, an old one."

"And where was this building?"

"It was over by Orchard Park. Tom and I just checked it out, and some of the neighbors confirmed it was just torn down recently and that it had a faded yellow advertisement painted on the side."

"There's plenty of old red brick in town. This is a long shot."

"I know. This one had a fence around it with an opening and a well-used path that had a lot of this type of material to stick to shoes with treaded soles."

"How is a vacant lot going to help us?"

"That path leads to a vacant building next door, and inside there's someone or more than someone living on the second floor."

Tom interjected, "It looks like homeless people have used this place for a while."

Brooks peered down at the sidewalk where he had dropped his cigarette butt and rubbed it out with the sole of his shoe. "You think a homeless person devised all of this?"

Tom responded, "We don't know, but it looks like they were keeping a baby there. No one was there when we entered the living area, but—"

Brooks asked abruptly, "But what?"

"A tea kettle started boiling while we were there, so we think they may have run out another exit. We may have scared them off."

Brooks ran his hand through his hair several times. "Great! We have a cold trail, and once the first lead shows up, amateur hour twins may have tipped them off. Isn't that wonderful?"

Angelo piped in. "If they saw us coming in from the window, it was pretty obvious that we weren't cops, so they may return—especially if they have no other home to go to tonight. Plus, the water and power to this building were still on, and that's hard to pass up on for people with nothing to lose."

"You two better hope you're right." Brooks grabbed the sleeve of Angelo's jacket as he started to walk. "Nice work, Salvato."

Angelo turned to make eye contact with him and nodded.

Brooks scowled. "But I'm still watching you."

Chapter 16

As Tom and Angelo stood outside the Boston Police station, neither one seemed sure where to go next. "Angelo, everything seems disjointed. Not knowing where Elizabeth is feels heart-wrenching to me—never mind how Erick and Addie are coping."

Angelo stood with both hands in his jacket pockets, listening and thinking things through. "If she was kidnapped for ransom money, I think we would have heard something by now. If she was held in that vacant apartment, they were either biding their time for selling her for adoption, or there's some personal angle to this we haven't figured out."

"Do you think your contacts might know anything about possible suspects in that neighborhood?"

"I already have some people checking. It's the only lead right now. Are you thinking of the other possibilities too?"

Tom glimpsed the dark gray clouds that had filled the sky. "How did you know?"

"Normally, I would say, 'Andare a fiuto.' That's Italian for 'follow your intuition,' but sometimes it can cause you to lose your focus."

"What do you think my intuition is?"

Angelo responded, "You're a priest. Your occupation is to care about people. I think you have found out a lot of things about the Comghans in the past forty-eight hours, that is—what's the word you used? Disjointed. I think you're split on where to focus your attention: their marriage, family, or finding Elizabeth."

Tom smirked. "How long have we known each other?"

As the sky grew darker, Angelo glanced up. "I think we should move along."

The two men only made it two blocks down Harrison before the clouds burst open, and it started pouring. Luckily, they were in front of the Boston Medical Center and made their way into the lobby while the heavy rain passed, watching with amusement as people scurried by, umbrellas being inverted by the sudden gusts, while others maneuvered around large puddles collecting on the sidewalk.

"You're right, you know. I've known Erick and Addie for longer than we've known each other, but I suddenly feel as if I don't know them at all. Maybe I don't really know you either."

Angelo shook his head. "I'm a single man, and that makes me simple to understand. You are dealing with relationships, and that digs up lots of emotional baggage."

Tom laughed. "Who's the trained psychologist here? Addie said that Erick has been different this past year. With the itinerary and paternity test we found, I wonder if he suspects Addie and Jack?"

"Having an affair? Huh. I guess that'd explain a few things and the lack of good alibis. Maybe Addie didn't go on a business trip, and maybe Jack didn't leave town on Sunday morning."

"I don't know. So many scenarios keep rolling through my brain. I do have a feeling Jack really liked Addie when they were younger. When I spoke to Jack, he seemed like someone who enjoyed family, including his brother Erick."

"And?"

"It's odd he would leave the area and move to England for so many years right after Erick and Addie married, and then when he comes back—"

"Erick starts acting strange, maybe suspicious or paranoid?"

"Maybe," said Tom. "Does he start tracking her whereabouts? You'd think he would have mentioned Jack to me at some point, especially when he moved back to Connecticut."

"Where did he move to?"

"Bridgeport."

"Huh."

"Don't 'huh' unless you are going to finish your 'huh,'" said Tom.

"Some of those places Addie stayed on that itinerary sheet in Erick's desk—Jefferson Point and Sag Harbor."

"What about them?"

"Most people would take the ferry to those towns from Bridgeport."

"And?"

"You told Brooks that Addie and Jack were having a conversation after the baptism off in a corner of the church. You also said that Jack came by to tell you something but never told you what," said Angelo.

Tom replied, "Yeah. He wanted to tell me something in confidence. He either knows something, or something is bothering him. Addie also got very short when the subject of Jack came up a few times. And Rachel is somehow mixed into this."

"Rachel? Addie's sister, Rachel?"

"Yeah. I saw her and Jack together at a pub, but their conversation was short and ended abruptly. Rachel seemed upset afterward. I think she's always had strong feelings for Jack, and my guess is some very strong feelings of envy and resentment toward her sister. I don't know if it has anything to do with Jack or not."

Angelo peered out the window as the dark sky started to lighten, and the heavy rain turned into a light mist. "I think Brooks was right, sounds like a soap opera."

"Yeah, a soap opera that could be killing what should be a strong marriage and four individuals in the process."

They walked out the lobby doors with a crowd of other people who had sought shelter from the downpour. "Well, you're going to have to solve that one after we find Elizabeth."

Just as they started down the entry courtyard, Tom noticed Jack coming toward them, his eyes wide with surprise. "Jack, how are you?"

Staring through them, Jack didn't respond.

"Are you visiting Erick?"

"I'm going to try to. Addie said he was doing well enough to see people for short periods of time. Did you just come from him?"

"Ahh, no. We were actually getting out of this downpour as we were passing," replied Tom.

Jack's coat and hair were soaked. "You were luckier than me." He shook raindrops off his jacket. "You weren't coming from the station, were you? It's only a few blocks away."

"Just checking in. Unfortunately, nothing yet."

Jack rubbed his forehead. "They had me come in for questioning. That Brooks kept badgering me about where I was every second. I don't know if he's getting frustrated with no leads, but he was talking to me as if I had something to do with this—with taking Elizabeth." Frustration edged his voice.

Tom said, "He's short on time and has to check everyone. I know it's hard, but they have to be thorough—especially with a missing baby."

"Yeah, yeah. I know. I just don't appreciate the tone and personal questions. Why aren't they out there looking instead?"

Tom patted Jack on the back of his sopping wet coat. "I think they are. They're looking everywhere. We just need to hope they find the right lead soon. Say hello to Erick."

"I will. Sorry to be testy with you. I haven't slept for three nights now."

"I hear you. I don't think anyone has."

As Tom and Angelo walked away, Jack entered the hospital lobby doors. Tom remarked, "He didn't seem like the guy I met on Saturday, but stress, no sleep, and a missing baby would have an effect on anyone."

Angelo nodded. "He said three nights."

Tom narrowed his eyes in thought. "None of us have slept, but it's only been two nights since the attack and kidnapping."

"That's right, but a hotel and emotional family stuff at the baptism. Maybe he was awake Saturday night too?"

"Could be. Just interesting."

Chapter 17

After a busy morning, despite there being plenty of work he had to attend to for the parish and the school, Tom felt compelled to sit in the church for a while. Inside, it was quiet and empty, but at the same time, there was the power of God's presence as he sat in one of the wooden pews in the center of the church.

He pulled the kneeler down to pray.

It's me. Thank you for all your blessings. Help us to trust in your plan for us. This tragedy that the Comghans are experiencing is a tough one. I ask that you give them strength as they endure this ordeal and please protect Elizabeth, wherever she is. Give the police the guidance to find her safe and sound, and touch the hearts of those who may be holding her. As you know, I'm concerned about the relationships between the Comghan and Kerrins families. If I have a role in this, please guide me to help them heal, and free them to love each other the way they were meant to. Amen.

Tom sat quietly for a good half hour in the presence of God, listening, which always centered him and gave him a sense of strength and peace. He didn't know what would happen, but he felt it was in God's hands, and he would be there for whatever role was needed.

Back inside the rectory, he grabbed a quick bite and was able to close his eyes for a needed nap to make up for the recent sleepless nights. As his sleep deepened, he could see himself winding through a maze of darkened hallways in the school, trying to find the class he was scheduled to teach. He moved along and had to make decisions about which hall to take, but he felt as if he were getting farther away from the room he was trying to find. The bell started ringing louder to signal the start of class, and then he woke to realize that his phone had been ringing. By the time he shook off the daze and made it to the kitchen, the call had already gone to the message machine.

Tom hit the play button. "Father Fitzpatrick—ah, Tom—it's Detective Brooks. Since it was your tip, I thought I'd pass it on that we found the woman who's been living in that vacant building. She claims to have no knowledge of any baby or anyone else living there with her. Of course, our information on the street is that there has been a man living there for longer than she has, and he hasn't been seen around since Saturday. Hopefully, this will lead somewhere."

Tom grabbed his jacket and found Angelo working in the garden. "Hey, Brooks just left a message saying they found a woman who's been living in that building we were in this morning. When they talked to her, she said no baby or man was living there with her."

Angelo leaned on his rake. "There's gotta be something she's hiding." Just a quick exchange of glances, and they headed down towards the station to find out. "You know, nothing is saying whoever did this was a man. The strike on the arm was low, and Erick said he hunched over before being hit on the head."

"It's against the odds but possible."

When they reached the front desk, Detective Mullen was chatting with Sergeant Doherty but stopped as he noticed them. "So, you heard?"

"Only that you talked with a woman who was living in that vacant building," responded Tom.

"It looks like the man living with her was a black guy named Jimi Johnson. He's got a tough past and into a lot of things—drug dealing, robbery, and such. He did some time in Norfolk but seems to have been clean since."

Angelo asked, "Any connections with the Black Market?"

"Not that we know of. So, we've been checking to see where he might have gone. There's been no sign of him since Saturday, so we checked trains and car rental places. Nothing in or around Boston. Then we checked South Station, and the ticket guy recognized his photo but didn't remember seeing a baby. The train was bound for Providence. No one stayed at any of the hotels in Providence matching the description, so we checked with the car rental places in the city—bingo, he rented a car."

"Did they see the baby with him?"

"Yep. The person at the desk remembered him clearly. She said he seemed quietly awkward and in a hurry. She remembers him holding the baby and getting a car seat for the rental."

"Was the baby white?"

"Yep. She noticed but didn't think anything of it. What stood out most was that he was going to Tijuana and only wanted the car for four days— one way, and he paid in cash."

Tom shook his head. "That's a lot of driving. I wonder, why Tijuana?"

Mullen responded as she pointed toward the detectives' room, "We don't know. It's awfully risky to keep a baby that long, and there's more money to be made selling a baby to adoptive parents in the Northeast or California than Mexico. She said they don't allow taking a rental into Mexico, so the drop-off was going to be on Friday in San Diego. That's three thousand miles of driving with a baby, so he'd have to do about 700 to 800 miles a day." She approached the map of the United States on the wall. Her finger started at Providence, Rhode Island, and as she traced it along the two possible routes, she said, "He could have either gone I-80 or I-40. They're about the same amount of time, but Maggie—the person at the car rental – mentioned some road work being done on I-80 to Jimi. So, we figured he might have made it to Columbus sometime Monday night. We checked all the hotels off the highway."

Angelo studied the map as Tom asked, "Any luck?"

"Not at any of the motel names you'd recognize, but there was a man with a baby fitting Jimi's description that stayed one night at the Roadside Motel. The woman who owns the place, Betts Hardy, said she tried to strike up a conversation with him, but he wasn't interested. He appeared tired and just wanted to know where the closest grocery store was. He was gone by early morning. Our guess is that he will make it as far as Missouri—maybe Springfield or Joplin by tonight, so we'll be checking those hotels and have the local police searching for that rental."

Tom watched her finger move along the map. "That would be halfway, but to where and why go such a long way?"

Mullen's hands now rested on her hips. "Hopefully, we'll know soon."

Tom responded, "I hope so too."

Mullen added, "We went back to talk to his companion, Mariana Perez. We have nothing on her in terms of a formal ID or a coherent story. Maybe she's from Tijuana? I don't know. She appears quite ill, though—bags under her eyes, fatigue, and in some obvious pain. It was hard to push her on this, and she offered no information, no knowledge of Jimi or the baby."

As they were talking, Detective Brooks entered the doorway. He rolled his eyes, rubbing his temples with his fingers, and said, "I was hoping a phone call would satisfy my new detective friends, but I should've known better. It looks like you have pumped my partner here already, so what do you have for me in return?"

Tom responded, "Nothing. We did see Jack after your questioning. He seemed a bit distraught by the interrogation and felt he was treated like a suspect."

"Maybe if he gave some better answers, the interview would have seemed more friendly. We are focusing on this Johnson guy right now. I'm not getting any intel that this is anything he's been involved with before. He may be panicking, or maybe he knows exactly what he's doing."

Angelo was still analyzing the route to San Diego on the map. "He must've stayed somewhere on Sunday night in Providence. It would be interesting to know if he was with anyone or met with anyone."

Brooks responded, "We're looking. We're checking everything." He glanced over at the empty pot of coffee and then at Mullen, "We're going to need to fill that up 'cause I don't see much sleep coming tonight. Do we have the word out to all the motels along the highway in that stretch?"

Mullen nodded. "Yeah. There are a lot of them. Local police are ready when the call comes in."

When Tom and Angelo returned to St. Francis, Tom noticed a black car parked out front, much like the one Jack drove. Tom walked out to the curb to see if anyone was in the car, but it was empty. As he circled the car, he noticed the Connecticut plates and then peered up and down the street, but there was no sign of the driver. As he started to walk back to the rectory, he noticed one of the large wooden entrance doors to the church slightly ajar. The church was always open for people to visit, pray, or just sit in any time of the day or night. Sometimes the door wouldn't close all the way, so he climbed the seven granite steps to close it but decided to check inside first. As his eyes adjusted to the dim light, he saw a man sitting in the last pew. It was Jack.

Tom genuflected toward the tabernacle and then sat next to Jack without a word. Jack smiled and laughed lightly to himself. "Two times in church in one week. I haven't done this in a long time."

"How does it feel?"

Jack paused for a few seconds. "I don't know. Part of it feels peaceful and protective, but the rest feels awkward and unsettling. Maybe it's just me who's been feeling unsettled."

"What about?" asked Tom, interested.

"Oh, life. Life's a mystery, isn't it? Jesus is a mystery, right? So maybe life is supposed to be a mystery? I came by the other time to tell you something but didn't think it was right. You know, confidentiality. But it's still bothering me."

"That's a dilemma. I'm not sure I can solve that one for you. I was wondering about something, though. You said you were close to your brother, that you loved him. But, things haven't been so close for a while.

What happened?"

Jack gazed up at the light streaming through the rose window, catching each particle in the air and creating beams of light that felt like the power of God shining down. He laughed again. "I wish I knew. I mean, I know, but I don't really know why it had to break the family up the way it has."

"Does it have anything to do with Addie?"

Jack smiled. "You are very perceptive, aren't you? We both liked Addie in high school. That was okay since neither of us was really dating her. High school was a great time. We hung out together and had fun. The basketball championship ride was such a blast."

"I heard about that. You won the big game."

"Erick won the game on a great shot at the buzzer."

"I understand that shot wouldn't have happened without a very unselfish pass."

"Okay, we won the game together. Who cares? We won."

Tom smiled. "I can only imagine how great that felt. My team was in the tournament here in the Garden, but we lost in the semi-final round. Still a great memory."

Jack seemed to drift off a bit. "It should've felt great, but things changed after that win. Everything was different somehow. Anyway, that was a long time ago."

"Yeah. Sometimes that 'a long time ago' stuff stays with us and impacts us for longer than we want."

"Things weren't too bad in college. We all ended up going to St. Joseph's in New York."

"Is that when you fell for Addie?"

Jack squirmed in his seat, sighed, and then nodded. "I did fall pretty hard."

"And you still love her?"

"I loved her enough to let her choose who she loved and wanted to be with. It wasn't easy, though, and Erick could always tell, so when they got married, I moved far away. I wanted both of them to have what I wished I had. Marriage, a home, a family and—Addie. I wanted them to have a good marriage. England was great but lonely, and I finally thought it would be okay to come back last year."

"Was Erick happy to see you come back?"

"I wish I could say that he was, but I think it was worse than when I left."

Tom hesitated. "This is a very personal question, so you don't have to answer."

"Okay."

"Did Addie ever come to see you on any of her business trips?"

Jack turned to face Tom. "You just go right for it, don't you? I told you that I was helping her to get connected with some of my clients who were looking for legal help. She's my sister-in-law, and I wanted to help. She said it was really important to her to prove herself and own something that was hers and not Erick's. It almost seemed like her self-esteem depended on it. I didn't want to see her like that."

"So it was business?"

"Absolutely. I'm her brother now too. There was one time when she was frantic. Something was weighing heavily on her mind, and she wanted to talk—or at least to have someone listen, which is the thing I struggle with. She didn't say so, but I think she told me in confidence."

"Did it have to do with being pregnant?"

Jack glanced down and pressed the palms of his hands against the top of his knees and nodded. "She wasn't ready for a baby. She was panicking and struggling with the reality of having a child and what that would mean for her career. She was just starting to really build something, and she felt as if it was now all over. She'd be trapped, and the business would die."

Tom peered up at the self-sacrificing love of Jesus on the cross. "Did she say what she was thinking of?"

"No. I don't think she could go through with abortion or anything like that. She'd seen the ultrasound, and it freaked her out that this was real. Erick was so looking forward to having a baby, and she was dying inside and faking her excitement to Erick. We didn't talk about options. She cried, and I held her. We just tried to forget about it, walked the beach, went to dinner, and took a long ride up and down Long Island. I think it helped to calm down her anxiety a little."

Tom asked, "But this has been on your mind because—?"

Jack responded, "Because it just has. I wonder if she's secretly relieved inside. I have asked her about how she's doing, but her answers are cryptic." Jack stood up. "Look, I think I need to go. I may drive home tonight since there is little I can do to help. Talks with priests are confidential, right?"

Tom stood up and into the aisle with him. "That's more for confessions, but you can trust that this is between you and me."

"Thanks." He strode past the baptismal font and out the front door.

Tom turned back to the pew and got on his knees. He was struggling with Jack's information. Addie had come to speak to him in confidence several months earlier. She wanted to understand if abortion was actually killing a real human being and a sin that couldn't be forgiven. Tom didn't know at the time that Addie was pregnant, but he guessed that she was. The conversation was difficult for Tom for many reasons, personal and professional. He remembered Addie seeming stressed and anxious, but she listened in earnest. She seemed to want to do the right thing, but it was obvious that a baby was not what she wanted at this time of her life.

Tom prayed for some time.

Chapter 18

It was close to eight o'clock at night when Jimi pulled his dark blue Toyota rental into the driveway of the Sunshine Inn in Joplin, Missouri. Everett Wilton stood behind the counter as Jimi entered the small reservation office. The man's voice cracked when he greeted Jimi, who was holding the baby to his chest. The baby had just woken and was making purring sounds as Everett nervously smiled and asked, "How can I help you tonight, sir?"

Jimi gently moved the baby into a cradle position. "Just a room for the night. First floor if you have one."

"No problem with that tonight. We have a crib if you need one."

"Sure. Also, is there a food mart or anything close by that'd be open?"

Everett pointed across the road with his pen. "You can have room thirteen over on the right there, and that will be sixty-eight dollars with the tax."

Jimi pulled some bills out of his pocket and gave him exactly sixty-eight dollars in cash. Everett handed him the key for the room with a yellow plastic shining sun on the end of the keychain. "Thanks," he responded and then pulled the car in front of Room 13.

The room had yellow wallpaper, a yellow rug, and a white bedspread with a picture of a smiling sun in the middle. Jimi was exhausted, but the sight of a room that hadn't changed for thirty years made him smile.

He took the baby across the street to the Shop-a-While Foodmart. Out front was a payphone, and Jimi noticed that it was exactly eight o'clock. He put in several quarters and dialed the number on a small piece of paper he kept in his shirt pocket. The number rang only once.

"Hello?"

Jimi answered, "Hey. It's me. How are you tonight?"

The voice answered, "I'm okay, but I think we've got trouble."

"What kind of trouble? What're you talkin' bout?"

She paused, and Jimi imagined her checking around to make sure no one was listening. "The police paid me a visit. They were askin' all kinds of questions about why I was there, who I was livin' with, and about the baby."

"What? How could they find us? Are you okay?"

"Yeah, yeah. How are you? All that drivin'. How's she doin'?"

"She's fine. Sleeping or cooing most of the time, crying the rest until she gets her fill and a change. What did you tell them about me?"

"Nothin'. I don't know no man or no baby livin' here. You take care of her—and you too."

"Call you tomorrow night. Same time."

"Love you."

"Me too. Don't tire yourself out," said Jimi, then he hung up.

At ten o'clock, when the lights were out in Room 13, two police cars quietly pulled in front of the office. No lights, no sirens, just a slow roll of the wheels until both stopped and opened and closed their doors without a sound. Everett Wilton met them in front of the office with a master key and pointed to the room. "That's the car over there. He's checked into room thirteen with a baby. I don't know if there's anyone else," he whispered. The only sounds were crickets from the wetlands behind the motel and an occasional passing car, but it was the quiet of the night that was most notable. The four Joplin police officers and two FBI agents quietly approached the door to Jimi's rented room with their guns drawn for the first time in many moons.

One of the officers gently pushed the master key into the door lock and turned it slowly until he could tell it was open. He glanced at the other officers and waved Everett back into the office as he gave three nods before pushing the door open and rushing the room. They didn't know if the kidnapper had a gun, so all had their colt revolvers pointed toward the bed as the lead officer shone his flashlight around the room. No one in the first bed. No one in the second bed. No one in the bathroom or under the beds. The room was empty. No Jimi. No baby to be found.

Chapter 19

Angelo slid his rook piece into place on the chessboard. "Check."

Tom studied the board, realizing he hadn't paid enough attention to give Angelo his usual challenging game. He moved his king one space to protect it.

Angelo moved his bishop. "Checkmate."

"Hey, it's not like you don't normally beat me."

"True. But not so easy as tonight. Still thinking about the Comghans, aren't you?"

"I didn't know I had a choice. I wonder if they caught that guy. It was Jimi, right?"

Angelo got up and put the pieces back in the cloth pouches. "I think there's only one way to find out."

Agreeing, Tom put on his jacket. "I'm sure we're testing Brooks' limits, but I don't think I'd sleep not knowing."

A handful of stars were visible in the night sky above the lumination of the city lights. As they approached the station, they could see Tony Brooks out front lighting his cigarette. He glanced up. "What a surprise!"

"We know." Tom studied Brooks' face to see if he could read anything into it. "We don't want to waste your time, but—"

Brooks blew out a long stream of cigarette smoke. "But you wouldn't be able to rest wondering what's happenin', right?"

"Something like that. Well?"

"We got a call from the motel Johnson booked in at. He still had the baby with him, and she appeared to be doing okay." There was a small sigh of relief on Tom's face. "Problem is he somehow knew we were coming. Something tipped him off because he was gone when the locals busted into his room. No baby. No bags. No Jimi. He left the car rental, so he must have found another ride. He's either very good, or there's a birdie tipping him off."

Angelo peered straight at Brooks. "It wasn't us, and we hadn't even mentioned this lead to anyone."

"Well, don't. We need to catch this guy before he makes that border."

Tom grabbed Brooks' arm. "You have to at least let Erick and Addie know that Elizabeth is still alive—right?"

Brooks put out his cigarette. "I know what you're saying. It's a tough call."

"Why is it so tough?"

Heading back into the building, Brooks pivoted and replied, "I told you I can't rule anyone out yet. Anyone. I don't have enough evidence, and for all we know, someone in the family may have paid this Johnson guy to take the baby. Or he may be working for one of those baby broker operations. Who knows?"

Angelo and Tom stood silent for a moment before Tom said, "I don't know if I feel any better than before we came."

"Well, knowing the baby is still alive and well is something positive, but finding her will be tough. Very tough."

"There's just so much up in the air right now; I don't know how Erick and Addie are coping."

Angelo started walking down Harrison Street. "Only one way to find out."

When they reached Erick's hospital room doorway, they found him sitting up in bed. "Hey. Thanks for coming by. Doing nothing but sitting here is getting to me."

Tom patted Erick's shoulder. "How is the healing process going?"

"Too slow. The swelling is coming down, but they're worried about infections in the brain, and we're waiting for the concussion symptoms to subside. I don't see why I can't do this at home, though."

Tom said, "There must be a reason to keep you here. Normally they're trying to get you out and free up the beds. Don't do anything crazy—even for you."

Erick winced. "I'm going to come out of my skin. Not knowing what's going on with Elizabeth is killing me—and Addie. Why can't they find this guy?"

Angelo said, "Do you know that it was a guy?"

Erick stopped and thought for several seconds. "I just assumed. Do you think a woman did this?"

"We don't know anything. I was just wondering if you knew if it was a man or a woman—you know, a voice you heard or something you saw."

Erick sighed and gently shook his head. "No. Nothing to tell me for sure. Just an instinct, but maybe not a good one. I don't picture women whacking people on the head and robbing houses or—"

Angelo interrupted Erick's emotional pause. "The odds are that you're right."

Tom changed the subject. "So, Jack came up to see you this morning?"

Erick pressed his lips together and shook his head. "I didn't see him. Maybe I was sleeping."

"Huh, it was right after that heavy rainstorm. We caught him in the lobby when we darted in out of the deluge."

Erick shrugged. "I remember the rain. Addie was here just before it came down but went down to the lobby to get a magazine. I never saw Jack. I haven't seen him since Saturday. I thought he went back to Connecticut."

"He's been around. He didn't want to bother you when you were first admitted. I don't know." Tom exchanged a glance of confusion with Angelo.

On the walk home, both Tom and Angelo were quiet.

Angelo finally said what they were both thinking, "Why didn't Jack go up to see Erick? He walked over during that rain."

Tom peered ahead at the dark sidewalk. "I don't know. Maybe he was afraid to see him and changed his mind? Maybe he saw Addie downstairs, and it changed his plans?"

"Or—"

"Or what, Angelo?"

"Or nothing. I don't know any more than you. I was just thinking of the other possibility."

"Which is?"

"He was meeting Addie all along and hadn't intended to see his brother."

Tom had thought of that same possibility but didn't want to say it out loud or think it was the case.

They didn't say another word for the rest of the way home.

Chapter 20

On Wednesday morning, Tom stared down at the morning newspaper lying on the kitchen table. Across the top banner read, "Sox Rout Yanks 14-3 to Take First Place." Normally, seeing news like that would have brought a smile to his face and a sense of satisfaction. Instead, he had to flip six pages before he saw a short article that caught his attention: "Baby Elizabeth Still Missing." Unfortunately, the article contained nothing new other than another plea from the police for neighbors to report anything they may have seen on Sunday afternoon.

Tom had learned to approach life with a sense of purpose. Despite difficulties and even tragedies that he encountered, God had a plan and would more than take care of any injustices or pain that seemed unfair or senseless at the time. Thoughts about Elizabeth and how her parents must be feeling made it hard to take comfort in that belief, but saying morning Mass did help him to rechannel his energy and rebuild his sense of optimism. After Mass, he no longer felt alone on the mysterious path in front of him.

Afterward, he headed back to Boston Medical Center to see how his friend Erick was doing. As he entered the hospital room, holding two cups of coffee, he could tell that Erick was agitated. He handed Erick a cup. "I'm not sure if you need caffeine right now, but here you go."

Erick leaned forward. "Have you heard anything? Any clues? Anything at all? I'm going nuts lying here not knowing."

"They are pursuing a potential suspect traveling with a baby girl. The suspect avoided them last night, but the baby seemed to be doing well. I'm praying they can find them today."

"Brooks told me that a half-day ago. I need to know what's going on today! Right now!" He took the coffee and peered out the window. "What if he's already reached his contact? What is he doing driving across the country with her, anyway?"

With fondness, Tom pressed Erick's arm. "I don't know what this guy's up to, but I have a strong feeling Elizabeth's going to be okay."

Staring at the ground, Erick didn't respond.

"We're holding a prayer vigil service for Elizabeth this evening. I hope that's okay. As Sister Helen says, 'the more prayers, the better.'"

Tom was back at the church at a quarter to seven as the church started to fill up for the evening prayer service for Elizabeth. Sister Helen had put out the word, and neighbors, parents, and friends were coming to offer their support. Despite the large number of people filling the church pews, there was a powerful silence that filled the air. Everyone held a candle, and slowly, from one candlewick to the next, the candles were lit until the entire darkened church took on a warm, golden glow. The congregation sang the first hymn. Tom was moved by the powerful community feeling as he proceeded down the center aisle with an altar server on each side.

Neither Addie, Jack, nor Rachel attended. Erick was understandably recovering at the hospital.

The songs, the readings, and Tom's homily all provided the community with a sense of strength and hope during an anxious time. It could've been any one of them going through this painful experience, so it felt uplifting to come together as one family in prayer.

After the service, Tom drove back to the hospital to let Erick know how many people showed up to pray for Elizabeth and support the family. "I know you're probably getting sick of me, but I wanted to let you know how nice the prayer service was. There must have been 500 people there, all praying for Elizabeth."

"That many. I wanted to be there. I even thought about breaking out," Erick cracked a half-smile. "I really appreciate you doing it. This has been like a nightmare I can't wake up from."

Tom sat down next to Erick and exhaled a long sigh. "I wish I could say everything you needed to hear right now or give you a guarantee. The only guarantee I can give you is that God will take care of her, no matter what. I just have a feeling she'll be okay, and this nightmare for your family will be over."

Erick nodded slightly and unsuccessfully faked a smile. "Can you tell me what I should be doing?"

"Yeah. Talk to God. Put your trust in him and listen with your heart. Try to be close to Addie. This is certainly trying on you as a couple. How are things going?"

"With us? I wish I could tell you. I think everything's great, and then I feel like I'm with a stranger. I don't always feel like I know her anymore. She seemed more distant and stressed during the pregnancy, and I wonder if she blames me for this. Maybe I didn't do enough. Maybe she never really loved me."

"Erick, don't do this to yourself. Addie loves you and needs to know you love her."

Leaving Erick to pray and sleep, Tom drove his Honda hatchback down the block to the police station.

Brooks was finishing his cigarette outside of the front entrance when Tom pulled up. He walked over to Tom's car with a smile. "I can't believe this still runs. It must be all those prayers, or it's a miracle."

"I think a little of both. Any news?"

"Hopefully soon. We have a roadblock set up just east of Albuquerque, New Mexico. We're expecting him to reach it in the next hour or so."

"Man, I hope you're right."

"Me too."

Chapter 21

The last stretch of highway seemed long and desolate as the sun set on the outskirts of the small town of Santa Rosa. The baby was cooing in the back seat of the new rental car, and Jimi slowed down on the shoulder of the highway. The last stop was a close call, and they'd surely be waiting for him along the way, possibly in Albuquerque. He sat for some time as he watched the traffic up ahead slow down. Rear brake lights began to shine. It could be an accident, but he thought it could also be a roadblock. He slowly backed the car along the shoulder until he reached the turnoff to the old Route 66 he had just passed.

On Route 66, the traffic was moving at a steady pace. A few miles along, he noticed a bright yellow '50s hot rod car up on a post outside of the Route 66 Auto Museum. With blue lights flashing far behind him, he quickly pulled into the museum driveway, a simple metal building with glass doors in front, and watched the police car drive past him. Relieved but tired and hungry, he stepped out of the car and strolled around a few of the old shiny classic cars out front and then peered in through the window to see what he could see. Inside the mostly dark building that had closed at five o'clock, there was a whole showcase of cars from the '30s to the '60s. He smiled at the brightly colored and well-maintained collection before backing up to see his reflection in the window. He stopped to look at himself, something he rarely did as there were no mirrors in his makeshift living quarters. He wasn't tall or good-looking. The lines on his face and the years of struggle and disappointment made him appear older than he thought he should.

Jimi thought about how he had gotten from his childhood to the man reflected in the window. Was there another path he could have taken that would have made things turn out differently? For a second, he wondered why he was here, but then he remembered. As he readied to turn towards the car, his heart stopped with the reflection of blue flashing lights in the window. He couldn't run, so he had to keep his composure despite the sudden rush of adrenaline running through his system and the almost audible pounding of his heart. He could feel a bead of sweat slide down his temple as he heard the officer, now visible in the window, say, "Are you lost?"

Jimi turned slowly. "No, officer. I was hopin' the museum would be open later tonight. I love that red Chevy on the right."

The officer peered in through the glass window. "'56 Bel Air. That's a beauty. What are you driving?"

"Oh, nothin' special. Just a rental."

"Mind if I take a look?"

Jimi panicked on the inside but remained reasonably cool on the outside. "Actually, I'm supposed to be meetin' someone and should be goin'."

The officer turned and asked, "Is this your car over here?"

Jimi didn't respond as the officer walked over to the rental car under one of the building lights. Jimi could see the officer's face now in the light. It was a little pudgy, and he must have stood six-foot-three.

As the officer shined a flashlight inside, he could see the baby in the back starting to fidget. He glimpsed Jimi and back down at the baby. "I think you had better come with me."

"Sorry, officer. Why can't I go with my girl? What have I done?"

The officer opened the back door to stare closer at the baby. "We had a report of someone fitting your description that's suspected of kidnapping a baby girl from Boston. Can I please see your driver's license?"

Jimi never gave up on the possibility that there was a way out of anything, as long as he stayed cool and used his head. The pounding in his chest hadn't stopped, but he never let on how nervous he was feeling. He pulled his wallet out of his back pocket and handed his license to Officer Barnes, the name he could see pinned to his jacket. "Here you go. Do you mind if I take care of the baby?"

The baby did not seem distressed. Officer Barnes hesitated for the longest time, probably contemplating the risks. He leaned over and inspected the back seat of Jimi's car, inspecting under the car seats and baby seat for any signs of weapons. He asked Jimi to hand him the keys and then nodded towards the baby. Barnes then got into his car and got on his radio, most likely checking the plate and name. He watched Jimi gently pick up the baby and lay her on the front seat to change and then held her as he gave her an overdue bottle.

Barnes continued to keep his eye on Jimi and the baby as he remained on the radio, waiting for confirmation. Finally, he got out of his cruiser and approached Jimi, who was still holding the baby. "I need to take a look at what you have in the car."

"What's the problem, Officer Barnes?"

"Can you pop the trunk, please?"

Jimi reached over and pushed the button. Inside the trunk was a spare tire and jack, a small suitcase, and a small yellow canvas bag. Barnes checked around and felt underneath, then picked up the canvas bag to see nothing inside, and finally asked Jimi to open the suitcase. Jimi held the baby close to his chest and unzipped the suitcase with one hand. There was little of interest inside: a change of clothes and underwear, a razor and toothbrush, and some powdered baby formula.

Barnes stared at the baby again and then at Jimi. The baby was clearly without a hint of having a black father or mother. He let out a long breath from his puffed cheeks. The officer stared him in the eyes. "You said she's yours. She doesn't look much like you."

"She's not my blood daughter, but she's my daughter and my girlfriend's. Kind of like a common-law marriage situation."

"Yeah, well, we've got those down here too. They don't seem to work out too often, though, especially for the kids."

Jimi shrugged.

"I'm going to have to take you to the station."

Jimi decided to ask no more questions and got in the back of the cruiser with the baby. At the station, they took his information, asked about his trip and where he was going. They took pictures of him and the baby. Jimi responded, "I haven't kidnapped any baby. This is Marie, and she's my baby. I'm headed down to seek some medical treatments for her."

"What hospital you heading to?" asked Police Chief Cranston. He was a large man with white hair and a mustache. His voice was raspy like an old country singer from Nashville.

"Oasis of Hope."

"Hmm. Is that the one in Tijuana?"

"Yes," answered Jimi. "Where's Marie?"

"She's doing just fine. A female officer is taking good care of her down the hall. So you live in Boston, with all those great hospitals I keep hearing about, and you decide to drive three thousand miles with a baby instead?

Jimi shrugged.

"When did you leave Boston?"

Jimi ran his hand across his forehead and down to the back of his head. He was beat-tired. "Um, Monday. I left on Monday."

"You must be doing 700 to 800 miles a day—with a little baby? That's tough driving." Cranston stared at Jimi for several minutes before Barnes came in and whispered to him.

* * * *

Cranston excused himself and went into his office to pick up the old black receiver. "Brooks? This is Chief Cranston. I've got your guy, Jimi Johnson, at my station. We have the baby girl too. She looks perfectly fine and healthy."

"I appreciate you guys setting up those roadblocks and helping us out on this. Did you find anything else in the car?"

"What in particular were you looking for?"

"I don't know. Weapons, money—anything that could help."

"Nope. Except for the most important item—the baby—it was pretty clean. Suitcase with just a change of clothes, baby stuff—and an empty canvas bag. Bright yellow. No sign of anything else."

"Any confession or information from Johnson?"

"Nope. He doesn't know why we picked him up. He says he didn't kidnap anyone, and the baby is his girlfriend's. Funny, he does seem fond of her—the baby, that is."

"Yeah, well, I just got the photos you faxed over. That's definitely the man we're looking for." There was a long hesitation before he continued, "I don't know. The complexion of the baby seems wrong somehow, and there's a birthmark on her neck I don't remember from the photos of Elizabeth. Chief, can you hold for a second?"

Chief Cranston kept the phone receiver to his ear and could hear Brooks' muffled voice on the other end of the line. "Mullen, can you bring me in the pictures of Elizabeth?" Several seconds passed before Brooks spoke. "I'm holding your photo side by side with our photo of the kidnapped girl. Damn! Chief, are you sure these are the pictures of the baby you brought in?"

"Who else's would we send? You said you were looking for a baby girl. What's wrong?"

"Does she have a birthmark on her neck?" asked Brooks.

"Yeah. Right side."

Brooks quipped, "It's not the baby we were expecting to find. Shoot! I sent someone over to the girlfriend's place to check out his story. Can you hold him for a few until we can confirm?"

"Will do, Brooks. Not too long, though. We like to welcome our visitors to New Mexico and not put them in jail for nothing."

Chapter 22

Detective Tony Brooks appeared highly agitated when Tom entered the detectives' room. "Did you find the guy?" asked Tom with anticipation.

Brooks nodded. "Yup."

But Mullen was shaking her head.

"That's good news then. So you found Elizabeth?"

"Nope."

"What? Did he tell you what happened to her?"

"Nope."

Tom ran his fingers through his hair. "What's going on?"

Mullen responded, "We found Jimi in New Mexico—with a baby girl."

"But not Elizabeth? Who was she? Does he know where Elizabeth is?"

Brooks glanced up. "You just asked me that. We confirmed the baby belongs to his lady friend, Mariana. He claims to be taking her to a cancer center in Tijuana. We checked with the hospitals, and it looks like Mariana had a baby a little over a month ago, named Marie. It also looks like Mariana has had a few bouts with cancer, herself, and there was an effect on the baby, who can't be treated here in the States. They have alternative treatments in Mexico that have been successful."

Tom stood in amazement. "So, what did you do?"

Brooks tapped his fingers on the desk. "We told the Santa Rosa police to let him go. We've been chasing the wrong guy and losing a lot of valuable time in the process. I was sure we had something."

"That's awful. Back to square one with no leads," said Tom as he sunk into his seat.

"Not exactly."

Angelo showed up at the door, and Brooks rolled his eyes at Mullen.

"Look," Brooks said, "we couldn't afford to follow one line of thinking at a time on this one."

"Who are you thinking it might be?" asked Tom.

Brooks responded, "If we weren't already bringing him in, I wouldn't tell you."

Angelo moved closer. "Him? Someone in the family?"

Brooks smirked. "Yes."

Tom was surprised. "You're not seriously thinking that Jack would do this, are you?"

94

Brooks got up and went to the board, and there were a lot more notes written around Jack's picture. "Remember that night your break-in parole-violating accomplice in crime took that bump to the noggin?"

"I'm sure Angelo does. That was Jack?"

"You said that you saw a cab driving away with a lighted ad on the back bumper."

Angelo said, "Boston Bottoms."

"Yup," said Brooks. "We checked all the cabs out that night with that ad on the back. There were three, and when we talked to the drivers, one remembered picking someone up in front of the Comghans' apartment area. They had called for a pick up a few minutes before. I showed him pictures of different people, and he slowed down at Jack's. He squinted and said it was hard to tell at night, and then he said, 'That's the guy. I remember that hair color. It was kinda different.'"

Tom shook his head. "I can't believe it. Wow. Is that enough to bring him in for Elizabeth?"

"It's enough to bring him in for breaking in, robbery, and assault. We have no good story for where he was on that Sunday when Erick was attacked and Elizabeth taken. That still goes for Rachel too, and Adelyn Comghan, for that matter. There are also some overlapping coincidences of them being in a few places in New York and Connecticut at the same time. With families, it wouldn't normally be odd, but there's definitely something different with this family."

"So, you are going to focus on Jack?"

"Yes, we are going to focus on Jack, but we're still working the professional baby brokers and other possible angles. Don't worry; we've done this before."

Angelo asked, "No offense, but how often do you find the baby in these situations?"

"We caught you for your crimes, and we'll catch this one."

As Tom and Angelo walked into the lobby, they saw two officers bringing in Jack, each holding an arm. Jack glared, but Tom couldn't tell if it was a look of fear or guilt.

Chapter 23

On Thursday morning, Tom stopped at the Eastside Cafe for a couple of coffees and walked past the Boston Medical Center on Harrison Avenue until he reached the police station. Sergeant Doherty was coming off of the night shift on the desk and opened the door for Tom. "Bringing treats now?"

"Just trying to be friendly. How did things go last night?"

"It didn't, so we kept him over to think about it."

Tom held out one of the coffees. "Would you like a hot morning brew?"

Doherty smiled and shook his head. "Save it for your bribe. Maybe you can get him to confess. That's part of your job, isn't it?"

Tom smiled back. "Only when they're ready and sincere."

"Maybe that's why people don't go anymore."

Tom entered through the glass doors. Right behind him was Mullen. Tom was surprised and reached out to hold the door. "Good morning, Detective Mullen."

"I hope so. Cases can often take a long time, but this kind can't."

"Doherty said you had to keep Jack overnight?"

"Yeah. Brooks lost his patience. No sleep, and Jack kept saying he didn't do it—but then offered no corroboration for where he was on Sunday or the other night. He went quiet and said he couldn't say anything. Hard to figure him out, but we found a few other items of interest. Maybe if you offer that coffee to Brooks, he'll let you in."

When they entered the detective's room, Brooks shook his head. "You back again?"

"Bearing pick-me-ups," replied Tom as he handed Brooks the large coffee.

"Okay, that buys you something. We found a few more things last night while you were dreaming. He's in the interrogation room right now." Brooks stared at Tom and thought for several seconds. "Look, I've been thinking that we may have a hard time getting through to this guy. When a baby's involved, I don't have time for that, so I may need you to talk to him later and see what he says."

Tom appeared surprised. "Sure. If he talks openly—but if it's a confession, I won't be able to help."

"Even if a baby's life is on the line?"

"Yup, but I could try to convince him to come clean."

Brooks squinted as he took a sip of the hot coffee. "I'll have to take what I can get." He glanced over at Mullen again and then back to Tom. "This is against regulations, but I need you to hear his answers so you can tell if he's playing you when you talk to him later. The interrogation room has a two-way mirror. You can see and hear everything in the next room. We can't hear or see you."

Mullen was rubbing her hands together. "Are you sure, Brooks? This isn't procedure."

"Neither are missing babies."

Tom entered the viewing room and could see Jack sitting nervously alone at a table as Brooks and Mullen entered. Jack lifted his head. "Why are you keeping me? I told you all that I knew last night."

Brooks sat down next to Mullen, across from Jack, and placed a closed manila folder on the table. "We'd be more than happy to let you go if you can help us out with some answers."

"What do you want to know?"

"Exactly where were you on Monday night between the hours of seven and ten?"

"I can't tell you."

Brooks turned to Mullen. "And he says he wants to go home."

Jack ran the palm of his hand across the table. "I can't tell you where I was, but it has nothing to do with anything criminal. What is it you think I did?"

"We have you ID'd, taking a cab on Commonwealth Ave. between eight and nine o'clock."

"I told you last night, I wasn't in that area and didn't take any cabs. I have a car of my own in town."

Tom was watching Jack's reactions to the questions and how believable he might be sounding to Brooks and Mullen. He could tell Jack was highly uncomfortable, but the next question caused him to noticeably adjust his sitting position.

"Let's move back to Sunday afternoon. Can you tell us where you were between one and three o'clock?"

"Sunday? I told you that I left for home early that morning."

Officer Mullen said, "Do you have any witnesses to that?"

"I was driving for a while, got home, and put my car in the garage. I don't know if anyone in the neighborhood saw me. It was pretty quiet, and I took a long nap."

Brooks nodded, but it wasn't in agreement. He opened up the manila folder to expose a grainy photo. "Is this your car?"

Jack took a peek at a photo of the back of a black BMW. The license plate was visible and clearly familiar to Jack as he responded, "Yes. What is this?"

"This was taken a little after two-o'clock—in Boston." Jack didn't respond as he seemed to be lost in thought. "We have a warrant to search your car. Is there any reason you'd like to have a lawyer first?"

Jack's head snapped back. "Warrant? Lawyer? What am I being charged with?"

"We haven't charged you with anything. Just wanted you to know what we were checking. If you haven't done anything, you have nothing to worry about."

Jack sat back in his chair and put his hands on top of his head. "I don't know what's going on here."

"The best thing to do, always, is to just tell the truth. By the way, that Father Fitzpatrick came by to see you. Are you interested in talking to him, or do you want me to send him off?"

Jack sat with his forehead buried in the palm of his hand. "Who? Oh, you mean Father Tom?"

Brooks nodded.

Jack said nothing for what seemed like several long seconds. "Yeah. I can see him. Do I stay here?"

Brooks responded, "No, there are cameras and a viewing room to this one. I would assume you'd want some privacy?"

Mullen escorted Jack into a small room, and then Tom was brought in.

"Jack, I wanted to see how you were doing."

Jack lifted his head wearily. "If you came for a confession, I haven't got one."

Tom pulled a chair over so he was facing Jack without the table in between. He put his hand on Jack's shoulder. "I'm not here for any reason except to see how you are and if there's anything I can do."

"Getting me out of here would be a good place to start. I really don't know what's going on."

"I can imagine. They've got a tough job to do and can't leave any questions unanswered. Did they say why they're holding you?"

Jack stood up and paced nervously. "I don't know. They think I was in town on Sunday. They think I took a cab I didn't take. Now they're checking my car. Do you have any idea why they're holding me?"

Tom shook his head. "I don't know either. Is there anything they're asking you that you can't answer?"

"Nothing that's important to them."

"It may not be, but not answering could look suspicious. They are grasping at anything to try to find Elizabeth. I'd just tell them everything you know and let them decide if it's relevant or not."

Jack sat back down and stared at the old wooden floorboards. "I wish I could."

"If you're protecting someone, you'll have to figure out if it's worth going to jail for."

"I feel like I'm already in jail."

"Is that how you've felt for some time?" inquired Tom.

Jack peered up into Tom's nonjudgmental eyes.

"I'm curious why you went to London for so long."

Jack's squinted. "I couldn't be here. It was good that I left. It wouldn't have been good for me or—or—or anyone else. It was an adventure in life, right?" Jack failed to sound convincing to Tom.

"Have those feelings or circumstances changed any?"

Jack half-smiled as his mouth twisted in a faint laugh. "Everything's changed—maybe not everything. Love is wanting the best for another person, right?"

"The real stuff is. You're right."

"It should feel good, though, shouldn't it?"

"Not always. Sometimes quite the opposite. You told me the other day you were worried about things Addie had told you."

"Yeah, I shouldn't have told you that. Please keep that to yourself."

"Okay, is there anything I can tell anyone for you?"

Jack stood back up. "I just hope they're done with my car soon, so I can be on my way."

Tom stood and shook Jack's hand. "I hope so. Don't hesitate to ask for me if you want to talk about anything—anytime." Tom opened the door.

Mullen stood outside, waiting. She escorted Jack back to the holding area.

Brooks came in from a side door that led to the garages. There was a renewed energy in his stride, and his eyes appeared dilated as he peered up at Tom. "I think we're bookin' this guy."

Tom asked, "For what? What happened?"

"Forensics is going through Jack Comghan's BMW. It's the same one we saw on video driving down the back alley behind his brother's apartment on Sunday afternoon."

"And?"

"The trunk has been obviously cleaned out, but we found some of that same gray gravel in the corner of his trunk. There was also a speck of blood on the lip of the seat. And—" Brooks held up a clear plastic bag. "And we found this pink bootie tucked down under the back of the passenger seat. It would have been easy to miss with the rug curled up."

Tom stared at the bootie and recognized it from the baptism. He remembered Elizabeth being fidgety and kicking it when he was talking with Erick, and they put it back on. A sense of dread shot through Tom's soul. He couldn't believe what Brooks had found.

"That's not all. We have a video from the hotel that Jack was staying at showing him there in the lobby area. He keeps telling us that he drove back home but has no witnesses."

Tom was stunned. "I can't believe what you're saying. This is really bad, except—"

Brooks lowered his hand that was holding the plastic evidence bag. "Except, what?"

"Except that he should be able to tell us where Elizabeth is," responded Tom with a more upbeat voice.

"Right. He has to first admit what he did before he does that. What did you get out of him?"

Tom was silent.

"Nothing?" asked Brooks.

"Nothing other than he's protecting someone."

"Who's he protecting?"

"I don't know, but there's someone or something he won't compromise on."

As Tom turned to leave, Brooks exclaimed, "Wait a minute. Wait a minute."

Tom turned back. "Did you want me to stay?"

"No, no. Something just hit me. Son of a gun. The Police Chief in Santa Rosa said they found an empty bright yellow canvas bag in the trunk of

Jimi Johnson's car."

"So?"

"Come on in and watch this."

Brooks took Tom over to the television in the detectives' room, which was full of other detectives and police officers, all engaged in different conversations. The detective closest to the television asked, "Hey, Brooks. Is it time for your favorite soap opera already?"

Brooks didn't bother responding as he put the tape into the VCR and started to fast forward to the spot he wanted. "Watch this and let me know what you see." They both watched people crisscrossing the awkward camera angle of the hotel lobby, with its burgundy and gold rug and arrangement of couches. "Here." The man entering the frame definitely looked like Jack, who stopped as someone bumped into him, exchanged apologies, and then moved on out of sight. "What did you notice?"

"The time stamp on the video was almost four o'clock on Sunday. Um, it clearly looked like Jack in the lobby," replied Tom.

"Okay, what else?"

"He bumped into someone. They looked like they were apologizing—and there was a yellow canvas bag the other man took. From the angle, it was hard to tell who had it first, but the other man left with it."

"Do you know who that man was?" inquired Brooks.

"No one I've seen."

"I should have seen it before. That was Jimi Johnson, the guy we just let go in New Mexico!"

"What are you going to do?"

"Bring him in—and more questions for Mr. Comghan."

Chapter 24

Tom stood in front of Boston Medical Center, hesitant to go in to visit Erick. He wasn't supposed to know anything that had just been revealed to him, and he couldn't say anything he had heard from the interrogation. As much as he wanted to see him, nothing good could come from saying too much, and he didn't have the poker face to avoid questions. He started walking south to clear his head and think about the morning's news. He stopped at the steps in front of Rosie's Place, the first women's shelter in the country. Tom had volunteered there many times and often brought students from the school to help out. Two women were sitting in front. The larger woman recognized him. "Father Tom, comin' to visit our home today?"

Tom smiled. "I was just passing by and had to stop when I saw two friendly, beautiful women. How are you doing today, Mavis?"

She grinned back. "You know what they say. 'Things could always be a whole lot worse.'"

Tom put his foot upon the first step as he leaned closer. "Who said that?"

Mavis laughed, "Well, I think I did—cause I've seen a whole lot worse."

Tom chuckled. "Do you want to introduce me to your friend here?"

"Oh, this ol' gal here is Theresa Simms. She's all right." Tom reached out to shake Theresa's hand that she tentatively offered. "This is Father Tom, Theresa. He won't bite none. She's quiet, which gives me a whole lot more airtime." Mavis chuckled. "Works out fine."

Grinning, Tom nodded. "I'm sure you have stories of your own. Hey, do either of you know a woman named Mariana?"

"I know two. What's her last name?"

"I'm not sure. Um—Mariana—"

"Asher? Perez?"

"That's it!"

"Well, which one, Father?"

"Perez. Mariana Perez."

"Sure, Mariana. She was here for a while when she was first havin' that baby. Bastard! Sorry, Father. She always hung 'round the worst guys until she met that new one. He treated her good. A little older than her but treated her with respect and dignity like they tells us here that we deserve."

"Jimi?"

"Yeah. Yeah. Jimi. That's his name. Had a tough life himself, but I hear he's been taking good care of her. Not too many men like that. I bet if you weren't a priest, you'd treat a woman right." Mavis started shaking as she laughed and waved her hand. "Well, you know what I mean. I think they're living over by Orchard. She had a tough time with the cancer too. Lots of treatments, but he took her to all of them, from what I hear. I think she had the baby."

"I think it was a girl. So the baby wouldn't be Jimi's?" Tom inquired.

"No. Her 'man' friend," she replied as she made quotations with her finger, "beat her good when he found out she had a bun in the oven. Jimi found her and nursed her back and has taken care of her since. Maybe it's his first girl, but he seems to know how to do it better than most men I've known."

Tom thanked Mavis and told Theresa it was an honor to meet her before continuing his walk down Harrison past a hodgepodge of old rundown buildings, new construction, and vacant lots. He found himself between Lenox Street and Orchard Park housing complexes that occupied some of the toughest street gangs in the city. Orchard Park was the neighborhood he walked with Angelo to find the vacant building where Mariana and Jimi were living. It was still early, and there weren't as many people out. Tom wove his way toward the empty lot and stood staring at the old building, considering his next move. For the second time this week, he squeezed himself between a chain-link fence opening to the lot filled with weeds and crushed brick.

Instead of intruding, he stood at the bottom of the darkened stairs and called up. "Mariana? Mariana Perez? It's Father Tom Fitzpatrick. I come as a friend." He waited for at least ten minutes before he heard any movement above him. "Mariana, I don't want to intrude. I just wanted to let you know that your baby girl is okay. Marie."

A faint voice came from beyond the top of the stairs. "You heard about Marie?"

"Can I come up?"

There was a long pause. "Okay, but if you're not a priest, I will shoot you."

As Tom ascended the stairs, he said, "I guess I'll be safe then."

When he got to the top, he could see Mariana sitting up in bed, appearing worn and tired. "Are you okay? Can I get you something?"

Mariana shook her head. "I'm okay. I want to know about Marie. I didn't hear anything last night. Is she okay?"

"She and Jimi were doing fine last night, and I expect today as well."

"How do you know?" asked Mariana as she winced, stiffly lifting herself to a higher sitting position.

Tom placed another pillow behind her to give her support.

"Thank you, Father."

He nodded as he took a seat. "The police were looking for another family's little girl who was kidnapped on Sunday. They thought Marie might be her and stopped Jimi last night to check. They said she seemed healthy and perfectly fine."

Mariana's eyes darkened, her voice dropping. "How did you find me? Did the police send you?"

"No. I was here with a friend the other day. We were wondering if another baby, Elizabeth, might be here."

Mariana lifted her head and squinted. "Why would you think that baby was here? Who are you? Priests don't go snooping around like detectives in people's homes uninvited."

Tom sat up on the edge of his seat. "I want to apologize for that. We didn't know if anyone was living here, but we had no right to intrude on your home."

She appeared even more dubious. "If you didn't think anyone was here, why were you looking?"

"Just a hunch my friend had."

"Is your friend a priest too?"

"No. He's a thief—or was a thief."

"Well, it sounds like he's still breaking into homes. What's a priest hanging around with thieves for anyways?"

"Jesus hung around with sinners, prostitutes, and tax collectors."

"Now you're Jesus? And I'm no prostitute!"

"I've heard only good things about you—and Jimi too."

"He's a good man. Who are you talkin' to about me and Jimi? Police telling you good things—I don't think so."

"No. I ran into some people that knew you from Rosie's. All good stuff, and I'm sure they're right on the money."

Mariana swung her feet onto the ground and slowly got up. "I have good days and bad days. Do you want some tea?"

Tom started to get up, but she seemed to want to take care of this herself. "That would be nice. You've made this very homey."

The kettle started rumbling as Mariana put two tea bags in the mug and cup she had laid on the makeshift counter. There was no sound of a whistle, but steam began coming out of the missing spout cover, and she poured the piping hot water into each vessel. "I don't have any milk or sugar. Is that okay?"

As she handed Tom the cup and saucer, he answered, "This is perfect."

Mariana sat back down on the edge of the bed and blew air on the surface of her hot tea, tightening her face as she took the first small sip.

Tom wondered if he was her first formal guest. Maybe she'd never had a chance to entertain before. Tom took a larger sip and said, "Hey, this is nice."

Mariana's eyes twinkled as she smiled. They sat quietly and took a few more sips.

"You like being a priest?"

"I really do. I like people, so it works out great. I'm at St. Francis, and we have a nice school. I love the kids."

"So, you believe in all that stuff, huh?"

"That stuff? Like God, and Jesus, and the Church stuff?"

"Yeah."

"More so every day. God's got a great plan for each of us, and it's great to see it in each person I meet."

"What if you never find out your plan? What if you don't have time? Why wouldn't he give us the time we need?"

"That's a good question to ask. I try to remember that the plan is there. It's not ours to come up with; it's his gift to us. God loves us so much more than we know and wants us to know it and share it. Sometimes that plan is difficult but has a huge impact on others—even if we don't realize it at the time."

"Are you saying, if I died tomorrow, I might still be doing something good for someone?"

"Yes. By how you live, how you love, and the example you set. God will take care of us, whether we are sick or there's an injustice. He will take care, and we will know real joy in him."

A crooked smile spread over Marianna's face. "You're really in, hook, line, and sinker—huh?"

Tom laughed. "Jesus did spend a lot of time with fishermen."

Mariana sipped her warm tea and closed her eyes as she swallowed. "So, why are you here today? Are you fishing for something?"

"I don't know. I was walking and thought about you. I guess I wondered how you were doing and wanted you to know about Marie."

"You weren't wonderin' if we took that baby—what's her name?"

"Elizabeth."

"You didn't come here wonderin' at all if we were the kidnappers?" She stared suspiciously at Tom.

"We thought about it when we came the first time. I didn't know what to think this time."

Tom finished his tea, and Mariana took his cup. "Well, thanks for telling me about Marie—and thanks for the company." Suddenly, she gazed into his eyes and nodded.

While walking back, Tom thought of all the lives going on that he would never know about, but then he thought about all the ones he had come to know. He felt like his decision to see Mariana was a good one and thanked God above for the guidance to take the chance.

Chapter 25

On his route back, Tom decided to see Erick again. When he reached the doorway of his room, he could see Erick and Addie in an intense conversation. Addie's eyes were red and puffy from crying.

Tom stepped back. "Oh, I'm sorry. I can come back."

Addie shook her head. "No. Come on in."

Erick said, "We just talked with Detective Mullen. They're booking Jack. This is all wrong. There's no way he would be responsible for this. No way!"

Tom came a little closer. "I think there's a lot of conflicting information. Whatever happens, I think the truth will prevail here."

Erick quipped, "Getting Elizabeth back is what needs to prevail, not being mad about conflicting information. I want to talk to the Commissioner about getting detectives who know what they're doing."

"I think Brooks and Mullen are good detectives."

"Four days, no Liz, and my brother in jail? Really? You call that good?!"

Addie glanced up at Tom. "They didn't even say why they were charging him or where Elizabeth is," she said as she wiped her eyes with a saturated Kleenex. Addie got up and excused herself, leaving only Tom and Erick in the room.

"This is ridiculous! How can they think Jack could do this? What happened to that guy heading to San Diego they were chasing?"

Tom paused. "I think they're pursuing every possible angle."

"Really? Someone can break into your home, try to kill you, steal the most precious thing, and no trace—so, let's just put some family members behind bars."

The nurse came into the room to check Erick's vitals. "Your blood pressure is high, Mr. Comghan. You need to relax if you want to heal and take care of that swelling in your head."

Erick snapped, "I'm not a robot with a turn-off switch for my feelings."

"I know. Maybe some deep breathing and something to relax too?"

When the nurse left, Tom said, "Do as you're told."

Erick tilted his head. "I've tried that, doing all the right things—it doesn't work."

"You do know the police have to be objective with everything, so they don't make any bad assumptions or miss anything?"

"Well, I think they are missing the mark by a longshot."

"They have to look at everyone—me, you, Addie, Jack, Rachel, friends. They can't assume if you're family, you're out of the question."

"I know, but they should've ruled people out days ago."

Tom took a seat across from Erick. "Everyone has to help them rule themselves out too."

"What does that mean?"

"Fill in the gaps. Provide witnesses for where they were."

"Hasn't Jack already done that?"

Tom replied, "I'm not sure. There must be something they aren't satisfied with. If you were them, you'd have to ask—what possible motive could each person have, no matter how seemingly unlikely. If Jack wasn't your brother, you would have to ask that question."

Erick gazed out the window. "I don't think I could do that. I couldn't undermine my trust in him."

"If he did it, what would you say the motive could be?"

"But he didn't."

"But *if* he did. *If* he confessed that he did it. What would you say?"

Erick shifted uncomfortably and changed his sitting position. Tom could see Erick's mind drifting and walking through the possibilities. "I can't think of anything. I can't."

"But if you were an objective detective and had to come up with something, what could it be?"

"Jealousy."

Tom was surprised to hear the utterance. "Jealous of?"

"I don't think he is, but we are twins, and I was first. I was stronger, more of a leader, had more character and did better in school and sports. I hit that last shot. I was successful in the family business. I have acquired things, and his life is empty. I married Addie and now have a family. He's alone. I don't know how I'd feel if I were Jack."

"Would you go this far?"

Erick responded instantly. "No, and neither would he. I don't think he could. I don't think he has it in him."

"Sorry to push that, but that's the type of question the detectives have to ask each of us."

"Yeah, while the actual kidnapper is getting farther away!"

Tom stood up. "Whoever it is, they will find the kidnapper. Let's make sure you heal too. You're not helping anyone if you don't take care of yourself."

"Yeah, yeah, yeah. I hear that all day long around here," said Erick as the nurse came back to check on him.

Chapter 26

Tom opened the side door to the rectory that led into the kitchen. Inside, Angelo was at the counter making up some pasta *Fagioli*, an Italian soup of beans, pasta, tomatoes, and vegetables. It was comfort food to Angelo and always tasted good to Tom. Tom breathed in the aroma that filled the kitchen air. "I did tell you I grew up with an Irish cook for a mom, so I feel like I'm getting spoiled in my old age."

Angelo kept stirring as he responded, "You don't have a clue what old age is yet, young man."

Tom took off his jacket and spotted the mounting pile of mail he hadn't kept up with during the week. He sat down as Angelo brought over two piping bowls of soup for their late lunch. Just as they finished saying grace, there was a rap on the door. Angelo answered it and saw Sister Helen standing impatiently outside. "Sister, just in time for some 'pasta va zoo'!"

Sister Helen shook her head and responded in her slight Irish brogue, "If you had some proper Irish stew, I might be interested, but we have work to do. Running around, as you have, I was just checking to see if you remembered that you still have a school and church to run."

Tom glanced over at Angelo and started to get up before he lifted his first spoonful of soup. Sister Helen quickly put her hand on his shoulder and pushed him down. "Now, I'll not be having you come over on an empty stomach and making all kinds of noises, but I do have a class that will be waiting for you in ten minutes."

"My guilt is greater than I can bear, Sister."

"Ten minutes, Father," said Sister Helen as she gave Angelo a smiling wink before heading out the door and back to the school.

Tom sat frozen at the table.

Angelo said, "That is five feet of someone you don't want to mess with." He waved his spoon. "Eat up before it gets cold."

"She's right. I've been neglecting things around here."

"I think you see a need and respond. That's your job."

"Yeah, I just told Erick we have to trust the police to do their job."

Angelo raised his eyebrows. "Now, I thought that always telling the truth was part of your job."

Tom smiled as he sipped his soup. "Yeah. Yeah. Maybe I haven't had the patience to trust them either. Brooks asked me to sit in the viewing room while they questioned Jack about the night you were bopped over the head. Well, it looks like they found some other concerning items putting Jack right in the middle of this."

"What's that?"

"They have a video of a black BMW driving down the back alley behind Erick's apartment Sunday afternoon around the time of the attack."

"There are lots of black BMWs in town."

"Not with Jack's license plate. It was clear as day. They also have a hotel lobby video of him in town when he said he was home in Connecticut."

"Still doesn't prove he did it."

"They searched his car during the interview and found a few things. Traces of the same gray gravel we found in the apartment were in the crease of his trunk, and—they found a baby's pink booty under the passenger car seat, and—"

Angelo stopped his spoon and raised his head.

"And, there was a trace of blood on the back seat, just under the leather cording. They are testing it for a DNA match. The booty was a match to the one I saw fall off of Elizabeth's foot at the baptism."

"That's not looking too good for Jack. Did he give any clues as to where the baby might be?"

"He'd have to fess up to do that. I talked with him after the interrogation. He seemed dazed. He denied it all, but he was also less than candid about certain things. It seemed as if he could give evidence for where he was on Sunday and again on Monday night, but he wouldn't do it. I don't know what to think."

"Well, that's a lot of things to explain."

"It is. I checked in on Erick on the way home. He was shocked and didn't think Jack would ever do this. He didn't think Jack even had it in him to do it if he wanted to."

"I still think it looks like a two-person job."

"Well, get this. The hotel lobby video of Jack showed him bumping into someone and that someone was Jimi Johnson. It was hard to see, but it looked like Jimi might have gotten a yellow canvas bag from Jack."

Angelo seemed interested. "Do they know what was in it?"

"No, but when they stopped Jimi last night, remember they said they found him with a baby, and in the trunk was—"

"His suitcase with his clothes and a bright yellow canvas bag. That's right, but it was empty, wasn't it?"

"It was. They're going to try to pick him up again."

"One. Two. Two people, two different types of gravel from different places in the apartment. One of them must know something."

"Well, someone knows something. I just—" Tom stopped as he heard another rap on the door. He quickly took another scoop of soup before getting up and opening the door.

Thirteen-year-old Michael Bernard stared up at him.

"Sister Helen wanted me to ask you if your watch stopped working. What does she mean?"

Tom reached out and patted the perplexed seventh-grader on the shoulder. "Let her know we got it going again, and I'll be right behind you."

Angelo smirked. "Priests should always tell the truth."

Tom sipped the last of his soup and wiped the corners of his mouth. "I'll have to remember that."

Chapter 27

After leaving Santa Rosa, Jimi avoided Albuquerque and took another route toward his drop-off destination of San Diego. In the morning, he planned to take a bus to get Marie Perez safely to the Oasis of Hope Hospital in Tijuana. He was surprised by how well she traveled, but then he thought of her mother, Mariana, who complained about almost nothing in her difficult life. He admired Mariana's resilience and positive day-by-day approach to life, especially knowing the reality of her health situation.

The drive through the Apache Sitgreaves and Tonto National Forests was a welcomed break from the boring drive. The forest parks had some of the most amazing scenery he had ever seen, but then, he had rarely left the confines of Boston for much of his life. He marveled at the green forested mountains, lakes, streams, and the rugged, spectacularly colored rock formations and terrain that made him feel as if he were in a western. He pulled over a few times to take in something he knew he would likely never see again. Those were the first moments of peace he had felt in a very long time, and he lifted up Marie, hoping she was soaking in some of that felt experience.

Coming out of the national park, Jimi figured he had another six hours to reach San Diego. Just off the highway, he pulled the car into the parking lot of Cindy's Arizona Café for a quick lunch and to refuel before the last leg of the trip. He sat in a booth and held Marie so that she could have some time out of the confining car seat. The waitress was happy to warm up a bottle for Marie while they cooked the cheeseburger he ordered. He had heard that the meat in the west tasted better than anything he had ever eaten in Boston. As he let the juices from his first bite trickle down his throat, he closed his eyes to enjoy the experience. They were right. Fish was better on the coast, and meat was much better out here.

Before he could take his second bite, a police officer came in, checking around before sitting at the counter. Jimi expected him to be wearing more of a wide-brimmed cowboy hat, but his hat was a flat-rimmed Canadian Mountie-type of look.

Jimi glanced out the window and noticed the police cruiser parked behind his car. Inside the cruiser, he spotted an officer glancing up through the windshield at his car while talking on the two-way radio. Without a baby, Jimi could always find his way out of these situations, but he wasn't without a baby today.

The officer sitting on the stool at the counter sat drinking a medium-sized Coke until the other officer came in, scanned the café, then approached his partner and whispered something in his ear. After a nod from his partner, he walked slowly over to the booth where Jimi sat and politely addressed him. "Cute baby."

Jimi nodded.

"Could you do me a favor and just put your hands, palms down, on top of the table?"

Jimi saw the gun in the officer's holster and made no sudden moves as he placed his hands flat on the table.

"I'm Officer Lopez. Are you Mr. Johnson?"

Jimi nodded again.

"I'm going to have to ask you to come with me and my partner, Officer Jenkins, to the station."

Jimi peered up at Lopez. "Any chance you can tell me why I'm being detained?"

"I think the chief can fill us all in at the station."

At the station, a female officer took Marie and promised to take good care of her while Jimi talked with Chief Fairbanks. Jimi was escorted into the Chief's office. "Mr. Johnson, please take a seat."

Jimi sat in silence.

"We got a call from the Boston Police, a Detective Brooks. They need you back in Boston."

Jimi stared into the Chief's eyes. "I'd be more than happy to go to Boston, but I need to get my baby to the only clinic that may be able to save her life. I don't know about you, but I think that's too important to delay. I've come almost 3,000—"

"I can understand your priorities. I can only comply with the legal requests to get you back to Boston."

Jimi closed his eyes and sighed. He thought about the long drive and being so close to his promise to deliver Marie to the cancer center in Tijuana that could provide alternative treatments. He failed her and he failed Mariana, but none of that mattered more than her life. Jimi pleaded for possibly the first time in his life. "Please. There must be some way you can let me do the right thing for that baby? It's her only chance for a cure."

The depth of sincerity in Jimi's plea would be obvious to anyone. Just as

Chief Fairbanks was ready to speak, Officer Lopez entered the room and called him out to the hallway. Jimi sat and could feel his heart thumping and the adrenaline rushing through his veins. There was no way he could complete his mission of love and mercy. As he was deep in thought, the chief surprised him when he opened the door holding a plastic bag that Jimi instantly recognized. His heart sank. Fairbanks laid the bag on the desk and sat down. "We found this in the lining of the back seat under the infant car seat. It looks like the lining had been cut open and pinned together. Do you know anything about this?"

"I just rented the car the other day. It could have been anyone."

Fairbanks took the bottom of the bag and dumped out the contents onto the desk. There lay at least forty brightly shining, solid-gold bullion coins, enough to make one's eyes dazzle at the sight. "What's that worth, thirty or more thousand dollars? Not like forgetting some loose change that fell out of your pocket. Maybe you just forgot?"

Jimi didn't respond.

He waited for his escorted flight back to Logan Airport in Boston.

Chapter 28

Tom spent the afternoon teaching and attending to administrative work he had let pile up, which felt good, as opposed to letting the Comghan case constantly spin in his head. While some of the students who stayed after school for clubs or to study were being picked up by their parents, Tom stood alongside to make sure the younger ones were off safely. Standing by his side was fourth-grader Billy Hynes, still waiting for his mom to pick him up. "Father Tom, you coach the high school basketball team, right?"

"I do. Do you like playing?"

"I haven't played too much, but someone on our street put up a hoop, and I started shooting a little bit. It's more fun than I thought. I'd like to learn how to play."

Tom gave Billy a big smile. "Your mom can't usually come to pick you up until late, right?"

Billy peered down, a flush working up his cheeks. "Sometimes, yeah—okay, usually."

"How about if we spend some of that time working on a few things each day and see how it goes?"

A white Toyota pulled up to the curb and, as Billy opened the passenger side door, he turned to Tom with a gleam in his eyes. "That would be great! Thanks."

His mother leaned down in her seat so she could see Tom's face. "Sorry, Father Tom. I keep trying to get here earlier."

Tom bent down with his hand on top of the car. "No problem, Mrs. Hynes. Billy and I will make good use of the time."

She turned to Billy. "You aren't in trouble again, are you?"

"No, Mom. Don't embarrass me in front of Coach."

Tom closed the car door and laughed to himself until he noticed someone coming out of the church entrance. It was Detective Tony Brooks. "Are you lost, desperate, or come to your senses?"

Brooks descended the granite steps and pulled out his pack of cigarettes. "I was just passing by. I haven't been inside for a while, and—you know."

"You can come by anytime and for any reason. I was just hoping it was for a good one. How are you doing? Any sleep?"

Brooks lit the cigarette dangling between his lips and took a long drag. "Not too much. It's too hard to stop when a case like this is open."

"I can imagine it's tough on you and your family."

"Maybe that's why we're both still single?" Angelo had spotted Brooks and made his way to where they were standing. Brooks said, "I could use a beer and something to eat. Anyone interested? It's on me."

Tom and Angelo glanced at each other. "And we know just the place."

There were more customers than the last time, but they were able to grab an open booth in the corner. Dempsey came over with menus and a smile. "Well, boys, are we thirsty this evening?"

Brooks said, "I'll have a Guinness, and the tab is on me for these two vagrants I found loitering outside your establishment."

Dempsey laughed. "A policeman offering to pay. That'll be the day in my pub."

Brooks responded, "I think you're mistaking me for your Gaelic-speaking men in uniform?"

Dempsey laughed loud enough for everyone to hear. "No chance of that."

Tom interrupted, "No Irish-on-Italian brawling here. Make it three Guinnesses, Demps."

When Dempsey delivered their beers, he said, "Since we're not arguing, those are on the house." Brooks raised his glass to Dempsey with a grateful nod and then took a long, refreshing sip of the dark red stout.

Angelo asked, "Can you drink on duty, Brooks?"

"Is this drinking?"

Tom asked, "Since you're working, anything new?"

"Still nothing out of Jack Comghan. All that evidence points to him, but he won't tell us where the baby is."

Angelo said, "Maybe he doesn't know that part. Maybe that was too difficult to handle, and that's where Jimi or someone else fits in? If you don't know, you can't tell or be charged."

Brooks eyed Angelo over his beer. "Did anyone think it might be too dangerous to let you out on parole?"

"Just trying to help and make my restitution to society."

Brooks smirked. "Well, I've been rackin' my feeble brain on the same question. There're too many things that don't connect, like how did they get together in the first place?"

Tom said, "Good point. Were you able to find Jimi?"

Brooks responded, "Yup. This afternoon, they picked him up with the baby in Mesa, Arizona—along with something else."

Angelo wiped the beer foam from his lips. "The money."

"Very good, Mr. Salvato," said Brooks, gesturing as if he were tipping his cap to Angelo. "He sewed 30,000 bucks worth of gold bullion coins into the back seat of the rental car, conveniently under the baby seat. Clever—like you?"

Angelo smiled. "And?"

Brooks stared his fellow Italian in the eye for several seconds and then nodded. "And, a hundred 100-dollar bills in his jacket lining."

Tom's eyes widened. "Ten thousand in cash? Forty altogether."

Brooks asked, "Okay, Sherlock and Watson, what does that tell us?"

Angelo said, "That the cancer treatment for the baby was pretty expensive, and—"

Tom finished his sentence. "And, that might confirm that they either sold or found adoptive parents for Elizabeth already."

Brooks nodded. "Maybe. Maybe. Jimi's on a plane right now and is desperate to take care of that baby."

Tom stared down at the table. "Which he can't do from jail or without the money he needed for the treatment. Where's your leverage to get him to talk?"

"I don't know, maybe jail time. I don't know his frame of mind or what makes him tick yet."

"Whatever you think it might have been, I have a feeling there's something different about him than his past would indicate."

Brooks quipped, "So, robbery, attempted murder, and kidnapping is your idea of a changed man?"

Tom scratched the side of his head. "I know, it doesn't make sense. Can we place any of them in the apartment during the time of the attack?"

Dempsey came by to take their orders. "Boys, how are we doing? If you're hungry, tonight we have burgers, burgers, or burgers."

Tom chuckled. "So you only have one offering?"

Dempsey shook his head. "Aren't you listenin', Tom? Burger rare, burger medium and burger burnt. That's three offerings in one—like the Trinity."

Tom smiled. "Not exactly. I'll take a medium."

Everyone ordered the same.

"So, as you were saying, Detective."

Brooks played with the unlit cigarette in his mouth. "Place them in the apartment? Well, not yet. We used the camera that captured Jack Comghan's car in the back alley and tried to see if we could identify any cars that came through between that time and when you showed up at three. There were three, but we could only make out the plates on two of them, so we're tracking those people down to see if they saw anything at the back door." Brooks turned to Angelo. "You still think it would've been more than a one-person job?"

Angelo sat with his forearms on the table. "Could be two or more. If it was Jack and Jimi, they had to get rid of the baby almost immediately. You said that you saw them on the CVT camera in the hotel lobby of Jack's hotel no more than an hour or two after the attack, without the baby, and they would've almost been certain to be seen bringing her into the hotel if they had."

"That's a good point. Hmm. One of the hardest parts of this job is waiting for the pieces to come together."

"One of?" asked Tom. He didn't have to wait for an answer from Brooks as they all sat in a moment of silence until Dempsey came back to the table with three burgers and a basket of fries. Tom said, "We didn't order 'burgers burnt,' did we, Demps?" Everyone chuckled as Dempsey started to pick the plates of burgers back up. Tom put his hand out to stop him. "Demps, nobody can beat your cooking. I was just giving you a hard time."

Dempsey responded, "I'm a sensitive man, you know. You can be shut off at any time," as he walked off.

Tom asked Brooks, "So, what are the possible avenues for moving a baby quickly?"

Brooks took a bite of his burger and held it out as the juice dripped onto the plate. It was easy to tell that he was hungry and enjoying it. "Um. We talked about some of these before: professional black market baby brokers, unscrupulous adoption agencies, directly selling to a ready couple willing to fork over ten or twenty thousand, or maybe a legit adoption agency."

Tom wiped this mouth with one of the napkins and asked, "How would a legitimate adoption agency take on a kidnapped baby? They'd have to think it's legit, right?"

"Sure. You find a young girl and pay her off to take the baby in as if it's hers. Lots of adoption agencies want to offer an alternative to her having an abortion, leaving the baby in a dumpster, or trying to raise her in a possibly drug-infested environment. We've got alerts out and have checked with all the agencies in the state. Nothing yet."

Tom shook his head with concern. "You know, if Jack was involved with this, I just can't see him going most of those routes, or why would he do it anyway?"

"Hey, you don't know all the deeply buried layers of emotions that exist in families. Lots of hurts that can build resentment, anger, and envy," responded Brooks.

That last item on that list reminded Tom of his conversation with Rachel. She seemed buried by her feelings of jealousy and envy for her sister, Addie. She had no alibi for Sunday, and what was that short and seemingly emotional conversation at the restaurant with Jack about? Tom was having a hard time thinking of any of the family capable of being involved in something as malicious as this, but he tried to think objectively as he considered the possibilities. Addie seemed emotionally unready to have a baby and even thought about aborting Elizabeth. Could she have set this up with Jack, who would do almost anything for her? Jack was covering for someone in his refusal to answer questions that might either implicate him or vindicate him. Maybe Addie had nothing to do with this, but Jack thought he was doing Addie a favor by freeing her from an unwanted baby. Maybe Rachel would help Jack with anything because she loved him and would be more than happy to take something, or in this case, someone, away from the sister she was envious of. Maybe it's somebody no one even knows yet.

Brooks stared at Tom. "You're doing it, aren't you?"

Tom tried to gather his scattered thoughts. "What? I'm doing what?"

"You're letting all the combination of possibilities race through your mind. I can tell the look. I haven't slept myself, replaying all the options with this family. Why can't they be straight and help make this right? Using a baby to solve your grievances is unconscionable—at least in my world, it is." Brooks turned to Angelo. "Your mind is cranking too. What's it coming up with?"

Angelo tightly pressed his lips together as he formulated his thoughts. "This had to have been planned, getting all the pieces together to pull it off and move Elizabeth quickly—and without a trace. Whoever did this was thinking about it for a while."

Brooks drank the last of his beer. "Let's hope they start having second thoughts."

Chapter 29

On Friday morning, Brooks stared up from his desk to see Tom standing there with two large cups of freshly brewed coffee and a wrapped breakfast sandwich. "Bribes are illegal, you know."

Tom handed him coffee and the sandwich. "Arrest me. I'm just trying to make sure you're keeping your strength up."

"Sure you are, and you don't want to know if there's anything new?"

"I haven't read the paper yet today, so—"

Brooks unwrapped the sandwich and took a bite. "This isn't bad. Jimi arrived late last night, and we are going to question him this morning."

"What do you think?"

"I don't think anything. I'm hoping a night in the holding cell will encourage his tongue to loosen up this morning. Yes, you can observe, but it goes no further than you."

Tom sat in the observation room for a long time, thinking something must have changed, or he was in the wrong room. Suddenly, the door to the interrogation room on the other side of the two-way mirror opened. The first man who entered was slightly less than a medium-height black man who was thin but didn't appear weak. He appeared more sullen than anything else. Brooks and Mullen followed and directed him to one side of the interview table.

Mullen said, "Mr. Johnson, we're going to record this interview. If at any time you'd like a lawyer appointed and present, we can arrange that. Just let us know."

Jimi didn't respond for a full minute until Mullen started up the recorder. "You don't need a lawyer if you didn't do anything—right?"

Brooks leaned in. "That's not for us to say, but I do want you to be completely honest with us. It's always better than trying to weave stories that fall apart and cause you more problems later. Agree?"

Jimi didn't respond or even glance at Brooks.

Mullen opened her folder to study the list of questions she had prepared. "Mr. Johnson, could you tell us where you were on Sunday—that would be May 7."

"Which Sunday was that?"

"Just this past Sunday. Could you tell us what you did that day?"

Jimi exhaled a long breath. "Let me see. Ahh, I got up and made some breakfast for Mariana. The baby, Marie, was up, and I got her a bottle. We all ate and talked about the trip."

"The trip?"

"I was going to drive Marie to the hospital in Mexico to get the treatments she needed."

"Couldn't you get treatments in Boston?"

"Ah—no. It's some rare kind of cancer. Mariana has been fighting it, but—" Jimi's eyes drifted away from the table. "They have an experimental treatment in Mexico."

"What else did you do?"

Jimi sat, shaking his head. "I packed what I needed, and then Mariana and I just spent the day together. She cried a lot that day."

"Did you go out at all?"

"No. Well, I did go for one walk."

"Alone? Where to?"

Jimi fidgeted in his seat, then buried his face in his hands. "This is one of those lawyer questions."

"Do you want a lawyer?"

"Like I said, you need a lawyer when you did something wrong. I needed the money for the treatments."

"Did you steal it?"

"Like I said, no, I didn't steal it."

"Where did you get it?"

"Someone tryin' to help us out. That's all."

Mullen glanced at Brooks, who said, "Come on, Jimi. Where did you get that kind of money from?"

"I'm telling you, I didn't steal it. I don't know where they got it from. I don't know anything about them or their business. But I didn't steal it."

"Were you on Comm Avenue at any time on Sunday?"

"No. I never stepped a foot on Comm. I can guarantee you that."

"Can anyone back you up on that?"

"That they didn't see me on Comm Avenue? How would they do that?"

Tom almost laughed out loud on the other side of the glass and wondered if they could hear him if he did.

Brooks stared directly at Jimi. "Did you kidnap Elizabeth Comghan?"

"What? Who's that?"

122

"Did you steal 30,000 in gold coins from Erick Comghan?"

"No."

"Why did you rent the car in Providence instead of Boston?"

"It seemed closer to Mexico and cheaper."

Brooks scoffed, "Come on, Jimi. We're not that dumb."

Mullen inquired, "Why did you abandon the first rental car? Did you suspect the police were looking for you?"

"How would I know they were the police? I've heard some stories about how the brothers are treated in the South."

"Okay. What were 30,000 in gold coins, exactly the amount stolen from Erick Comghan, doing stuffed in the seat of your rental?"

"I told the police in Arizona that I don't know anything about that. I wished I did, 'cause it would certainly help." Jimi glanced up at the wall Tom stood behind, as if he were looking right through the glass and directly into Tom's eyes, begging to be believed. "Look, I have a sick girl to take care of, and you guys pulled us back just as we were almost there. I get the mistake if you thought I had this other girl, but I didn't. Where's Marie?"

Mullen responded, "She's with her mom."

"Mariana was here?"

Brooks answered, "We got her to take the baby, but we didn't want you two talking yet."

"Yeah, I know why."

"Well, your stories are pretty close. When they are too close, it's more suspicious, but that doesn't mean you didn't rehearse it before you left."

Jimi put both palms on the table and stared directly at both Mullen and Brooks. "I've got nothin' to hide."

"Well, if gold coins start magically showing up in rental cars, I'm going to buy the whole fleet. You're hiding something—and that little girl better not be one of those somethings!"

"I don't have her, and I don't know where she is. What are we going to do about my little girl?"

Mullen leaned toward the recorder. "Johnson interview, ending at 8:54 a.m." Then she clicked the button and got up and escorted Jimi back to his holding cell.

Brooks stared directly at the glass of the two-way mirror. "See what I mean. Nothing fits."

Outside of the interrogation room, Tom and Brooks stood in the hallway. Tom said, "He didn't sound like he was lying."

"I know, but he's a professional. He's had to lie his entire life, so these answers don't represent truth or lies to him, just a means to an end."

"Do you think he's lying?"

"I don't know. About the gold—of course. But the rest? I really don't know. He wasn't any more helpful than Mr. Jack in the other room."

"Do you mind if I see him?"

"Jack? You can, if you want to."

The officer let Tom into Jack's holding cell. He wondered if there were any viewing rooms in these cells.

Jack lifted his head to see Tom. "This is crazy. I had to call my lawyer to drive down from Bridgeport. He's mainly a real estate and small business guy."

"Jack, there's a lot of evidence they have questions on. If they don't get answers, you might want to think seriously about a lawyer who deals with this kind of stuff."

"So, you don't believe me either, do you?" Jack stood up and put both palms of his hands behind his neck. "It's kinda funny. You have all these dreams about what your life is going to be like, and then none of it happens. It happens to other people." He paused for a few seconds. "Did you really come by just to see me?"

Tom stood by Jack. "I wanted to see how you were doing. Did anyone come by to see you?"

Jack smiled. "I don't really have anyone. I don't think anyone has told my parents, or else Mom would have called."

"Have you heard from Erick or Addie?"

"No. I don't think Erick could see me yet, and who knows what he's thinking about me right now. I don't know if he'd believe I could do this or not."

Tom put his hand on Jack's shoulder. "I spoke to Erick, and he said there was no way you would or could do this, if that's any consolation. Hey, do you know anyone named Johnson?"

Jack let out a puff of air from his cheeks. "Johnson? From where?"

"Jimi Johnson."

"Oh. They already asked me about him and something to do with a yellow bag. I don't know him or anything about a yellow bag. Why are you asking, too?"

"I don't know. Maybe he had something to do with the robbery or possibly the kidnapping."

"Then why am I still in here? I hope my lawyer can sort this out. This is crazy wasting time on me when Elizabeth's still out there!"

Tom stared Jack in the eyes. "If she were your daughter, you'd want them checking every possible lead and piece of evidence, right?"

"You're right. Seems like you usually are. I heard you had a prayer service for Liz the other night. I really appreciate that."

Tom shook hands with Jack. "She is in God's hands—and so are you."

"I'd like to think that's true."

"Then it's a good thing that it is true, whether you think it or not."

Tom called the attending officer and left Jack's cell, asking, "Would it be possible to see Jimi Johnson while I'm here?"

"If he's up for it. Let me check."

Jimi must have been okay because Tom was being brought to his cell. As Tom walked in, Jimi looked up at him as if he had seen him before. Tom thought maybe Jimi could have seen him through that mirrored wall in the interrogation room. "Mr. Johnson, I'm Father—"

"Fitzpatrick. I know who you are, but why are you coming by to see me?"

"Is that okay?"

"Depends on your answer."

"I don't know exactly why. I was here to see someone else and was moved to talk to you. I met Mariana the other day. She seems like an extraordinary woman."

Jimi sat up on the edge of his steel-framed cot. "She is at that. God hasn't given her much of a shake, though. She's been through a lot in her life, might not have much time left, and now I can't even save her baby girl."

Tom sat in the chair next to the cot. "You really care about her, don't you?"

"No one else ever has. Yeah, I do. More than anyone she's known. She's too young, and it ain't fair. It just ain't fair. Tell that to God when you talk to him next."

"I will, Jimi. I will. She seems to care about you too. I can tell that she trusts you. That isn't always easy to earn when a person has had tough experiences in life. We protect ourselves from getting hurt again."

"Look, it may seem like we're desperate for Marie, and we are, but I can tell you, I've done nothing wrong. I didn't steal anything. I don't know where that baby girl is. I just know I need to get out of here to help another baby girl before it's too late."

Tom stood up. "I will see if I can help. Do you want me to pass anything on to Mariana?"

"No. She'll come by. I'm just tryin' to do the right thing here—for the first time in my life, maybe, but I'm tryin'."

"I believe you."

Tom was confused. He didn't know what to think, other than the fact that the facts didn't line up with the stories. Was he too trusting and gullible? He was a priest and had heard straight from the lips of so many people how weak the human condition was. He was also a psychologist and knew how deceptive people could be, even subconsciously, to avoid difficult things in their lives. What was the truth?

As he walked down the hall in deep thought, he bumped into Brooks.

"Hey, thinking too much can be dangerous," joked Brooks.

Tom frowned. "Sorry. I have been thinking a lot."

"Welcome to my world."

Chapter 30

As Tom was leaving the station, he instinctively held the door for the woman entering with eyes focused on the ground. It took him a second for recognition to dawn on him. "Mariana!"

Mariana turned. "Sorry, Father. I wasn't paying attention."

"I wasn't either, so we're even. Where's Marie?"

"She's with a friend of mine, well, a family that took me in for a bit before I met Jimi."

Tom felt relieved. "You coming to see him?"

"Who else would I see here?" she quipped, then regretted it. "Sorry. Not feeling well and worried, that's all. It's not you."

Tom met her gaze straight on. Her face showed a tough life but a tenderness behind her misty eyes. "What can I do to help?"

"Help me get Jimi out. Marie needs him to take care of her. She needs a parent." Mariana seemed more upset as she projected Marie's future. "She can't go through what Jimi and I did. She deserves better."

"She certainly deserves love and care, just like you deserved it."

Mariana dropped her gaze and shook her head. "You don't have to worry about me. My time is up, but she needs Jimi—and Jimi needs her. We need to get him out and get her well."

Tom leaned forward and tilted his head to make eye contact again with Mariana. "That's going to be a tough one. If they have evidence from the crime scene on him and he's not cooperating, it's not going to help him get out unless he has a credible reason. He needs proof that he's innocent."

Mariana rocked back and forth a few times, letting Tom's words sink in. "Okay. Father, thanks. I'm going to see Jimi now."

Tom was back at the rectory, talking with Angelo in the kitchen, when the phone rang. Before he could even say hello, Brooks started talking.

"Did you see Mariana Perez when you left the station this morning?"

Tom glanced across the room at Angelo as he responded, "Yeah, I met her at the front door coming in. Why?"

"Did you say anything to her?"

"Like what?"

"Did you give her any details on the evidence we had on Johnson?"

Tom ran his hands through his hair as he recalled the short conversation.

"Nope. I asked how she was and how I could help. She wanted to know how to get Jimi out. I think she believes she's dying, and Marie will need Jimi. She seemed desperate to know Marie wouldn't be alone. Oh, I did say that Jimi would need proof that he was innocent and to cooperate with you guys. Something like that."

"Well, she wanted to visit Jimi. I told the desk sergeant to make sure I talked with her first. I wanted to get her story before she could coordinate anything with Johnson."

"Did her story match with Jimi?"

"We didn't get that far—she confessed."

"She confessed? To everything?"

"She said she was desperate to get Marie the treatments she needed, and the only place that could offer something that may work would be in Mexico, but the cost was high. She needed 40,000 to begin treatments. She said she had talked to someone who knew the Comghans from one of their grocery stores. They knew he was rich and had a new baby girl. She said she didn't have a gun, so she brought an old baseball bat as a weapon and went to the Comghans' apartment, where the door was open. She entered quietly and snuck up on Erick Comghan, struck him on the head, and took the baby and the gold coins. She said she didn't want to hurt him."

Tom was almost speechless. "She—did she say where Elizabeth was?"

"She says that she doesn't know."

"How can she not know?"

"She said there was a guy that approached her in the street when she was pregnant and asked if she wanted to make a lot of money legally. He told her there were really good couples who wanted to adopt and could give the baby a home, a family, good schools, clothes, and a life."

"This was a while ago then."

"She said around November. She had been through a lot of cancer treatments for quite sometime before and didn't want to hurt the baby. She wanted the best for her but was now living with Jimi Johnson. She said she thought long and hard about it but couldn't do it. The guy gave her a card—no name, just a number to call."

"And?"

"She kept the card and called the number. She says she never saw the guy who called himself Homeboy. She met him at the end of the alley that ran behind the Comghans' apartment complex. He handed her 10,000 in cash and took Elizabeth."

"She must have seen him then?"

"She said, 'No,' because of the black hood, and he got right into a black car that took off."

"Does that sound high—10,000?"

"Parents will pay 20 to 30,000 or more for a white baby from good stock. If it were the mother who was giving up the baby, they might have offered her a couple of thousand, but Mariana was doing their dirty work and held out for more because of the medical costs for Marie, if—"

"If, what?"

"If this story isn't just a story."

Tom shifted the phone from one ear to the other. "Do you think she's making this up to cover for Jimi?"

"It would make sense. I checked her medical records. She went through a lot of treatments, but her form of cancer is highly resistant. If my time to live was short, and I was desperate to make sure my daughter would be taken care of, I might do the same."

"What if she did do it? Desperation can make you do some drastic things, and it would make sense she would do anything to get that money for Marie's treatment."

"There're a lot of things that don't fall into place here—but that's true for everyone we are suspecting right now. We're damn well going to find out, though. Now, did she say anything to you, or you to her, that would help to understand how real her confession is? You do specialize in confessions, don't you?"

"Not these kinds. I can't think of anything, but I'll let you know if I do."

"Do that. By the way, she did ask to see you, though, when you happen to be in the neighborhood again."

"Why would I be hanging around the police station?"

Brooks laughed. "I've asked myself that same question all week."

"Let me know when you get an answer. Thanks for the update, and I'll drop by later." Tom hung up and turned to Angelo. "Did you hear that?"

"Mariana confessed?"

"She did, but she has no idea where Elizabeth is." Tom explained all Brooks had related about Mariana's story.

Angelo asked, "Does Jimi know she confessed?"

Tom responded, "I don't know. I don't think so, since Brooks didn't let her see him first, and she just finished confessing to the crime."

"It's obvious she could do it."

Tom asked, "Do what? Confess or make up a story about doing it?"

"Either. The angle Erick was hit at could have been done by someone shorter, which could explain the initial low blow to the arm. It makes sense she may have been approached by a baby broker when she was pregnant. That would give a lead to someone that operates in or near her neighborhood. Even if she and Jimi were involved, that part about her selling the baby to someone she doesn't know would still make sense—but there are a lot of other things that don't."

"I'm going to see if I can find out the truth."

Chapter 31

Tom stopped by the hospital before making his way back to the police station to see Mariana. When he arrived at Erick's room, the bed was empty. He asked the nurse, "Did Erick get released already?"

She smiled, "He'd like to be released. The doctor said he needed another day or two before he'd be ready. He hasn't been healing as quickly as we'd like, and he's been too antsy to take it easy. You'll find him walking around somewhere."

Tom walked up and down the halls, finally finding Erick sitting in one of the family visiting rooms watching a replay of the Red Sox-Yankees game from the night before. "Erick. Is this last night's game?"

"Oh, hey, Father. Yeah, I didn't get to watch it last night. They gave me something to sleep—saying I'm bouncing around too much."

"Yeah, they were down three to one but won five to three. It was a good game."

Erick's eyes rolled toward Tom. "Thanks."

Tom smiled. "Anytime. They said your swelling has been slow to go down. Sounds as if you need to take it a little easier."

"I can't sit still all the time. I'll be fine. It's not me we should be talking about."

"You're right. I do have a question for you. I know you said that you didn't see the assailant."

"I didn't."

"Do you think it could have been a woman?"

Erick hesitated to respond. "Like I said, I didn't see who it was."

"Understood, but do you think it *could* have been a woman? Any chance?"

Erick was shaking his head but said, "I guess so. I never pictured it being a woman. Why are you asking?"

"No perfume, sounds, or anything else that might give you a clue?"

Erick paused at the possibility. "I don't know. I can't remember smells or sounds other than Elizabeth. She's all I saw and all I want to see." Erick winced with apparent pain. "What's happening? Why're you asking me about a woman?"

"I'm sorry. Just trying to think of all the options. Did you know your brother was still in custody?"

"What? Addie said he was getting a lawyer to come in."

"Addie spoke to him?"

"She must have. How can he be the prime suspect? He's my brother and Elizabeth's godfather, for cripes sake!"

"They also have two other possible suspects; one is a man and one is a—"

"A woman. Who is she?"

"Her name is Mariana Perez. She confessed this morning to the entire crime."

Erick's head snapped up. "What? Then they know where Elizabeth is?"

Tom shook his head. "No."

Erick stood up and winced again. "No? I thought you said she confessed. How can she not know where Elizabeth is?"

Tom responded, "Erick, I don't know, but I'm going to see if I can find out. Keep praying, and we'll find her."

Erick dropped back down to the leather chair he had been sitting in. "You keep saying that, but the days keep passing. What day is it today?"

"Friday, May 12."

"Five days. Five days! It feels like a lifetime. I've got to get out of here."

Tom patted Erick's shoulder. "The sooner you start taking care of yourself, the sooner they can let you go home."

"Home to what?" Erick responded in a defeated tone. "Tom, do you honestly feel like we are going to get Liz back? Sometimes I don't know. I know Addie's as upset as any mother would be, but—I can't always tell where she is anymore. What's she's feeling? Is she feeling anything? Heck, I don't know what I'm feeling all the time. I'm climbing out of my skin one minute, and then I'm just numb."

"I would focus on what you can do. Get healed, and pray for guidance."

Erick nodded.

On his short walk to the police station, Tom thought about how heart-wrenching this emotional punch must be for Erick. Tom felt emotionally torn apart himself, and he wasn't even Elizabeth's father. He thought how much more Addie must be going through after carrying Elizabeth for nine months and losing her such a short time afterward. The bonding hormone for mothers is five times as strong as it is for fathers, and now her baby was suddenly gone.

As he approached the entrance door to the station, he thought that Mariana must know exactly how strong this bond is for a mother. Could she do this to another mother and not be profoundly conflicted? Was the desperation to save her own daughter so strong it drowned out incompatible thoughts like that?

Tom was escorted down a different hallway to a room where Mariana was being held. It appeared to be an interrogation room. Tom stopped and asked the officer, "Is this room where you question suspects?"

"Yes. Ms. Perez is still being questioned, but they're taking a break."

"Is there a viewing room behind the room she is sitting in? Can someone watch or listen in?"

The officer responded, "No one is in there, but it's possible, yeah."

"Would it be a problem to have a room with privacy?" asked Tom.

"I don't see why that would be a problem for you, Father. Just don't slip her any files or anything," chuckled the officer.

When Tom walked into the room to speak with Mariana, he could tell how distraught she was. "Mariana, they said you wanted to see me. Are you okay?"

Mariana looked up with tears in her eyes, but there was a sense of purpose in them as well. "Father Tom, I didn't know if you'd be able to come. I'm not okay, but that's not important right now. Marie's important, and telling you my confession is important."

Tom walked over and pulled a chair to sit face to face with Mariana. "Are you Catholic?"

"My father was. Not a good one, but he was Catholic and had us baptized. Is that important? Doesn't God love all of us?"

"He does."

"And wouldn't he want to forgive all of us?"

"Yes. He has open arms for all of us who want to accept them, but our asking for forgiveness has to be sincere; it has to be real."

Mariana's forehead tightened. "Of course."

"Did you want to talk or make an actual confession?"

"I need to make a confession. I don't know how things will go for me, so I think it is a good time to come clean."

"Okay." From his jacket pocket, Tom took a purple stole with gold trim and a cross on each side and put it around his neck so that it hung down on both sides of his torso. "When was your last confession?"

"I don't know. Probably when I was a kid. Maybe only when I first received the sacrament—that's what it's called, right?"

Tom nodded.

"Oh, wait. I went again when I was a teenager and was on my own, sort of. I don't remember what to do."

Tom smiled and gazed at her with tenderness and without any sign of judgment. "Just take your time and think about things that you may have done, or not done, that you believe are not what God had planned for you. We can walk through each commandment, or you can just tell me what comes to mind that you feel sorry about."

Mariana sighed. "That could take us a very long time, and I don't think I could even remember all of them."

"Just do your best."

"Well, I know I haven't loved God with all my heart and soul, and I know I haven't used his name the way I should. I haven't always told the truth."

"Who do you think you lied to that hurt them the most?"

Mariana thought for several seconds and then responded, "Myself. I don't think I have always been honest with myself, and that has made me lie to others to cover up or hide."

"You're doing fine. What else?"

"I think...all of the commandments. I've been jealous. I've stolen lots of things. I've used drugs. I've had sex with guys I didn't love. I had a baby without being married, and now that's hurting her."

"Mariana, you love your daughter very much, right?"

Mariana bit her lower lip and let a tear roll down her cheek. "Yes."

"And you would do anything for her, right?"

"Yes."

"And you would teach her and give her guidance, not to hurt her, but only because you thought it was best for her, only because you loved her more than yourself."

"Yes. Yes."

Tom leaned over and looked into Mariana's eyes. "I know you didn't have a good experience with your dad, but think of God as the loving, doting, and proud father you dreamed your dad should have been. A father with unconditional love who would run to you and welcome you back with open arms, no matter what. You'd do that for Marie and would long in your heart for her to come home if she strayed. That's the kind of loving parent God is. You are his beloved daughter. He so loves you and wants to be close to you. We are the only ones who can separate ourselves from our relationship with God. Confession or reconciliation carries us back home."

Mariana began sobbing.

Tom took out a handkerchief and gave it to her.

She wiped her tears and blew her nose. "I can't believe he would want me. I can't believe anyone would want me that much."

"Do you think Jimi cares about you? Would he do anything for you?"

Mariana nodded, wiping her nose on each side.

"So you can believe that someone would want you that much. God wants you even more. He made you beautifully exceptional and for a purpose."

Mariana shook her head with the conviction that this couldn't be true for her. "I don't know."

"But you can know. I'm letting you know that you can know."

"Well, I don't think he could forgive me for what I did."

"What you told me? Yes, he can."

Mariana rocked back and forth while shaking her head. "No. It's what I haven't told you."

"I'm in no rush. Take your time."

Mariana struggled to stand up, her movements slow and tentative. "Look, I know I don't have forever to live, and I won't see Marie—" She hesitated to gain her composure. "I won't see Marie grow up. I can't give her what she deserves, but I might be able to protect her from having somethin' she doesn't deserve. She doesn't deserve cancer. I never had nothin', and she may never have nothin', but at least she can have a chance. I know I was wrong to do what I did, but this couple has everything—money, time, each other. They can have another baby. They will always have more money than they know what to do with. I watched them walking that baby and arguing one day—arguing hard. I was thinking about how their baby's goin' to have what I lived with—angry, arguing parents. I didn't feel bad about it when I walked into their rich place and hit that man. I was taking that baby to parents who wanted her—really wanted her. Neither of them appeared as if they wanted her much when I watched them. I knew the money would give Marie a chance. Jimi doesn't know how I got it. I just made him promise he'd get her there and take care of her. He did his part, and now I've gotta do mine and make sure he doesn't go to jail—for somethin' he never did."

Tom saw the sincerity in her eyes. He couldn't tell if it was for the confession or Jimi and Marie, but there was a raw honesty to her words and expression. "So you're saying that you knocked out Erick, took the money and Elizabeth, and then sold her to get money for Marie's treatments?"

"I didn't say that I sold her. I got her to parents that wanted her, that wanted to adopt her. I wish I could've been raised in a home where people wanted me."

"Okay, I see how you were processing this. But you don't know where Elizabeth Comghan is now?"

"Hopefully, in a happy, loving home."

"But you don't know how to find her or the people you worked with?"

"No. I never knew their name or met them."

"And you believe all this was okay to do?"

Mariana tilted her head downward. "No. I know that hitting someone and knocking them out is wrong. I know that stealing is wrong, even if it was for Marie. I want to confess these sins. I'm sorry I did it."

"And everything you have told me is the truth?"

Mariana let out a soft chuckle. "I guess lying during confession wouldn't be too good, right?"

Tom smiled. "No. Is there anything else?"

"Isn't that enough for you? For God?"

"Of course. Are you sorry for all of your sins?"

"I am."

Tom made a Sign of the Cross with his right hand, "I absolve you from your sins, in the Name of the Father, the Son, and the Holy Spirit."

"That really works?"

"Only if you are truly sorry. Jesus gave his apostles the power to forgive sins in his name, and those apostles were the first priests who handed it down."

"So, you're an apostle of Jesus?"

Tom smiled. "We all are."

Mariana glanced up at Tom with a surprised expression.

Tom asked, "Did you want to talk about anything else?"

"No. I think I've talked enough today. I just want to make sure Jimi gets out."

"I'll see what I can do."

Tom entered the hallway where the escorting officer was standing and pointing Tom to the exit from that area of the station. At the end of the hallway, Tom ran into Tony Brooks. "Hey, Padre. I heard you were in with Perez. What did she say?"

Brooks' body slumped when Tom said, "She wanted to make a confession."

"You mean a confession-confession?"

"Yup."

"You mean an 'I can't tell you anything' confession?"

"Yup."

"Big help you are. Hey, we did finally track down the drivers of those two license plates that were filmed driving down that alley behind the Comghans' apartment complex after Jack's black BMW."

Tom's eyes widened. "Really. Any information they could provide?"

"Yup."

"But you're not going to tell me to get back at me, right?"

"Yup!"

"Yours is by choice."

"Okay. The first one didn't remember seeing anything that afternoon, but the second one believes he did. He had a wide truck, so he remembers going slow through that section to make sure he didn't scrape anything— like a parked black car."

"Did he see anything else?"

"He remembers seeing two people coming out of some door. He doesn't remember if they were female or male, short or tall, black or white, skinny or fat—but he does remember one of them cradling a baby. He didn't pay much attention because he was checking back and forth between his two mirrors."

"He couldn't ID anyone if he saw them in a line-up?"

"I pushed him on this, and he said, 'No.' He could barely remember what he did."

"Huh, two people—well three with the baby," said Tom as he tried to reconcile this in his mind compared to what Mariana had just confessed to him.

Brooks could tell that he was trying to connect the dots.

"Yup. Two changes the dynamics of the possibilities. I hate to say it, but it also fits Salvato's theory about this being two versus one and the different gravel samples we found on the rug, but who are those two? Jack and Jimi? Jack and Mariana? Jimi and Mariana? Or someone else altogether?"

"You mean like Jack and Rachel?"

"Or Jack and Mrs. Comghan?"

Tom shook his head. "Almost like being back to a different square one."

"And no closer to finding Elizabeth," said Brooks as he headed down the hallway, leaving Tom to find his way out.

Chapter 32

Angelo spotted Tom as he took the turn down the St. Francis driveway. "We're no closer, are we? I can tell from that walk of yours," Angelo quipped.

"Angelo, you can always tell when something's up—or not up."

"I'll bet you haven't had anything to eat today. Let me heat some spaghetti with meatballs. Sound good, Father?"

"Sounds good." They entered the rectory, and Tom took out the well-worn plates and silverware as Angelo heated the homemade leftovers that always seemed to taste even better the second day. Tom reached into the refrigerator. "Angelo, do you want some Moxie to go with your lunch?"

"Moxie? I only use that to clean out the gunk from the engine in the car," responded Angelo with a smirk as he stirred the sauce heating in the pan over the gas flame burner. "Sure, I'll have one."

Tom laughed and took out two bottles and opened them with a swooshing sound of the escaping gas. He got out a pen and opened up a large notebook to a blank page. "I'm going to write down all the tidbits of information to see if this puzzle makes more sense in black and white."

Angelo said, "Good idea," as he brought the piping-hot saucepan over to the table. He ladled the tasty-looking food onto each plate. Tom cut several slices of bread, and they were ready to get to work on the food and the case. "Let's write down everything, big or small, and see if it connects to anything or anyone. Okay, so we don't have a great alibi for early Sunday afternoon from anyone on the radar so far. We know Jack lied about where he was from the hotel video."

Tom added, "Erick must have left the door unlocked for me, but the assailant was able to enter and sneak up on him without Erick hearing or seeing anything. That's not easy. There were traces of two types of gravel or stone on the rug. We think the gray matches fragments found in Jack's car. The reddish stone with the yellow paint matches the crushed brick in the vacant lot outside of Jimi and Mariana's place. You think there were two people, so that would match up with the two tracks."

Angelo said, "Jack also had the trace of blood that matches Elizabeth and a lost baby booty that matched the one she was wearing at the baptism. That's tough evidence to explain away—especially since he lied about his whereabouts during the time of the crime. There's also a video of Jack's black BMW and a license plate match heading down the alley behind Erick's apartment complex just before the attack. He might have a motive, depending on his relationship with Addie and jealousy of his brother. Or maybe he thought he was doing Addie a favor since she wasn't sure she wanted a baby now. Was her relationship with Erick in a bad place after Jack returned from London? He must have ordered the paternity test because he was suspicious, and even though it turned out that he was the father, who knows what feelings or levels of distrust festered in his mind and soul?"

Tom replied, "Technically, all we know from the DNA test is that Elizabeth may still be Erick's baby. Man, I don't want to believe Jack could ever do this—almost kill his brother and kidnap and maybe sell his goddaughter? Jack's covering up something, and I can't tell if it has anything to do with Addie, Rachel, or who knows."

Angelo said, "The crime itself. There was nothing else disturbed in the house, so they must have come for Elizabeth or the money, and the other was a bonus. It's impossible to know until we know the assailant and their motive."

Tom interrupted, "Oh, and I just found out there was a witness that saw two people leaving Erick's apartment with a baby, not just one, so we have to figure out a likely, or unlikely, pair."

"Did he have any description at all? Man or woman?"

"Nope. He was too focused on squeezing his truck through the tight alley to notice any details," replied Tom as he twirled his fork in the sauce-covered spaghetti.

"Two people. Two men, a man, and a woman, or two women? We haven't thought about that last combination much."

"Mariana confessed to the police that she did this alone, which conflicts with there being two witnessed people. She may be covering for Jimi or someone else. I guess she could've been involved in this with—no."

Angelo asked, "With Addie, or Rachel, or some woman working the black market baby-selling business, or maybe a friend of hers trying to help her save Marie?"

Tom said, "Maybe. She confessed for some reason. If Jimi did it, she could be covering for him or did this with him. If Jimi didn't do it, but she thinks he's going to be indicted because of the gold coins and money on him, she could be trying to take the fall for him—especially since she believes she is dying and wants desperately for Marie to be taken care of."

Angelo stared at the half meatball on his fork. "There's that desperation word again. So, she has a strong motive, either way. Jimi has a strong motive because he would do anything for Mariana and for Marie, which he has demonstrated. Jack may have a strong motive. We really can't know yet for sure. Addie could have a motive, and Rachel could have a motive we don't know about outside of jealousy—or if she somehow thinks Elizabeth is Jack's? A black market agent would have the obvious motive of money."

Tom was trying to organize each item on the paper to align with a possible subject. The ink in the pen was starting to run out, and he got up to grab another one. "You know, I keep thinking about the crime itself. The doctor said that he was probably hit on the arm first, then on the head twice—a lighter blow and then the harder one. I know why Erick says he instinctively hunched his body to protect Elizabeth, especially if that first blow wounded her, but it would seem like he wouldn't have stayed in that position for two blows to the head. You said the angle of his body would've allowed a shorter person to do this, but it didn't have to be anyone shorter. What else do we have?"

Angelo replied, "A potentially paranoid brother or husband, checking his wife's itineraries and doing paternity tests. Oh, yeah, the money. Erick had received a delivery of 30,000 in gold coins. They could've been out or in the safe. I checked the safe, and there was no tampering, and it was closed. Even if you had the combination, you probably don't bother to close the safe if you're robbing it. How would they know about the delivery and the timing? If Mariana or Jimi needed more than the ten grand they could get for the baby, how did they know the gold would be there?"

Tom stopped mid-chew. "Huh. Good point. Remember, the video camera shows Jack bumping into Jimi in the hotel lobby and seemingly receiving the yellow canvased bag, the same bag found in Jimi's rental car. Were the gold coins in that bag before he sewed them into the lining of the rental car seat? Also, if Jimi didn't do it, why did he head down to Providence to rent the car with Marie?"

Angelo stared at the long list of items Tom had written. "The worst part about this list is that it doesn't get us any closer to finding Elizabeth. And Mariana didn't give any clue as to whom she would've sold the baby?"

The phrase "sold the baby" sent shivers up Tom's spine. He responded, "Nope. Never knew their name or saw their face." Tom started rinsing off the dishes in the kitchen sink and noticed someone coming down the driveway. He opened the door before the man could knock. "Detective Brooks, I presume." Tom let Brooks into the kitchen. "What brings you here so soon?"

Brooks glanced at the spaghetti and meatballs Angelo was putting in a plastic container. "I guess I missed a feast?"

"I'll make you up a meatball sub if you're nice," offered Angelo.

Brooks smirked. "I need to go to Providence and didn't know if you wanted to go for a ride."

Tom laughed, "Should I get nervous when two Italians want to 'take me for a ride' to Providence?"

Brooks replied, "You've been watching too many movies, Father. I got a call from a sister that runs a Catholic pregnancy center in Providence."

Tom jumped in, "Visitation House. Was that Sister Gerard?"

"Yeah. You know them?"

"They do great work there for pregnant women who need medical support, counseling, housing, training, meals, and help with taking care of the baby or finding a home for adoption. Does this have anything to do with Elizabeth?"

"Could be the break we've needed."

Angelo handed Brooks a spuckie roll full of meatballs and sauce, wrapped in some paper towels. "Let's get going."

Tom grabbed his keys. "Since you can't properly dine and drive, let's go in style."

Brooks only shook his head as they stood outside of Tom's old beat-up Honda Accord hatchback. "Hey, it still goes—most of the time, and we don't have to worry about it being stolen."

Angelo slid into the back seat. "He's definitely got a point."

Brooks got into the passenger seat, and they were off for the fifty-minute drive to downtown Providence. On the way, Tom and Angelo rattled through all the items they had been discussing and how some pieces were at odds with each other. "Tell me about it," said Brooks. "This Sister Gerard said she normally would watch out for kidnapped babies being dishonestly funneled through Visitation House, but this one didn't connect until she saw the photo of Mariana on the news earlier in the day."

"Mariana?" asked a surprised Tom.

"Yup. A young woman named Katie O'Donnell arrived at Visitation House early Sunday evening with a baby she said she gave birth to a month prior and decided she wanted to find a good home for adoption to give her a chance in life. The girl had come into the house alone, but Sister Gerard recalled seeing Mariana parked in front, waiting for her."

Chapter 33

Tom pulled up to a large old Victorian-style home with a sign outside that read: Visitation House, Where Every Life Has Dignity. The home had been donated to the mission to provide support, resources, and alternatives to pregnant women. Many of the women who came here for support were often poor, homeless, and physically, emotionally, or financially incapable of taking care of a child without help.

They were met at the door by one of the resident girls, smiling warmly with one hand on her hugely pregnant belly.

Brooks took out his ID. "I'm Detective Brooks. Sister Gerard called me to talk."

"Yes. She's expecting you, but we didn't know you had a posse."

"Oh, this is Father Fitzpatrick and Mr. Salvato. They've been helping out with the inquiry."

"Come on in and let me see if Sister's available."

After a few moments, the young woman came back out with a short, sturdy nun wearing a light gray veil that partially covered her blonde and gray hair. She greeted her guests with a welcoming smile. "Detective Brooks, you found us okay, I see. I'm Sister Gerard."

The young woman who had shown them in said, "St. Gerard was the patron saint of mothers. I don't think he had anything on Sister, though."

"Oh, Hope. See if you can get these gentlemen some coffee or lemonade."

Brooks put his hand up. "No. No. I'm good but thank you, Sister. Thanks for seeing us on short notice. I hope you don't mind my bringing a few people also trying to find the baby girl we talked about."

Tom reached out his hand. "I'm Father Tom, from St. Francis, in the South End of Boston. It's a pleasure to meet you, Sister Gerard. I see you're a Dominican?"

"Oh. Father Fitzpatrick, what's a Jesuit such as yourself doing at a Dominican church?"

"Have we met?"

"No, but I know your Sister Helen, and she's told me all about this young Jesuit priest running the parish and school."

"Well, it's really Sister Helen who runs the school. She does a great job. I hope she's had at least one good thing to say about me?"

Sister Gerard smiled. "I'll have to think on that."

Brooks interrupted, "I don't want to break up a holy reunion, but—"

Sister Gerard nodded. "But you're here on more serious business. Come to my office where we can talk in private."

The walls in her office were full of pictures of young women holding their babies and volunteers that had worked at Visitation House over the years from its founding in 1970. Some of the frames on the walls had encouraging quotes of wisdom.

As they all sat down, Sister Gerard asked, "Are you sure you're all okay for a hot or cold drink?" They all nodded. "So, I called you about a baby whom I think may be the girl you're looking for. I'm not completely sure, but I did recognize that woman, Mariana Perez, from the news."

Brooks said, "First, thank you for calling. Can you tell us everything from the start? Don't worry about too much detail; the more, the better."

Sister Gerard sat with her hands folded on her desk. "Well, we encourage women who are in a pregnancy situation that is less than ideal to come in for help – everything from talking to staying with us until they've had the baby and they know how to care for him or her. We don't judge the situation; we only offer help and encouragement. For those girls, young women, who, for whatever reason, don't want the baby or cannot care and raise this new person, we offer an alternative to abortion. Many couples want to adopt, so we do help them in making that choice.

"Early Sunday evening, Katie O'Donnell arrived at our door with a young baby girl in her arms. She said that she gave birth to her about a month ago and tried to care for her, but felt as if adoption would be the right thing to do for her baby." Sister Gerard glanced up. "You might be surprised how many girls go this far, only to abandon the baby. The responsibility is too overwhelming for girls who often cannot cope with even taking care of themselves. The romantic image of being a mom takes on the realness of the work, dedication, and self-sacrificing love, so some end up at our door, asking if we can help to find a good home for the baby."

Brooks asked, "What did this girl Katie say?"

"I don't know if she knew what to say. She's eighteen and homeless. She held the baby next to her chest and cried. We asked what she needed, and she said she wanted to find a couple who couldn't have a baby of their own and wanted one to love and care for. We asked her if she had the baby's birth certificate, and she said she didn't know how to get one. There were no reports of missing babies in Rhode Island, and we hadn't heard about the girl you're looking for yet—Elizabeth, you said?"

"Yes, Elizabeth Comghan. So, you agreed to take the baby and help her find a family?"

Sister Gerard responded, "Yes. In this case, there was a perfect couple already waiting. They had come to us earlier and offered a donation of support for Visitation House. We talked, and they were anxious to start their family through adoption because they were not able to conceive naturally. They're devout Catholics and a couple I'd be honored to help to adopt. They wondered if we could call them if we ever had a young mother wanting to place her baby girl up for adoption."

"So, they specifically asked for a girl?"

"Yes. It's not unusual. When Katie showed up at our door only days later, I figured it was the Lord's hand in this, and I gave them a call. They came immediately and met Katie and the baby. I've never seen a couple so happy, and Katie seemed more than pleased with them."

Tom asked, "Sister, would the couple take the baby immediately in a situation like that?"

Sister Gerard replied, "No, we took the baby in and made sure all the legal and government paperwork was in order, and the couple was checked out first. That went very smoothly, and we were able to let them take the baby home on Wednesday."

Brooks interrupted, "Back to when this couple came after your call. What happened after they met Katie and Elizabeth?"

"They talked in private for a short time, then we told them how the process would work, and everyone seemed happy. At the end of the visit, Katie was picked up by someone in a car. The Larsens – that's the couple's name, Sam and Becky – walked her to the car to say goodbye. They talked to the woman driving the car, and at one point, she turned and looked at me and then quickly turned away, but I remembered the expression on her face. When I saw the news, there she was in the photo. I have no doubts about it being the same woman."

"Nothing else?"

"Not anything remarkable. The girl has no record or home. I'm not sure you could even find her. The Larsons just seemed like a wonderful, generous, and loving couple. I almost hate to think about them having to lose Esther."

"You mean, Elizabeth?"

"Sure. But they called her Esther after Becky Larson's grandmother. There wasn't anything that raised red flags. Unfortunately, there are a lot of young girls in this situation, and more often than not, they opt for ending the baby's life as their only choice. It's sad."

Brooks took out a photo of Elizabeth and placed it on the desk in front of Sister George. She stared at it for several seconds and then said, "That's her."

"Are you certain?"

"I remember the pretty auburn hair and that smile. She's a beautiful baby."

Brooks pulled the photo back. "Would you still have the address of Sam and Becky Larson?"

"Yes, of course." Sister George got up to find their folder and opened it up. "Here it is, 10 Allen Lane, Wickford, Rhode Island. It's a pretty town on the coast, just a half-hour down I-95."

Tom said, "Thank you, Sister. There's a very anxious couple in Boston who'll be so glad to know their baby's okay. Have you seen Katie or the Larsons since?"

"Katie, no. The Larsons? Not since Wednesday."

"And the woman you saw in the car. Anything about how she appeared that stood out?"

"Just the way she quickly looked away when we made eye contact. It was across the drive, but she didn't look comfortable."

They all stood up and thanked her again before getting back into Tom's old Honda. As Sister Gerard waved goodbye, she said, "Let me know if there's anything else I can do to help."

Brooks leaned his head out of the open car door window. "You can pray that this Jesuit's car makes it there in one piece." Everyone laughed as they headed down to the coastal town of Wickford.

Chapter 34

The ride from Providence to Wickford was a welcome break from the bustle of the city. As they got closer to the historic town on the ocean, the salt air was refreshing. Brooks said, "This is crazy."

"What's crazy?" asked Tom.

"That I am doing official police work in this car—with the two of you! That's crazy."

Angelo called out from the cramped back seat. "Hey, we can go without you, if that helps."

Brooks laughed out loud and pointed out the window. "Sure, I'll take out one of these yachts while you solve the case. Just let me know when you're close." The harbor was quaint and picturesque, as were the old rose-colored brick storefronts and antique homes dating back to the early 1700s. It was the kind of town that inspired people to quit the hassle of city life and breathe a little. Each turn Tom took led them down another tree-lined road bordered by charming, antique houses and peeks of the waterfront. They finally pulled in front of 10 Allen Lane. The home was newer but architecturally appropriate for the town and appeared to belong to a well-off family.

Brooks asked Tom and Angelo to stay in the car as he approached the front door and used the brass shell knocker to announce himself. No answer. He knocked again. No answer. He peered in through the door window. There was no sign of life. No car in the driveway. Returning to the car, Brooks said, "Looks like no one's home. Maybe they're both at work, but it seems odd with a new baby."

Angelo said, "Maybe they're out for a stroll?"

Brooks ran the palm of his hand across his mouth. "No car. A few days of mail in the box. I'm not so sure." As he stood outside of the car peering up and down the sidewalk, a woman approached, walking her small armpit-sized dog. Brooks asked her, "Do you live close by?"

Her head pulled back a little, and she answered, "Two doors down. I don't think the Larsons are selling. They just got a new baby."

"Did you see the baby?"

"Sure did. A very sweet little girl." The woman's eyes narrowed. "Why are you asking?"

"We're just friends who came to visit Becky and Sam—and Esther, of course."

The fact that Brooks knew the baby's name seemed to put her more at ease. "It's wonderful, isn't it? I think they'll be perfect parents. They're so excited."

"I know. They've tried for so long and to find a baby girl like Elizabeth—"

"You mean Esther?"

"Sorry, slip of the tongue. Well, would you know where they might be today?"

"I might."

"We just wanted to know if we should wait or not."

"Probably not. They asked me to check up on the house. They took the baby to Becky's mother to show her off. I bet she'll just be beside herself—Becky being her only child."

"Do you know when they planned on returning?" asked Brooks.

"Sunday afternoon, you know, so they could spend Mother's Day morning with her mom."

"Hmm. Maybe I can reach her there. Do you have the mother's address?"

The woman appeared perplexed as she glanced down at her dog for any help. "Well, no. We don't know. I should find out someday. Good to know these things. I just came by to get the mail, and I do have to get going on my walk. Captain Parker here is fairly regular."

Brooks smiled as she strutted off with Captain Parker enthusiastically tugging her along. When he sat back down in the car, he said, "Nothing in this case is going to go smoothly, is it?"

Tom started up the engine. "Tell you what. We are going to hit traffic at this time of the day. Let me take you to Gregg's for some fried clams and any dessert you want—although the chocolate cake they make is hard to beat."

Brooks agreed, then called his partner Mullen to ask her to find out Becky Larson's parents' address. During dinner, they tried to think of all the reasons that their current suspect candidates could or couldn't be the guilty party. Since it had to be two people, it made it even more complicated. Mariana's confession seemed to have some truth to it but not all. As they left the restaurant feeling stuffed and satisfied, Brooks received a call. "Mullen, what've you got? Okay. Okay. Thanks." Brooks turned to Tom and Angelo. "We've got the address and phone number for Becky Larson's parents. I'm going to try to reach her."

Angelo asked, "Where do they live?"

"New Britain, Connecticut. Why?"

"That's an hour and a half from here. Maybe this is news better delivered in person?"

"Well, I don't think waiting till tomorrow to find out if this is Elizabeth is a good idea," replied Brooks.

Angelo opened the car door. "Then let's not wait till tomorrow."

Tom glanced at Brooks, shrugged his shoulders, and got into the car. After driving to New Britain, they found the residence of Becky's parents. Suddenly, as Brooks rang the doorbell, the thought of telling the parents that their new baby was no longer going to be theirs seemed like a daunting task. A man in his mid-sixties greeted them with a broad smile. "Hello, gentlemen, what can I help you with this evening?"

Brooks replied, "We were wondering if your daughter might be here?"

"And who would you be?"

Brooks took out his badge. "Boston Police. We have some very important questions for your daughter and son-in-law."

"They can't be in trouble. What's wrong?"

"It's about Esther."

"Oh, come in. Let me see if I can get them."

Brooks, Tom, and Angelo were escorted to the living room, where Sam arrived moments later. They all stood as Sam entered.

Sam stared at them, bewildered. "What's this about Esther?"

Then Becky stepped in and stood behind him with an anxious expression on her face.

Brooks said, "It might be better if you both sat down."

Sam held Becky's hand as they sat close to each other as everyone took seats.

"There was a kidnapping of a baby girl in Boston this past Sunday. We think she may be the same baby you're in the process of adopting."

Becky screamed, leaned her head onto Sam's shoulder and began crying.

"We would need to see her to confirm this."

Becky continued to cry. She ran out of the room, sobbing, "No! Not Esther!"

Sam remained in the room, his eyes blank. "She's asleep right now."

Brooks took out a picture of Elizabeth, and Sam's whole body drooped. He sat with his eyes closed as he nodded in affirmation that this was the same baby.

Brooks said, "I'm so sorry about this. You can imagine what the parents have been going through this week, but I can also imagine this is no less difficult for you and your wife right now."

Sam appeared shell-shocked as the painful reality set in.

"I need to ask you a few questions."

Sam nodded mechanically as Brooks inquired, "Did you know about Visitation House before this week?"

Sam took a deep breath. "Um, we first heard about it a month or so ago."

"Do you remember who you heard that from?"

"Um. Becky and I were at a fundraiser for Multiple Sclerosis. It's an annual event of the New England Small Business Association. Small and mid-sized company owners get together. Um, it's a large gathering, so we normally end up socializing with people we know from Rhode Island. We started talking to someone we hadn't met before. He asked about kids, and we told him we had tried but couldn't have any children." Sam paused to collect himself. "We were interrupted by some other couples we knew, so there wasn't much more to our conversation."

"So, he told you about Visitation House there at the fundraiser?"

"No. He must have looked up our number or something because he called us a few weeks ago, reminding me who he was, and said he was thinking about our conversation. He said he met this young girl who recently had a baby and wanted to find a good loving home for her. He said the girl and her mother would be taking the baby to Visitation House on May 7. He offered to speak to the girl about us as adoptive parents and that we may be able to help her financially since she was homeless. We've been very fortunate, so when he recommended that we give the daughter 2,000 in cash and the mother 10,000, it seemed like the right thing to do. He said that keeping that between us and the daughter and mother would be better for them. I agreed and talked to Becky about the possibility. She was so hopeful when we talked. I couldn't believe how happy she was. I forgot how happy she used to be."

"Then what happened?"

"Ah, well, we got another call from this guy telling us that everything would be ready for them on the seventh if we were. We were more than ready. Becky and I both agreed to give a nice donation to Visitation House that week before, and Sister Gerard seemed very grateful. The guy we met at the fundraiser told us that it would be better not to mention anything to Sister Gerard about our conversation or knowing about the baby coming. It seemed a little odd, but we figured it was about protecting this girl's privacy. We followed the recommendation, but let Sister Gerard know our desire to adopt an infant girl, if possible."

"And on May 7?"

"Just as he said, the girl showed up at Visitation House with her beautiful baby girl, and Sister Gerard called up immediately. I had taken cash out earlier that week and placed it in two envelopes, one for the girl and one for her mother. I gave the girl, Katie O'Donnell, her envelope when we met her. She seemed very pleased, and I gave the other to her mother, who was waiting in the car."

Brooks took out a photo of Mariana and held it up for Sam to inspect. "That's her. Looking at her now, she appears nothing like Katie."

"Thank you, Mr. Larson. Last question, who was the man that you met at the fundraiser?"

"That is the odd part. I don't know. We only got the name Jacob. I don't recall him ever telling us his last name. Funny, in a sad way, how you only pay attention to certain things when you want something so badly."

Brooks took out photos of Jimi and Jack and showed them to Sam.

Sam nodded, pointing to the photo of Jack. "That's Jacob, the man we spoke with."

Tom introduced himself. "Sam, I'm Father Tom, and this is Angelo Salvato. We're close friends with the parents of baby Elizabeth."

"Father, maybe you wouldn't mind talking with Becky? It's going to be very hard to give up Esther—I mean, Elizabeth. She felt like ours."

Tom spent at least a half-hour with Becky and her parents talking and counseling. Becky seemed able to collect herself and let Tom take Elizabeth in his arms while Sam put the baby seat in the back of Tom's car. Tom promised to come back to visit them in Wickford and work with Sister Gerard to find them a baby girl they could raise and love as their own.

On the way home, they all agreed that the evidence pointed to Jack and Mariana being the two accomplices in the assault and kidnapping. Jimi must have been telling the truth about not doing anything wrong and probably trusted Mariana when she gave him the cash and a plea to save Marie. Questions swirled through their minds as they neared home. How did Jack and Mariana know each other, and what was Jack's motive?

Chapter 35

When they reached Boston, Tom drove to Boston Medical Center. They called ahead and arranged to take Elizabeth in for medical testing to ensure that she was okay. Addie waited at the entrance in tears, with her arms outstretched, waiting to hold her daughter for the first time in almost a week. "I can't believe it. Thank you so much for finding her. She's so precious." The tears flowed freely as she hugged Elizabeth close as if to say, "No one is taking her again!"

Tom smiled, his hand on Addie's shoulder. "I told you God would take care of her."

Addie looked up, mascara mixed with the tears rolling down her cheeks. "He had some angels working for him here. I can't thank you enough. I'm going to take her up to Erick if that's okay?"

Brooks replied, "Sure. The doctors are expecting her when you're ready just to make sure everything is okay. I'll let them know you'll be with your husband in his room."

Tom and Angelo walked Addie up to Erick's room. Tom walked in first. "How're we doing, Champ?"

"No better than yesterday. Maybe if you could bring me some good news, I'd be doing better."

Just then, Addie stepped into the doorway, holding their baby girl.

Erick swung his legs across the bed and onto the floor. "Is this— Elizabeth? What? How?" He got up and reached Addie and Elizabeth in two quick strides, resting his head next to Elizabeth's, breathing in her scent. "I forgot how tiny she was. Can I hold her?"

Addie was still crying as Erick's eyes filled with tears, holding his lost daughter. "I can't believe this! Is this a hallucination from this bump on my head?"

Everyone laughed while attempting to wipe their tears away.

Erick gave Addie a big kiss and then gazed deeply into her eyes. He had been oddly estranged from Addie – rather than closer – while Elizabeth had been missing, but now it was obvious to Tom that something had changed.

As they were hugging with Elizabeth between them, a female doctor entered the room. "I hear we have good news? I'm Dr. Hartzel, pediatrics. I'd like to take a look at your daughter—Elizabeth, correct?—to make sure she's as healthy as she appears."

Erick held Elizabeth as the doctor checked her vitals. Then they laid her on the bed and undressed her while she cried for a second before smiling, bringing bigger smiles to everyone in the room. She looked very healthy. There was no evidence of bruising or cuts. "I think she's as healthy as she is beautiful. Please let me know if anything changes in her condition or behavior, but I think she's A-okay."

"Thanks, Dr. Hartzel. I appreciate this," said Brooks as he walked her out of the room to ask a few questions.

Erick turned to Tom and Angelo. "How did you ever find her? This is a miracle! I still can't believe it. Maybe prayers do work, after all?"

Tom smiled. "Prayers always work, but the answer might not always be what we have planned. Hopefully, you'll be going home yourself, and you can all be together again."

Erick replied, "If you found Elizabeth, does that mean we know who did this?"

Tom exchanged glances with Angelo. "Unfortunately, there is evidence pointing to your brother, Jack, and another woman."

Erick dropped onto the bed. "I can't believe this. I've been racking my brain, and it doesn't make any sense."

Tom said, "I know. I haven't been able to figure it out either."

Erick glanced over to Addie and then back at Tom. "In my bones, I can't believe Jack would do this. It's just not in him to do something like this."

Addie took Elizabeth to hold as she shook her head in disbelief.

Angelo stepped forward to caress Elizabeth's head. "At least you'll have Elizabeth for Mother's Day on Sunday."

Addie gazed at Elizabeth. "I was thinking all week that I'd be without my baby on my first Mother's Day. Thank you for thinking of that—and thank you for making it happen. I really can't thank you enough."

Erick smiled and then turned back to Tom. "Who's this woman you mentioned?"

"Mariana Perez."

"Do you know who she is?"

Tom replied, "I met her early this week for the first time. Angelo helped to track down the location of a possible assailant. I met her again at the police station when she was visiting her friend that we thought had taken

Elizabeth."

"Her friend?"

"Jimi Johnson lives with Mariana near Orchard Park. Mariana has a baby girl of her own who needs cancer treatments. Jimi was taking her to Mexico for those treatments, and we thought she might have been Elizabeth. It ended up being Mariana's baby girl, Marie, but the police found 30,000 in gold bullion coins in the rental car, so they brought him in. Mariana ended up confessing to kidnapping Elizabeth and must have given the coins and money from the adopting couple to Jimi to pay for the treatments."

Addie interjected, "Adopting couple. There was a couple already adopting Elizabeth?"

Tom replied, "Yes. That's where we were tonight, breaking the news to this couple who thought they were legally adopting her from a Catholic pregnancy support agency."

Addie said, "No! Did they already have her?"

"Yes, for several days. They were heartbroken by the news, but they knew Elizabeth belonged with her mother and father."

"I feel horrible. I can't imagine how that would feel if you finally thought you had the baby you dreamed of. I hope they'll be okay."

Tom said, "I think it will take time, but we'll pray they find a baby they can give a good home to."

Erick asked, "Tom, if this Mariana confessed, why are they still holding Jack? Why do they think he did it?"

Tom replied, "I don't know what will happen, but there's a lot of things pointing to Jack that need to be explained. Someone saw two people leaving your apartment with Elizabeth that afternoon. There was a lot of evidence in Jack's car and other things he can't or won't explain. The adoptive parents identified Jack as the person who set up the adoption and—" Tom glanced over at Addie before responding. "And he broke into your apartment this past Monday night and took something from your desk drawer. He hit Angelo over the head to escape."

"What? Why would he be in our apartment? Why would Angelo be in our apartment?"

With a guilty expression, Tom responded. "He was with me."

"What were you doing in our apartment?"

"We were trying to find evidence to help find Elizabeth. Every second mattered."

Addie was still holding a cooing Elizabeth. "Nothing is more important than this one." She got up to feed Elizabeth in the common room.

Erick remarked, "I've got to get checked out of here today."

Tom said, "I don't know if you've got medical clearance to be bouncing around town yet."

"It's been almost a week in this room. I can't have Addie and Elizabeth sleeping alone tonight in our house after what happened!"

"I completely get that, but you won't be much good if you end up back here again for longer."

Erick rubbed the side of his cheek. "I know. I want to talk to Jack, too. I need to know what he was thinking. Something tells me this can't be his idea or something he would do. I mean, why would he do it? I don't know about this woman or if she could do this alone, or maybe she had someone else that looked like Jack helping her?"

Tom grimaced. *Great, another amateur sleuth on the case. Brooks will just love it.* "Promise me you'll talk to the doctors to get a real assessment of where you are. If you need help at home, Angelo or I would be more than happy to help or stay with Addie and Elizabeth."

Erick paused and, in a quieter voice, said, "You're a good friend. I don't know that I have had one, since—well, since a long time."

Tom and Angelo said goodbye to Erick and caught Brooks in the hallway. Tom clapped his back. "You must be feeling a heck of a lot better with Elizabeth safe with her parents. I know I do."

"I do, but we have a long way to go on this one."

Tom said, "I was hoping you felt like we were close."

"I wish. The doctor said that Elizabeth had no signs of cuts or bruises, so where did her blood come from at the scene and in Jack's car? While we were sightseeing in southern New England, I had Mullen search Jack Comghan's hotel room. He had a dark blue sportscoat, and we found two spots of blood on the left sleeve. We also found a receipt from a Providence gas station in his pocket from a few weeks ago."

Angelo remarked, "If you are right-handed and swinging a stick or bat at someone, your left arm would lead and be more likely to get hit with blood. Why does your case seem so solid but not feel so solid?"

"I don't know. I really don't know."

Chapter 36

Though he was exhausted, Tom tossed and turned in his bed as he tried to sleep. He should've felt great about Elizabeth being safe, and he did, but something didn't seem right. It was bad enough that it was Friday night, and he hadn't prepared his homily for the weekend Masses, but he couldn't stop thinking about what could have driven Jack to the point of kidnapping Elizabeth. Was it envy or anger that skulked under Jack's friendly and easy-going manner? Was he still in love with Addie and couldn't let a baby bond her to Erick more? Was he having an affair with Addie and believed it was his baby and not Erick's? Was it just a lifelong case of building resentment, coupled with a lonely life that pushed him over the edge? As a psychologist, the often-complex factors that drove behavior, good and bad, were always of interest to him, but this behavior had him flummoxed.

At morning Mass, Tom's heart rejoiced at the sight of Addie with Elizabeth sitting in the front pew. After he greeted everyone and wished them a good day, Addie was the last to come out of the church. "I can't tell you how happy I was to see you here today," Tom said as he smiled at Elizabeth. "You too, Liz."

"We owe you and your boss an unpayable debt of gratitude."

Tom smiled, "My boss is your boss, and he'll always look out for you and Elizabeth. It's always good to say, 'Thank you,' though. He's a generous God, and I find myself thanking him all the time. How did you two do last night?"

"It was a little spooky at first, but she slept in the bed with me, and we were so tired we both slept well. What do you think's going to happen with Jack?"

Tom paused to think about his answer. "Right now, I don't know. There's a lot of things to account for. Do you think he's capable of doing something like this?"

"Jack? No. He'd have to have lost his mind to do something like this."

"Addie, I'm going to ask you a very difficult question. There's no judgment intended, and you don't have to answer."

"What is it?"

"You remember our conversation early in your pregnancy?"

Addie turned away and stared into space.

"I'm sorry. I shouldn't have brought this up."

Addie gazed at Elizabeth and said, "I remember. Go ahead. Ask your question."

"I was wondering if there was any chance that Jack thought he was doing you a favor by finding a good home for Elizabeth and freeing you to pursue your career until you were ready for a family."

Addie continued to gaze at Elizabeth as if to say, "How could I have ever not wanted you?" She answered, "I did talk to him about my conflicted feelings during the pregnancy. I just don't think he would—I don't know. I don't know."

"Addie, we all have doubts along the way about things. We can't beat ourselves up or be ashamed of every conflicted feeling we have. We're all human, and the idea of a child is different from the real thing, isn't it?"

Addie nodded as she lifted Elizabeth and placed her cheek against her own, breathing in her sweet scent.

"I'm going to try to see Jack this morning. Is there anything you'd like me to tell him?"

Addie hesitated before responding. "I can't think of what to tell you to say—maybe to be strong?"

"I will. You take care of yourself and that beautiful girl of yours. Call me any time you need anything. Really, anytime."

Tom went to the rectory to peel an orange for breakfast before heading to the police station.

Jack appeared fairly depressed but brightened at seeing Tom. "Father Tom, thanks for coming. Outside of my lawyer and being questioned by the police, I haven't seen anyone else since I was brought in."

"You heard that Elizabeth is back, safe and sound?"

"I did. Thank God she's okay. I understand you were there?"

"Yes, with Detective Brooks and Angelo. We were lucky."

"Lucky?" Jack laughed unconvincingly. "At least someone's lucky." Jack closed his eyes as his face tightened, and his voice shook as he continued, "My lawyer was here and believes I have a high risk of being convicted. 'Too much evidence without explanation,' he said. He recommended that I get a good criminal lawyer. I keep believing the truth will come out."

"Neither your brother nor Addie believe you would do this. I don't think you would do something to hurt anyone, but convince me you're innocent."

Jack appeared disappointingly surprised by the question.

"If you can't convince someone that believes in you, how will you convince the police—or a jury?"

Nodding, Jack replied, "I see your point."

"Despite all the circumstantial evidence that needs to be explained, I think they'd also look for motive."

"What motive would I have to try to kill my brother and kidnap his baby?"

"The question is—what motives will they consider or question you on?"

"Huh. If you thought I did it, what would you be thinking?"

"You really want to do this?"

"Not really, but I think you're right. I need to think about this. I don't want to, but it's sinking in how real this is and what could happen to me. Ask me."

"Okay, I will be like a lawyer, so don't take this personally. When did you first fall in love with Adelyn Kerrins?"

"What?"

"Mr. Comghan, just answer the question—and remember that you're under oath."

Jack frowned and answered, "Senior year of high school."

"And did you still love her when you attended the same college with Adelyn and your brother?"

"Yes."

"How about when your brother married her?"

There was a long hesitation in Jack's response before he finally replied, "Yes. Yes, I did."

"And is this why, just after the wedding, where you were the best man for your brother, you moved to London for six years?"

"Yes, but it was because I wanted my brother and Addie to have their marriage and life together. I didn't just love her for me. I wanted her to have what she wanted in life."

"But you came back a year ago?"

"I missed my family, and I thought it was time."

"But you still loved Adelyn?"

"I didn't think so, not in the same way."

"But, when you came back, was it different? Had your feelings changed?"

"Maybe. Maybe we were better friends."

"But you still loved her?"

"Yes."

"And you still do?"

"Yes."

"And you would do anything for her?"

"Probably, yes, I would."

"You've seen her on some of her business trips, is that correct?"

"Yes, but—"

"A yes or no is enough. And during one of those connections, she talked about having conflicted feelings about having a baby at this time—is that correct?"

"She did, but—"

"And you wanted her to pursue her dreams, correct?"

"Sure—"

"And you said you would do anything for her? Would you do anything for the woman you loved?"

"Okay. Okay, Father Tom. I can see where this is going. You missed your calling."

"I hope not. I think they'll be a lot tougher than I was in pushing a believable motive, and that's only one."

"There are more?"

"Probably several, but I don't want to overload you."

Jack peered around his holding cell. "Where else am I going?"

"True. Um, okay. Mr. Comghan, you are a twin, correct?"

"Yes."

"Twins often have intense rivalries. Can you say that your relationship with your brother has been without any issues of envy, jealousy, or resentment?"

"I don't think any relationship is without some of those feelings at times. We were very close growing up. Erick was my best friend."

"But things can change as we grow, and there's more at stake—like a woman you both love, one getting more recognition or love from a parent, one achieving more in business, sports, and life in general."

"Things do change, but I think you can work through them."

"What if one had the life the other always wanted? The wife, the friends, the business success, the wealth, and then a new baby—a family of his own?"

Jack didn't respond.

"What if the other was feeling as if his life had passed him by and his brother had stolen it from him? Would he be resentful, angry, even envious?"

Jack sat on his bunk motionless.

Tom thought about how Jack must feel sitting in this cell as if everything were now literally taken from him. "I'm sorry, Jack. I went too far."

Jack stared at the ground.

Tom nodded. "I should go now. I'll come back later."

Jack remained silent as Tom returned to the desk.

The desk sergeant let Tom know that Mariana had been moved to a woman's security facility in Framingham. Tom stepped outside to see Brooks crush a cigarette butt before glancing up to speak.

"It might be easier for you to just move in."

"No, thanks, I've seen your accommodations, and your room service isn't up to the lifestyle I've become accustomed to."

"Since Jack Comghan is the only one left, I assume you talked to him?"

"I did. We talked about motives. I really pushed some possible angles a prosecutor might question."

Brooks quirked one eyebrow. "And?"

"I can't tell you what was discussed in a confidential conversation."

"Then, what good are you?"

"Hopefully useful if I can get Jack to tell the whole truth."

"Well, we know he hasn't done that so far. I don't know if anyone has. We let Jimi out of custody, but he still needs to account for the stolen money in his possession. Mariana Perez only wants Jimi cleared, so she'll say anything to take the blame. Jimi says she didn't do it. Neither Mariana nor Jack has made any connection to the other being involved, but we know it was two people. Who said this job wasn't going to be fun?"

"Do you think the two of them will go to prison?"

"With all the evidence and witnesses to connect the dots, I don't see how they don't. The prosecutor is looking at attempted murder, kidnapping, breaking and entering, robbery, fraud, and a long list of other charges. This is no small deal."

"Even though Elizabeth wasn't harmed, and all the money has been returned?"

"That doesn't make the law any less broken."

Chapter 37

Tom continued to wrestle with his unsettled feelings. Despite his fondness for Jack and Mariana, he knew that both Jack and Mariana faced terrible prison terms.

As he approached the Boston Medical Center, he thought about what he'd say to Erick. What family dynamics could have brought these brothers to this point? When he arrived at Erick's doorway, there was a travel bag on the bed, and Erick was dressed in his street clothes. "Erick, healthy enough to go home?"

Erick replied with a half-smile. "They were waiting for the swelling to go down, but then they realized this is the normal size of my head."

"I was thinking the same thing. I should've said something earlier. Is Addie taking you home?"

"She wanted to, but I told her to stay with Elizabeth, and I'd take a cab. I think I might walk, though. It's only a mile, and the rain's stopped."

"Mind if I join you?"

"Only if you buy me a cup of coffee on the way—and not from the hospital," Erick replied, with a look that would accept no compromise.

Tom laughed. "Deal—but only if I get to see Elizabeth."

Fifteen minutes later, after stopping at the corner coffee shop, they walked slowly down Massachusetts Avenue.

Tom peered at Erick with concern. "You feeling okay walking?"

"Feels great to finally be out. That was the longest week of my life. It felt like an eternity."

"How do you feel about having your family together again?"

Erick's gaze turned inward.

"Erick?"

"Yeah. Sorry. Of course, it feels good—I mean great."

"You sound hesitant?"

"No, no. I was just thinking. I guess I still feel numb about this whole thing. One second, you think you're a dad, and in a snap, it's taken away from you."

"But, Erick, parenthood hasn't been taken away from you. You're a very lucky man. Many couples who lose a child never recover. The loss devastates them."

They walked quietly for a few minutes until it started to rain, and they ducked into a covered doorway of a small shop.

"I can understand that," said Erick.

"Understand what?"

"Being devastated by losing a child you thought you had."

Tom replied, "Seems as if you could only really understand it if you actually experienced it. Do you still feel like you've lost Elizabeth? As if it's not real yet?"

"I know it's real, but it still doesn't feel like it."

They stood in silence, watching the rain pour down for several minutes until the shower let up some, then trudged onward the last few blocks to Erick's apartment.

Erick stood and glanced at the door for several seconds before Addie opened it holding Elizabeth. "I thought you were taking a cab home. You're both all wet. Come in and dry off."

After unpacking his bag and taking care of a few things, Erick started a fire in the living room fireplace, and Addie made some tea to warm them up on the extra-chilly day in May.

Tom said, "It's so good to see Elizabeth back in her mother's arms."

"Thanks to you. Maybe you can get some sleep now. I've heard you've been burning the candles at both ends lately, worried about this little one."

"Can you think of anything more important?" Tom asked as he sipped his tea then dried his hair with a fresh towel.

Addie gazed at Elizabeth. "I don't think I knew that as much as I know it now."

Erick stared into his teacup.

Addie continued, "Somehow, it's not all right with Jack sitting in jail."

Erick shot her a look of surprise.

Tom nodded. "I saw Jack this morning. He's plenty nervous right now—I'd say terrified about where this could go."

Addie said, "Surely, the truth will come out, and Jack won't be charged for something he didn't do?"

Tom glanced at Erick and then back at Addie. "Both of you should know that Jack is facing some serious charges, everything from attempted murder and robbery to kidnapping—along with a long list of other charges. If he were found guilty, he'd go to jail for a very long time."

Addie's voice rose in alarm. "Guilty? Do you really believe he's guilty? Erick, do you believe Jack could have been involved with this?"

Erick glared at Addie with confusion. "The Jack I grew up with? Never. But I don't know if I know Jack any longer. I hope to hell this isn't his doing, but how do we explain everything the police have found? Could Jack do things to me that I never thought possible? If you asked me that a short time ago, I would have sworn on my soul that he couldn't and wouldn't ever break our trust in each other. I truly wish I could say that now."

Addie stood open-mouthed in astonishment. "Erick! Do you know what you're saying? He's your brother!"

"That's what makes it worse. I want to know that he would never betray me, but if there's proof that he has done it, how do I just dismiss that? How would I ever forgive that?"

Addie took Elizabeth into the study and placed her in the bassinet for her nap. She came back into the room. "Erick, do you honestly believe Jack's guilty?"

Glaring, Erick responded, "Jack is guilty!"

Tom stood up. "Maybe I should go. I hope we can trust that Jack could be innocent until—"

Erick interrupted, "Until proven guilty? But there's proof!"

Addie walked Tom into the hallway as Erick sat staring at the yellow-amber flames in the fireplace.

Tom peered into the study where Elizabeth was sleeping and then down at the spot where he had found Erick unconscious after the attack. The bloodstained rug had been replaced, and everything was back in order.

Suddenly, Erick came up behind him. "Scene of the crime?"

"This is where I found you, right over there."

"It was terrifying, trying to protect Elizabeth." He walked in to see Elizabeth sleeping peacefully, with momentary twitches in her legs, as if in a dream. Tom smiled as he watched her. "Hey, I never gave you that donation check for the baptism service."

"Really, Erick, don't worry about it. Very honored and happy to do it."

"But the Church needs money to keep doing its work." He sat down at his desk, unlocked it, and opened one of the drawers to pull out a checkbook. He wrote out a generous check, tore it out, and handed it to Tom. "That's not enough for all you've done."

"Thanks, Erick. This will go to good use," said Tom, folding the check into his pocket. "Please take it easy. This is your first day out of the hospital."

Erick let Tom out the front door and thanked him again for everything.

As Tom walked home, he thought about how emotional the conversation had gotten. When he returned to the rectory, he went into his office to put the check in a strong box he kept in one of the drawers of his desk. As he closed it up and slid it back in the drawer, he stopped short, a realization coming to him. When he was in Erick's study and Erick opened the drawer of the desk that held his checkbook, he saw the same thin, metal box that Angelo had found Sunday night, which was then stolen the following night by the assailant who hit Angelo over the head. How had it gotten back in the drawer?

Chapter 38

Normally, Tom would have a well-thought-out homily prepared to help touch the minds and souls of those attending the vigil Mass before Mother's Day. He considered talking about his mom, a moving story that would tie into the Gospel reading that included, "Abide in me. I am the vine; you are the branches. He who abides in me, and I in him, he bears much fruit, for apart from me you can do nothing."

He closed his eyes and thought of his mother for a moment. He loved her dearly and admired her strength, spirit, and undying faith. To her, blessings and challenges made sense and had meaning only because they were connected to God. His mother suffered from Multiple Sclerosis and had been bedridden for the last decades of her life, but she never lost her love for life, her family, or for God. In fact, she believed her handicap only made it stronger.

After Mass, Tom had a quiet dinner with Angelo and tried to catch up on some reading, but he kept thinking about his visit with Erick and Addie. He expected them to be ecstatic about being back together as a family, but something uncomfortable remained between them. He walked over to the gym and turned on the lights to shoot some baskets. Physical activity seemed to help when his mind was racing, and it always felt good when he hit shot after shot. He finally missed a jump-shot, which hit the back of the rim, bounced past him, and then rolled towards the dimly lit doorway until it was stopped by the foot of Tony Brooks. "Are you up for a game, Brooks?" Tom shouted across the court.

Brooks approached Tom and replied, "I know a hustler when I see one. I hope you don't mind my coming over on a Saturday night, but I saw the lights on."

They met at half-court. "Do you ever rest?" asked Tom.

"Do you?"

"So, what brings you over tonight?"

"What do you think? The Comghan case should be a solved crime on the way to an easy verdict for the jury."

"What happened today?"

Brooks bounced the ball a few times. "Comghan came by the station."

"I thought you were still holding him at the station?"

"Erick Comghan. Erick came by to see his brother at the station."

"I'm surprised. I walked him home from the hospital today, and he got a little heated when talking about Jack. I think he believes Jack's guilty."

Brooks half-smiled. "Well, he is—the evidence is pretty overwhelming. You know that."

"I know. I just think it would take even more than that to convince me my brother could try to kill me and abduct my baby and give her, his goddaughter, away to strangers."

"Yeah, well, maybe he knows more about Jack Comghan than you do? When did you first meet him?"

"On the Sunday of the baptism. Prior to that, Erick never even mentioned he had a brother."

"I guess that should tell you something about friction in their relationship. Erick came by my office and asked if he could visit Jack. It's not unusual for someone to want to visit a family member in jail, but it is odd to have the victim of an attempted murder sitting in a room with the alleged murderer. You can see all the possible problems that could present if any anger or hostility continues to exist."

"Yeah, I do. So, did you let him visit?"

"He wanted to visit one-on-one with Jack, who agreed. We allowed them to use the interrogation room while we sat in the viewing room, watching to make sure nothing happened to either one of them. Who knows the level of animosity that could exist?"

"How did it go?"

"They were quiet at first. Erick seemed extremely angry, while Jack pleaded with Erick to believe him. He kept saying that he had nothing to do with hitting him and would never risk hurting Elizabeth. Erick questioned him about all the evidence, and Jack kept saying he didn't know anything about any of it. At one point, it was obvious that Jack was highly stressed about the possibility of going to jail. He pleaded with Erick to trust him as a brother, but Erick seemed very removed as he watched him. It was like someone watching a wounded animal die in front of him more out of interest than empathy. It was sort of surreal seeing two brothers that looked so identical seem like such strangers as they engaged."

"Did Erick finally respond to Jack?"

"Not really. Jack's emotional torment seemed to only grow with Erick's silence, and he screamed at Erick at one point. That's when Erick gave us the sign that he wanted to leave the room. It seemed kind of heartless, but maybe sitting in the hospital all those days and hearing more of the evidence against his brother made him angrier at Jack, and he just wanted to watch him suffer for what he did. He certainly didn't come to offer any brotherly love."

"So, he just got up and left him in this state?"

"Yup. He didn't say much to us afterward, either."

"It just doesn't sound like the Erick I know—or think I know. What about Jack? What did he say afterward? Anything?"

Brooks sighed. "It took him a while to calm down. I think he was surprised by his brother's response. I don't know what he's thinking. Maybe he's been in denial about what he did? Maybe he thinks his only chance to get out is to continue to deny his guilt and hope his brother and sister-in-law are convinced he's a wrongly charged man? If he confesses, he knows he still goes to prison for a long time, so he's taking a chance. If he cooperates, it will help him some—only because we have so much evidence against him, and now he thinks his own brother is against him. Hope took a big hit."

"What if he didn't do it?"

Brooks laughed and stepped towards the basket, stopping at the foul line to hold the ball above his head, slam it to the floor, and have it bounce high enough to actually go through the basket. "This case is solid. If we can get Mariana or Jimi to break and tell us about Jack and account for what happened, it will be over for Jack."

"Wouldn't you feel better if, not just the evidence, but your gut told you this was a certainty?" Tom picked up the ball, took a very long shot, and sank it.

"You mean with as much certainty as you had that that shot was going in?"

Tom turned out the lights and, as they exited together, replied, "I felt pretty good about hitting it, but I wasn't certain until I did."

Brooks acknowledged his point with a smile. "So, I'm guessing you don't feel certain or even pretty good about our charges?"

"I really don't know. I feel like something doesn't fit. It's as if there are pieces of the puzzle we've forced into places they don't go."

"Well, we wouldn't even have some of those pieces or the baby if it weren't for you and Angelo. The link to Jimi Johnson and Mariana Perez was critical. I don't think Perez will give up anything on Johnson. She believes her time is short and wants to protect Jimi and Marie at all costs, but maybe she can give us something on Jack. Jack is simply denying everything and still hiding something, so he's not going to help with any connections to Mariana."

"If we find those missing pieces, this may all make more sense."

Chapter 39

Tom was surprised to see Addie at the early seven a.m. Mass on Sunday morning. After Mass, she stayed seated in her pew as Tom wished everyone a good day on their way out. As he re-entered the church and saw her sitting there alone, he approached and sat next to her. "No mother should be without her family on Mother's Day."

She sat still, staring at the altar. "Most of me feels alone."

He let silence stretch between them a few minutes before responding. "How can I help?"

"I don't know. I think I want to make a confession."

A flood of thoughts raced through Tom's head as he worried about what Addie had to confess. Would it be an affair with Jack? Did she have something to do with the kidnapping? "If you have something weighing on your conscience, this is the place to be. Would you like to do this face to face or in the confessional?"

"Can we just stay here?"

Tom glanced around and saw no one in the church yet for the next Mass. "Sure, wherever you're comfortable. Here is fine."

"Bless me, Father, for I have sinned. It has been a long time since my last confession. I have lied many times."

"Lied to whom?"

"Myself and to Erick, mostly. I haven't loved Erick in the bad times as I have in the good. The biggest thing weighing on my heart is that there were times that I wh—" Tears began to stream down her cheek as she tried to collect herself. "There were times where I wished the baby wouldn't— wouldn't make it. I feel so awful. I feel as if all this is my fault, and now nothing will ever be right again."

Tom put his arm around Addie's shoulder as she shook and sobbed.

She turned her head into his shoulder, taking short breaths. "I think I caused a lot of this. How can I celebrate today, when—"

"Addie. Listen. We're human beings with weaknesses; our thoughts aren't always under our control. If someone got me mad and I wanted to beat them but resisted that feeling and didn't—is that a sin? Feelings are feelings. Many feelings aren't even based on rational thinking—just emotional impulses. You aren't a bad mother or committing a sin because you had feelings and thoughts that you aren't proud of. It's good to say them out loud, but you didn't do anything wrong."

"What if it made someone else do something wrong?"

Tom peered up at the high-arched ceiling. "That would depend. Was it your deliberate intent to convince them to do something you knew was wrong?"

Addie sat quietly as she thought about Tom's question.

"Addie, if you're truly sorry, you can be absolved from your sin of lying, but you need no forgiveness for having feelings—no matter what they are. If we wish harm to someone, that's something to feel natural guilt about, but simply having a range of feelings that may come from fear, doubt, or even selfishness is not a sin. That's something you might need to let go and forgive yourself for."

"I'll have to think about that."

"Is there anything else you'd like to confess today?"

"I guess if I tell you everything I feel bad about, we could be here all day. I think that's it for sins I feel ready to confess today." Addie recited the Act of Contrition.

"Okay. You know, you can come back anytime to talk. As far as your sins." Tom held out his hand and said, "God, the Father of mercies, through the death and the resurrection of his Son has reconciled the world to himself and sent the Holy Spirit among us for the forgiveness of sins; through the ministry of the Church may God give you pardon and peace, and I absolve you from your sins in the name of the Father, and of the Son, and of the Holy Spirit."

"Thank you, Father. I appreciate that and your offer. I may need to take advantage of it. I might sit here to think and pray for a bit if that's okay."

"Absolutely. Take all the time you need and see if you can lay some of those heavy burdens down. I often find that talking to Mary can be of real help." He got up and started to walk away. He stopped and turned, saying, "Addie, you are a good person and a good mom. You've taken the time to be a strong person for Elizabeth, nurtured her for nine months, and have taken care of her. I know you'll make a world of difference in her life as she grows up. I know you'll let her know how loved and cherished she is."

Addie gazed up at Tom with tears still filling her eyes. "Thank you."

After the nine- and eleven-o'clock Masses, Tom headed back to the rectory for lunch. Angelo was already there with two sandwiches ready to be devoured. Tom changed into more comfortable clothes and sat down at the kitchen table. "Angelo, you spoil me."

"Someone needs to."

Tom took a big bite of his sandwich and smiled. Then he caught Angelo up on his conversations with Erick and Addie and then with Brooks from the night before. Tom could see Angelo's mind working as he listened to the details of the conversations. In the end, Angelo said, "Well, a few people believe Jack is guilty. Why do you think Addie is convinced he's not?"

Tom replied, "I think it's more personal. Jack's family or maybe more. I don't know. Do you think Jack's guilty?"

"Based on the facts or how I feel?"

"Okay, so what makes your gut tell you something different than the facts?"

"The evidence is pretty strong. Almost too much to argue against without looking stupid. Let's think of the pieces that don't seem to make sense." Angelo took a sip of iced tea while Tom thought about the pile of facts the police had uncovered so far. "Blood."

Tom asked, "What about blood?"

"Blood at the scene. Erick's blood is consistent with the wound on his head, but the other blood on the rug, the door, Jack's trunk, and now his jacket is confirmed to be from Elizabeth."

Tom said, "And Elizabeth showed no signs of cuts or even bruising. Where did her blood come from?"

"Exactly. The doctor also said Erick received three whacks, one to the arm that made him hunch over to protect Elizabeth from a blow and then two to the head."

Tom added, "A lighter one first and then the one that knocked him out. The first one makes no sense." Tom paused for a moment, thinking, then added, "And wouldn't Elizabeth have been crushed or at least bruised by the fall?"

Angelo stared wide-eyed at him, putting pieces together as he nodded, then poured more iced tea for Tom. "Now for the motive. What would bring a brother to plan out and commit a crime that could have killed his brother and basically sold off his goddaughter?"

Tom replied, "I have a hard time believing that much resentment and envy had built up within Jack against his brother. He doesn't seem like the type. I think he loves his brother—but that's a gut feeling and not anything I know for a fact to be true or false. Now, it might be his feelings about Addie that drove this emotion. I believe he's still deeply in love with Addie and would do anything for her. She expressed some reservations about having a baby with her career and with how Erick has been acting this year. Jack may have thought he was doing a good thing by securing a good home for Elizabeth. You have to admit that the Larsons seemed like a solid couple who would love Elizabeth, so he took care to ensure that."

"That's true. But what if his love for Addie and the life he might have had did drive resentment and envy? As Erick told you, he was always stronger, smarter, more accomplished, and successful, and then Erick ended up with the woman he loves and the family he was cheated out of."

Tom sighed. "Definitely a strong candidate for the motive, if that's what Jack believes."

"He definitely didn't do it for the money since that all went to Mariana to take care of Marie, which oddly was a very thoughtful and caring gesture."

"You know, this could be a crime of sudden emotion, except there are parts that seem too well-planned-out, if you know what I mean. Despite the evidence, this took some thought and coordination. He had to invest time into this, so the motive has to fit that reality," said Tom, finishing the last bite of his sandwich. "Mind if I make us another?"

Angelo shot up. "No, no. I'll make them. I like them to be made right."

Tom laughed. "I think we both do. You know what's odd, though?"

As Angelo laid down two more pieces of bread, he said, "Lots of things."

"Yes, but Erick must have been suspicious of Jack and Addie to check on her travel itineraries and then to order that paternity test. I wonder what he thought when the doctor confirmed that he was Elizabeth's father? You would think it would've made him less suspicious, but I'm not sure if it did."

Angelo brought the two smaller sandwiches to the table. "There's still a mountain of evidence Jack needs to explain. His whereabouts, the evidence in his car and on his jacket, the camera video of him in the hotel that conflicts with this story about going home, Erick's blood, the camera footage of his car at the scene during the time of the attack, the ID from the adoptive parents, the yellow bag being passed to Jimi that was found in the rental car, and this bump on my head when we were breaking into Erick's apartment. Why would he need to steal that metal box?"

"Hey, that reminds me. When I was at Erick and Addie's apartment yesterday, I was in the study with Erick. He insisted on writing me a donation check for the baptism. When he opened the desk drawer, there was the metal box back in the place you found it. Now, maybe it was a different box, but Erick had just gotten home. Who put the box back?"

"Huh."

"I think we need to find out Mariana's connection to Jack and more about Jack's family."

"What are we waiting for?"

"Are you saying to see Mariana? Or Jack and Erick's parents?"

Angelo picked up the now-empty plates. "It's a good day for a drive."

"That's three-and-a-half hours of driving—one way!"

"Like I said, it's a good day for a drive," laughed Angelo. "I hope that car of yours can make it that far."

Chapter 40

The route to Southbury, Long Island, was mostly easy highway driving. As Tom drove, he asked, "Angelo, I was wondering about something. When you were in prison, how many men claimed to be innocent?"

"Just about all of them."

"How many were innocent?"

"Not many."

"How many of them thought they were innocent?"

Angelo laughed, "Now, that's a good question."

"Do you ever think about any of the guys still there? It's been four years now, right?"

"You know, Gianni Fidele was a great man and the best friend I ever had. Since he died, I haven't thought a lot about the pen, but there are some guys over those thirty years I miss. Most of them are out and living their lives. I stay in touch."

"Well, you've been a good friend to me." Tom drove past signs for Bridgeport, Stamford, White Plains, The Bronx, Queens, and then finally onto Long Island. "I've actually never been to Long Island. I don't think Southbury is very far."

They got off the main highway and onto quainter roads until they stopped at a roadside country store to ask if anyone knew where the Comghan Farm was located. After a series of back roads, they came upon a dirt road with a sign for the farm. "I feel a little funny showing up unannounced."

"It's never stopped you before," Angelo retorted with a half-smile.

The road ended at an idyllic-looking farm with a large old maple tree standing sentry in the front yard, a white fence running along the driveway to the house, and an old red barn that looked over acres of land with fields of vegetables and fenced areas with hens, pigs, cows, and sheep. The only sound they heard was the light breeze bending back the tall grass and an occasion squabble from the chickens in the background. On the porch sat an older man shucking corn. He raised his head to peer down the driveway as they approached. They sold produce, berries, meats, and other items you might find at an old-fashioned farm, so they were most likely used to people stopping in to buy something or see the animals. As Tom and

174

Angelo climbed out of the car and ambled up a footpath to the front door, the man stilled his hands and smiled. "What can I help you boys with today?" There was a slight hint of an Irish accent in his voice. He appeared strong and able-bodied, but as he stood, the wear and tear of his age and years of hard work showed.

"Mr. Comghan?"

"You can call me Zak. Have we met? My eyes aren't what they used to be."

Tom stepped onto the porch and shook his hand. "Only through your sons. Their description of how beautiful and peaceful this spot is didn't do it justice. I'm Father Tom Fitzpatrick, and this is my friend, Angelo Salvato."

"All the way from Boston, you come? Addie has mentioned you many times. St. Francis, is it?"

"That's right. I've heard about you as well."

Zak scratched his head. "Well, I'm not sure what you've heard." He handed Tom and Angelo some ears of corn. "Here, take a seat and help me shuck a few more of these, and we can have dinner." He yelled in through the window, "Becca, we'll need two more places at the table."

Becca Comghan stepped out onto the porch with a ladle in one hand. "Who have you invited to our table today?"

Zak nodded towards them. "This is Father Tom. He's the priest at St. Francis, where Erick and Addie go, and this is his friend Angelo." Zak turned to Tom. "Did you baptize Elizabeth, Father?"

"I did. We missed you."

"Erick wasn't all that keen on us coming out. I can't drive anymore with these eyes of mine, and Becca never bothered to get her license. We wanted to be there, though. Over a month, and we haven't met our granddaughter yet. Imagine that? Erick keeps saying he'll bring her soon, but I'm beginning to wonder."

Becca's eyes held a quiet sadness as she stared out over the sun-filled fields. "It would've been nice to be with my sons and new granddaughter on Mother's Day." After a quiet pause, Becca wiped her hands with a dishtowel and held out her hand. "Well, it's very nice to meet you, Father—and, Angelo, is it? It'll be good to have some company."

Tom wondered why neither Zak nor Becca had mentioned the attack on Erick, the kidnapping of Elizabeth, or the incarceration of Jack. Why hadn't Erick, Jack, or Addie called them or kept them apprised of how things were going? But Tom was quickly questioning that assumption. He was also trying to assess how much to reveal without permission from their children.

As they shucked the corn, Zak asked, "So then, what brings you boys all the way to Southbury? It can't just be getting out of the city."

Tom glanced at Angelo before responding. "Well—we were in Connecticut and remembered your sons talking so fondly of this farm, so we decided to take a drive. We certainly didn't intend to impose on you for a free meal."

"Who said it was going to be free? I need some help unloading that trailer of hay into the barn—that's if you're hungry."

The men stood and followed Zak out to the barn. With all three of them working, the full load disappeared quickly. Zak exclaimed with a laugh, "Maybe we should have you over for dinner more often."

Becca was at the porch door waving them in to wash and sit at the farmhouse table for pork loin, roasted potatoes, corn on the cob, and some freshly baked bread.

Tom eyed the table of food. "Mrs. Comghan, we should be cooking for you today."

"Are your own mothers no longer with us?" inquired Becca.

"Sadly, no, but I'm praying they are happily in the arms of the Lord."

"Well, let's say grace and wish them a good Mother's Day, anyway."

Tom smiled, "That would be nice. I appreciate that. And let's also pray for the entire Comghan clan." Tom made the Sign of the Cross and said grace silently, asking God to grant the grace that this family needed to get through the coming tribulation.

As they shared their meal, Tom asked, "I'm curious, what were Erick and Jack like growing up?"

Becca grinned. "I always liked the name Jacob better, but the man here started calling him Jack. The boys were so close right from the start. After our troubles with having a family, it was a blessing to have the two of them. They may have looked alike, but it was easy to tell them apart."

"Erick was more like me," Zak said with a grin. "A bit of a perfectionist, more ambitious and demanding of himself."

"And of others," added Becca. "I think you were too demanding of those boys sometimes."

"The world can be a tough place if you're weak and lack the character and spine to face its challenges," quipped Zak.

"Erick and Jack were born with different strengths and gifts."

"Ah, you always overprotected Jack, didn't give him a chance to struggle through things and find out what he could do. It's when we push past what we thought were our limits that we grow and find out what we can do, who we really are."

Becca shook her head. "I think you can break a young boy by pushing too hard, expecting too much. A challenge is good, but encouragement and love are more important."

Zak lifted his glass of local red wine. "And this is why kids have both mothers and fathers. There are different ways to care, love, nurture, and help someone grow."

Tom said, "I think you're both right. I see a lot of parents overmanaging their kids, and, as a result, their sense of confidence and self-worth goes down as their anxiety and inability to deal with life go up. I also see parents pushing too much for superficial accomplishments instead of helping them discover who they are through those challenges. Rarely does one approach work for everyone. Of course, this is easy to say since I don't have kids of my own."

Everyone smiled.

"But I do work with kids and their families. So, what were your boys like growing up?"

"They were good boys," Zak replied. "Really good boys. They changed our lives and gave us a family. They were so close—best friends. They fought and competed, of course, but they really loved each other." Zak glanced at Becca. "Remember that fort?" He turned back to Tom and chuckled at the memory. "They worked on it for a month, hauling wood and figuring out how to build it. And they loved spending summers here on the farm with their grandparents, even with all the hard work. It was a good life."

Becca said, "It was. Jack wasn't as strong or competitive as Erick. He needed a little more encouragement and more hugs."

Zak laughed. "He had no shortage of those from you."

"They could've used a few more from their father, too," Becca replied. "You pushed them."

"Only to be their best."

"I think you pushed Erick harder, though."

"He was stronger and had more potential."

Angelo asked, "I heard they loved to play sports, and you coached?"

Zak grinned. "I loved coaching them. It was fun to watch them learn the game—especially basketball. They played so well together, always knew where the other one was going to be at all times. Did you know they won the State Championship one year?" Zak pointed to a trophy on the top shelf of the hutch.

Becca shook her head. "He stares at that darn thing every day. It looks silly here in the dining room."

"It makes me think about being with them. It brings them here when I see it."

Tom said, "I heard about that win. I imagine that was a pretty exciting game — winning on a last-second shot like that."

Zak grinned. "Erick was our best shooter, and he showed it there. I was so proud of him—of both of them."

Tom said, "I saw the headlines from the local papers. It seems like Jack's pass got all the praise from the press?"

Becca glanced at Zak with an expression of concern. "Erick was crushed."

"We've been over this a thousand times. Erick was the best player. Erick made a clutch shot and won the championship for us, but he wanted to take that shot and get the recognition for the wrong reason—for himself and not for the team. I called the play to give Jack the last shot, and Erick didn't support him. He argued with me in front of the team and his brother—twice on that last play. Jack knew the right thing to do for the team; he knew Erick was the better shooter. Jack deserved the recognition. He deserved it not just because he made a really great pass, but he made the right unselfish decision for the team and his brother. The game wasn't more important than Erick's character."

Becca glanced at Zak. "You could have given Erick something. That headline in the paper devastated him. He wanted your approval, your recognition."

"I tried to give him my love instead. Something that would last longer than sending him a conflicting message."

Tom politely interrupted, "How were Erick and Jack after that game?"

Zak stared down at his plate. "Jack was fine afterward, but Erick changed. He was angry and hurt. I tried to talk to him, but he pulled away. He put up a wall between us where there was none before. I always thought it was temporary, but I think it has only gotten worse over time. Then, they were both off to college and busy with jobs. Everything seemed to have literally changed overnight when it should have been a great memory for everyone."

Becca said, "We thought there was an opportunity for healing when Erick married Addie. Addie's been a blessing, but I think she may have created more separation between the boys. After Erick and Addie's wedding, Jack left for London without an explanation, and we didn't see much of either of them. Erick was busy building his business and being married in Boston, and Jack was simply gone until a year ago. Luckily, he's close now, and he visits, but Erick has remained distant."

Zak added, "I think he's still angry."

Tom responded, "Angry is one side of a coin that usually has fear on the other side. Children often pull back and seem like they are rejecting the very thing they want so badly, but they don't feel like they can take the risk of disappointment. They are hurt and vulnerable and put on a thick armor of protection to avoid the pain. Problem is—it never really works well and only keeps us from having the relationships we crave."

Zak asked, "Do you mean you think Erick might not hate us but love us and be too afraid to risk feeling rejected?"

Tom responded, "Could be. You may have all the right intentions in the world as a dad, but each child receives that lesson through different filters, different needs, and different abilities to tolerate difficult emotional situations. Emotions with parents are always the most sensitive and deep— not because they hate you, but because they see their sense of self-worth in your eyes, your affection, your recognition, and your unconditional love."

Zak shook his head. "I don't know. I can see that as a young boy, but he's been a grown man for a long time now."

Becca chided, "Isaac!"

Tom said, "Mr. and Mrs. Comghan, I'm just tossing out thoughts. I don't know your family well enough to know the dynamics, so I apologize for talking as if I did. You seem like very decent, generous, and loving people, and I care greatly about Erick and Addie. I'm just getting to know Jack a little, but I think there's a good person there who has been affected by some of the family dynamics. I don't know that for certain; it's just a feeling I have."

Zak replied, "I can see you care, but you're right to say that you don't really know our family, so maybe we should talk about something else."

Becca exclaimed, "Isaac! The Father's just trying to help."

Tom said, "I'm the one who should be sorry. We have enjoyed your gracious hospitality and an outstanding meal. It is a long ride, and Angelo and I should be heading back to Boston. I'd like to come back and visit again, though."

Out on the porch, Tom, Angelo, and Zak stood watching the sun set on the newly planted fields.

Zak said, "I know you meant well. I do. I just need time to think about things. Losing connection with the boys has been so difficult for Becca and me, but I still love them and want the best for them. I don't want my hurt and pain to be the reason we stay apart."

Becca stepped onto the porch with two containers in her hands. She handed them to Tom and Angelo. "Sorry you have to rush off, but I'm not letting you go without some homemade blueberry pie for the road."

Angelo said, "Thank you. If it's anywhere as good as your dinner, we'll have a happy ride home."

With a half-smile, Becca said, "Well, here's some napkins to keep from having a messy ride, and please tell the boys we love them."

Tom peered into her eyes. "We will. I think there's an opportunity here."

A few miles into the four-hour ride home, Tom said, "I like them. I think they both genuinely care."

Angelo shrugged. "Seem to, but there are a lot of layers of emotion and hurt there too."

"We all suffer that, at times. Never being a twin or even having a brother close to my age, my guess is that being a twin creates more intense dynamics from comparisons and being lumped together as if they were one person."

"Makes sense. I would think parents might make sibling rivalry worse sometimes."

"I think you're right, especially if they treat one child differently from the other. I don't know if parents always consciously know when one child gets more attention, recognition, or love than the other and how it can impact that sibling relationship without even being aware of the dynamics," said Tom.

"So, what's your conclusion with the Comghan brothers?"

"It's hard to tell. The mother seems as if she may have been over-protective toward Jack growing up. It's not always the stronger or more gifted child that receives praise or special treatment. Some parents think they are doing the right thing by protecting and supporting the one who doesn't have the same strengths or gifts, but that can leave the other child feeling less loved when they perceive less attention relative to the other one."

"I didn't think of that. Do you think it still has that kind of impact even as adults?"

"It definitely can. The greater the difference in parental affection perceived by the child, especially from the mom, can cause resentment, envy, hostility, and conflict between the siblings. And Mr. Comghan's withholding of the recognition Erick felt he earned may have pushed Erick over the edge, but there may be some maternal dynamics to pay attention to as well."

Angelo stared out the passenger side window, apparently thinking about the things Tom was saying. "I never had a father around. I'd imagine a child getting pampered or overindulged by one parent while getting criticized or rejected by the other would cause issues —so, with brothers, if one gets pampered and the other gets criticized, I could see how that would affect their relationship."

"I think you've got it! You can also grow up to disrespect the parent that pampers you and despise the one that rejected you. One child's interpretation of favoritism or indifference definitely throws off the dynamics of the whole family. It can create distrust, dishonesty, resentment, and anger. Love can't grow without trust and honesty."

Angelo said, "I wonder how much this plays into this case?"

"That is the $64,000 question."

As the setting sun painted the cotton clouds in Tom's rearview mirror with spectacular colors of red, orange, and yellow, Angelo nodded off for most of the trip home, while Tom tried to think of the answer to that very question.

Chapter 41

At the end of the day, Tom and Angelo pulled down the quiet street and into the church driveway. Angelo headed to his tiny quarters, but Tom decided to see Jack Comghan.

When he arrived at the station, Sergeant Doherty glanced at the clock on the wall behind him and then back at Tom with a curious smile on this face. "Are we havin' trouble sleepin' now, Father?"

"I just missed that smiling Irish face of yours, Sergeant," replied Tom. "I know it's late, but is there any chance I could visit Jack Comghan—if he's awake, of course."

Doherty squinted his eyes a bit as he pondered the request. "I don't know. It is kinda late for visiting. Comghan is being moved to the Norfolk facility tomorrow until his trial. I guess that would make this kind of an exceptional situation. Let me check on him and see if he's up for it."

When Tom reached the holding cell, he could tell Jack hadn't been sleeping, and the uncertainty of his future appeared to be taking its toll. Tom considered the stress could be the same whether he was falsely accused or actually guilty. Either way, he might be worried about a long and tough prison sentence defining his existence for the prime years of his life. "Jack, sorry for the late visit."

"I wouldn't have any idea of what time it is—and I haven't been flooded with visitors either, so no apologies necessary. Hopefully, you brought a key with you."

"No physical key for the bars, but maybe we can figure out a better answer." He paused. "I saw your folks earlier today."

Jack squinted. "In Boston?"

"No, in Southbury. The farm was as beautiful as you described."

"What? You drove all that way? Why?"

Tom replied, "I don't know why. I just felt an urging that I needed to talk to them, so I followed through. There are some strong dynamics in your family, and I didn't think I had a full picture, and I needed to talk with your folks to get a better grasp of your past." He let the statement settle between them, then looked him in the eye. "Your parents don't seem to know anything about Elizabeth's disappearance or that you are in jail."

"Yeah, I haven't had the heart to call them. I'm not surprised that Erick hasn't told them either. I guess none of us wanted to worry them until this was sorted out. Mom would freak out, for sure."

"She might have done just that. I liked your folks, though they seemed saddened that the close family relationships you had in childhood have been lost."

Jack met his gaze for a few seconds, then concentrated on an imaginary spot on the table.

Tom shifted strategies. "So, you're looking pretty beat yourself. Are you getting any sleep?"

"How can I? This is a nightmare. I didn't do this!"

"Then help me to help you."

"How can I help from behind these bars?" snapped Jack.

Tom rubbed his fingers across his lips as he thought. "I've been racking my brain trying to think of that. What about walking through each piece of evidence to see what stands out for you?"

"Evidence? That would mean I'm guilty, wouldn't it?"

"Only if you were guilty."

"So, you're not so sure, are you?"

"To be honest, Jack, I don't know what to be sure of. What about your whereabouts on Sunday?"

"What I told the police is true. I got up early on Sunday and drove home to Connecticut. It took just under three hours."

"Okay. What time did you get home?"

"Let's see—about ten, maybe a little after."

"That still gives you time to drive back to Boston before Erick was attacked and Elizabeth was taken."

Jack shook his head. "But why would I do that? Why would I want to hurt my own brother?"

"The problem the police and the jury will have is that your car was seen on a video driving down the public alley behind Erick's apartment just before the attack."

"Aren't there a lot of cars that look like mine?"

"Not with your license plate. Jack, you can't be the least bit dishonest here, or they'll bury you. You need to be credible."

"Okay, I need to prove that couldn't have been me. Is that what you're saying?"

Tom nodded. "Yeah. At least, something to raise doubt."

Jack peered up at the bars. "Let me think. I didn't stop for gas— Wait a minute. I had an accident on the way."

"But you drove over to the church during the week. I didn't notice any damage."

"I know. It was a small dent to the back fender when a woman bumped my car with hers. I didn't think it was anything until I saw the dent, and then we exchanged insurance information and numbers. It must be in my jacket pocket."

"Okay, now that's something we can check that would help. It would still have been possible to make it back to commit the crime, though. That video footage makes this tough. You were also seen in the hotel lobby on their video camera bumping into Jimi Johnson and seemingly handing him a yellow canvas bag that may have held the gold coins."

Jack ran his hands through his now-stiff auburn hair. "They showed me that guy's picture. I don't recall meeting him, and I don't know anything about a yellow canvas bag."

"But you were at the hotel not long after the attack, meeting the man with the stolen money from Erick's desk, and who lives with the woman who happens to have confessed to facilitating an illegal adoption. This was all when you claimed to be home in Connecticut."

Jack let out a long breath as he sighed, but he didn't respond.

Tom tried to give him plenty of time to come up with an answer, but Jack remained silent. "Okay, what about the blood, pink bootie, and gravel that matched the gravel from the crime scene being found in your car?"

"I honestly don't know how any of that got there. I just don't."

"Was your car gone or out of your sight for any of that time?"

"Only when it was parked in a garage or in town."

Tom said, "Another tough one would be Sam and Becky Larson."

"Who are they?"

"The Rhode Island couple who said they met you at a fundraiser. They talked about not being able to have a baby, and you called them back, recommending them to go to Visitation House for help."

"What? What fundraiser? What's Visitation House?"

"It was the New England Small Business Association or something like that."

"Sure, I attended that, but I don't remember any couple from Rhode Island."

"The problem is that they found a receipt in your pocket for gas or something you bought in Rhode Island not long before the kidnapping."

"In my pocket? What?"

Tom replied, "Yes. The jacket you wore the weekend of the baptism had a spot of Elizabeth's blood and this receipt in the pocket. These are things you'll have to explain or provide convincing evidence that you couldn't have been there."

"Oh, my gosh. I'm more stressed than ever. How can I answer these questions?" responded Jack, slumping down on the metal-framed cot.

"I think we're going to have to get Mariana or Jimi to shed some light on who they were working with if it wasn't you."

"If?" Jack shot back. "If?"

"They'll go through those possible motives we discussed last time. Your responses were very shaky. There was also evidence that you took a cab from Erick's apartment after a break-in."

"I thought you said they saw my car?"

"I'm talking about the next night. After dark, someone was in Erick's study and stole a metal box out of Erick's desk. Whoever it was, hit Angelo on the head with it before escaping and catching a cab. The cab driver identified you as the person taking that ride to flee the scene—and you don't have an alibi for where you were."

Jack sat silently, running his palms along the sides of his head. He let out several long breaths but didn't offer any help.

"Jack, don't take this the wrong way, because I'm making no judgments, but if things got really bad for you, even if you thought you were doing a good thing, it would be better for you and everyone to just be completely honest. It's always the best way to go, no matter what, and the healing process can begin. Even if it's rough for a while, it could oddly be a new beginning."

Jack buried his face in his hands for a moment, then gave Tom an unreadable expression.

Tom couldn't tell if the stare was from anger, betrayal or fear. Tom checked for any warning signs of possible suicide, brought on by overwhelming stress and anxiety.

Jack narrowed his eyes at Tom. "I need to be alone. I need to figure things out."

Tom stood up. "Jack, nothing is too great to keep us from getting to a better place. All relationships can be healed. All sins can be forgiven, and all people redeemed. Please don't give up hope. We'll be there for you, no matter what."

Jack hung his head and said, "You're not my family."

"No, but I could be a better friend if you'd trust me enough to be honest with me."

Chapter 42

After saying Monday morning Mass, Tom went back to the rectory and made a phone call.

"Hello."

"Erick, can I buy you some breakfast to make up for our last conversation?"

"Is it a sin to turn down a breakfast invitation from a priest?"

"I think it is. Let's meet at the Eastside in fifteen?"

"I'll probably regret this," replied Erick before hanging up the phone.

Tom headed out to the Eastside Café, an old stomping ground for many of the local neighbors.

Erick entered the door just in front of Tom, oblivious to the waitress, Linda, giving him her usual hard time. "Well, well. I'm glad to hear the good news about your baby, but I don't see what all the fuss was about you."

Erick smiled. "And good to see you too, Linda."

"Well, that's not much of a newsflash."

As Tom stepped forward, Linda rolled her eyes. "Oh, boy, isn't this going to be a fun morning?" She pointed her order pad towards a table in the corner. "Two coffees, coming up."

Tom shook Erick's hand and smiled as they sat down. "Thanks for coming on short notice. It seems like ages since we've had breakfast together."

"It has been a long few weeks. Thanks for the invite. It's good to get out for a bit."

"How are you feeling this morning?" asked Tom.

"My head's doing pretty well. I'm taking it slowly. The rest is so-so."

Linda brought over their coffee and stood with one hand on her hip and an impatient expression on her face. "Two usuals this morning, or are we going to go for something wild today?"

Tom laughed. "Sorry to be dull, but I'll have my usual today."

Erick agreed, and Linda didn't bother writing down their order as she left, shaking her head.

Tom took a sip of his coffee. "Why only so-so today?"

"I guess it's my brother and Addie."

"You still believe your brother's guilty?"

"If there's evidence to say so, what am I supposed to believe?"

"I heard you visited him the other day."

Erick stared into his cup of deep-brown coffee as the steam rose from it. "I guess this is a smaller town than I thought. Yes, I went to see him."

"So, why did you go?"

"I wanted him to convince me he was innocent or to apologize. He did neither. I could read the guilt in his eyes—in his soul."

"What if he were guilty? Could you ever forgive him?"

"What?!"

"Could you ever forgive Jack?"

Erick hung his head as he shook it. "No. I don't think I could ever forgive him for what he did. I know that's wrong to say, but I have to be honest."

"How did you feel when you saw the expression on his face in that cell, contemplating possibly spending his prime years in a dangerous prison?"

"I don't think anyone would want him to go to prison, but there has to be responsibility. Justice has to mean something. What if we just said to 'forget about it'?"

"You're right that he would need to repent and be sincerely contrite, to be sorry and make amends. Could you forgive him then?"

Erick glanced up, shaking his head with a half-smile on his face. "You're a tough one, aren't you? What would you do?"

"I'd be very hurt and angry for a while, but I'd hope I could try to step out from letting that feeling consume me and try to assume the best in him."

"Assume the best? How could I ever trust him again?" replied Erick, trying not to raise his voice despite the pain contorting his face.

"If he was my brother, I'd try to believe that deep down he loved me and his falling happened for a reason—maybe not a good one, but because something was broken inside. We have turned our back on God, spit in his face, not trusted him, and even killed him—and what does he do for us?"

Erick didn't respond.

"He gave us his life out of nothing but self-giving love. He forgave us and gave us another chance. We hate, lie, kill, cheat, and disrespect—does he forgive us and give us another chance because we deserve it?"

Erick reluctantly replied, "No."

"Exactly. He did it because he loves us and puts the relationship ahead of the hurt. It's easy to love someone who's doing right by us, but it's often those who aren't who need it most. Forgiveness, hope, redemption, love.

We're called to give those to others who don't deserve it, and even if I take my priest collar off for a moment, I think there's some real upside to our relationships when we do this."

Seething, Erick stood up, pulled some bills out of his pocket, and tossed them on the table. "You don't know what you're talking about. You don't know what he's done!" Then he stormed out of the café, letting the wooden door slam behind him.

Linda approached with two plates of eggs, bacon, and toast. "I hope you're hungry this morning."

"I've lost my appetite. Could you box those up for me?"

On his walk back, Tom was giving his boxed breakfasts to two homeless men in the park when he noticed a familiar face approaching him. As she got closer, he could tell it was Addie. "Addie, are you okay?"

Catching her breath, Addie replied, "Yeah. Maybe not. I don't know. Erick came home distraught, but he wouldn't talk. I just wanted to get out for a bit and see Jack before they move him today."

"Do you mind some company for the walk?"

"No, it'd be good to have someone to talk to. I told you that Erick had been different this past year and then really different the past month or so, but he seems even worse since coming home. I don't know if it's the head injury or what, but it hasn't been easy."

"Do you think it's just possible this has dredged up a lot of buried feelings from earlier in his life? Resentments, disappointments, and hurts?"

Addie mulled it over until they reached the front entrance of the station. "Maybe jealousy."

Inside they sat and waited for permission for Addie to visit Jack.

Detective Brooks came out and asked them to come into the detectives' room for a few questions. He pulled up a chair next to his desk for Addie to sit, then retrieved a folder that had grown during the case. "I appreciate your coming by. I know you wanted to visit Jack, but he was moved earlier this morning to the corrections facility in Norfolk."

Addie responded, "What happened to 'innocent until proven guilty'?"

"I understand your concern. Mr. Comghan is charged with physical assault with the intent to kill and kidnapping. Those are deemed acts dangerous to society. He'll go through some psychological testing while he's there."

"Jack's not crazy or dangerous."

"Do you think those are things a sane person would do? There's got to be some reason for these extreme actions—actions that were not a spur-of-the-moment act of passion, by the way. It took a good deal of time and planning to do this."

Addie shook her head. "Jack's not ambitious enough to plan something like this. I don't think he has this in him, and I can't think of any reason he'd ever do it. Don't you need a motive? A weapon? A witness?"

"Mrs. Comghan, we have quite a bit of evidence. I was wondering if you could help?" Brooks watched Addie's eyes as they fixed on the large whiteboard linking all the evidence and potential suspects. "Sorry. Are you concerned that your picture is on the board?"

Addie stood up slowly and walked over to inspect another picture. She squinted and turned her head to the side as she pondered the face. "Who's this man?" she asked, pointing to the picture with the name "Jimi Johnson" under it in blue marker. "I know this face."

Brooks joined her at the board. "Any idea where you may have seen him?"

"I don't know. I just know that I've seen him before."

"On the sidewalk?"

Addie shook her head.

"Here at the station?"

She shook her head again.

"At your apartment?"

Addie stopped and closed her eyes to imagine this man's face. "My home. I saw him at my home."

Brooks exclaimed, "What? When? Why was he at your home?"

"He came to the apartment to give us an estimate for wallpapering Elizabeth's room. He wasn't talkative. He just looked around the apartment as he walked down the hall and then into Elizabeth's room. He said he would send us an estimate, and he left through the back entrance."

Tom asked, "Had you met him before or seen him since?"

"No."

"How did you find him?"

Addie thought for several seconds. "We looked up contractors and called several. Most were busy, but he must have been one that was available. I don't remember, but I remember his face. He seemed quiet but nice. Why is he on your board?"

Brooks scratched his eyebrow with his fingers. "He was our prime suspect for the first several days. He was transporting a baby girl to

Mexico, who we thought was Elizabeth. I think you knew about that. This was the guy. It just so happens that he lives with the woman who confessed to taking Elizabeth and arranging her adoption. There was red brick material in your apartment that matched the crushed brick outside of the building where they live."

"Why isn't he being held instead of Jack?"

"We had a witness that saw two adults leaving from your back entrance at the time of the attack. One was holding a baby. We have witnesses that tie Mariana to the crime and a list of evidence that tie Jack to this. We don't have anything pointing to Jimi, except that he had the money on him when we apprehended him in Phoenix. Mariana claims that she gave Jimi the money to pay for medical treatments for her daughter, and he had nothing to do with this. Suddenly, I'm not so sure."

Tom stepped closer to stare more closely at the photo of Jimi. He had believed him when Jimi said he didn't steal the money or do anything wrong. No one saw three adults coming out, and there was no evidence that he was involved with the adoption, but there was evidence that Mariana and Jack were. Tom's eyes drifted from one photo to another, trying to let things come to him versus overthinking. He found himself now staring at Jack's photo and all the evidence tied to him—the blood, the bootie, the matching gravel, the Larsons' witness, the receipt, the question marks on his whereabouts, the photo from the hotel lobby, the yellow canvas bag, the photo of his car in the alley just before the attack. He stared at the pictures, trying to tie them together in a logical order, then looked more closely at the grainy photo of the back of Jack's black BMW and the confirmed license plate number, and thought, *How does he explain all of this? He couldn't even do it when I asked him, and I'm no prosecutor.*

Brooks glanced at Tom. "You've seen those photos a bunch of times. What's so interesting now?"

"Nothing, I wish there was. Looking at the same thing and trying to get a different answer is like banging your head against a brick wall."

Brooks turned back to Addie. "Let me know if you can think of anything else, no matter how small, about Jimi when he was at your apartment. I still need to account for where you were last Sunday and if you've had any conversations with Jack that could shed light on this case. I don't care whether it clears him or convicts him, but we need to understand everything to know what happened that day."

"Bumping my head," said Tom in a muffled tone.

Brooks asked, "What are you mumbling about over there?"

"Just thinking about—" Tom glanced back at the photo of Jack's car. "Are you sure this is Jack's plate number?"

"One-hundred-percent sure. Why?"

"The bumper," replied Tom. "The bumper isn't right."

"What?"

"The bumper. Jack still says he drove home on Sunday morning."

Brooks shook his head. "We have evidence he was in Boston on Sunday. Who does he think he's convincing?"

"But he said some woman bumped the back of his car, and he had proof. He said there was a small dent on the back bumper, and I don't see it in this photo, so that means—"

Brooks interrupted, "He's lying, or the accident happened after the assault and kidnapping, or—"

"Or this photo isn't of his car!" said Tom.

Brooks laughed. "Don't get overexcited, Sherlock. That option isn't very likely."

"But possible?"

"Possible."

Chapter 43

The train from Boston to Framingham took about forty minutes. Jimi sat and watched a myriad of people getting on and off at each stop. At one stop, a large woman with several bags sat next to him while a younger couple sat across the aisle, seemingly lost in thought. For the most part, Jimi had lived a solitary life without feeling bad about that aspect, but now that Mariana was in his life, he had a hard time thinking of life alone, without Mariana. He had come to know friendship and then love through her.

Jimi stepped onto the platform and asked the ticket inspector where the Framingham woman's prison was located. After a twenty-minute walk, he arrived at the main gate with his pre-approved papers allowing him special permission to visit because of his own prison past. The thought of even being near a prison still sent shivers through Jimi. He had promised himself he'd never see the inside of one of these inhumane cages again, but here he was, arriving at one on his own power.

When he finally sat down on the visitor's side of the glass, his anxiety grew, but he tried to maintain his composure while Mariana was escorted to her seat opposite him. He smiled, but worry and sadness filled him, for he knew she most likely only had a short time to live. "Are you okay?" he asked.

Mariana seemed more concerned about Jimi than herself. "I'm okay, but you don't look like you have slept at all. How's Marie doing?"

"She's good. She's happy, but I know she misses her mamma. I can bring her next time."

"I see her in my dreams every night, but I'd really like to hold her and breathe her in. I'm worried about her. We were so close, and she needs that treatment. It's tearing me apart thinking about her having a mother in prison."

"Mari, the only thing she has because of you is life and lots of love. Don't go blamin' yourself for things like that. We'll take care of her."

"How're we going to afford it now?"

"Remember what we talked about. We had Plan A, and we had our backup Plan B. It's not the one we wanted, but I made a promise—and with that promise came our insurance policy for Marie."

Mariana grimaced. "I don't like it. She needs you." Tears flowed down her cheeks.

Jimi wanted to reach through the glass to wipe the tears as he gazed at her with all the affection he had to give. "You shouldn't be here. A baby needs her mamma."

"But—"

"No buts. You should be with her, and you're not going anywhere," said Jimi.

"Jimi. You know what I have. We need to think about Marie. We can't deny reality, no matter how painful, or it will end up hurting her."

Jimi leaned forward and gazed into Mariana's eyes. "I don't like to think about it. I don't believe it's true, but if that happened, I think Marie deserves parents like the ones we had for that baby—a home, a mom and dad, good schools."

"And love. She needs to know she is loved and has worth. Fancy houses and money can't give her that."

"I know, but she can't have either without the treatment. I need to be a man of my word and keep my promise—then she can have what she needs to live."

Mariana sat, shaking her head. In her entire life, nothing had ever been easy, but this was the hardest. Jimi could see that in her eyes more at this moment than in any other since he had known her.

Chapter 44

Tom walked Addie back to her apartment. The streets rumbled with traffic, and the sidewalks bustled with people heading in various directions. "Addie, how do you think Elizabeth is doing? She seems very content when you hold her."

"I was frightened to think she might be traumatized, but she's been very good, almost as if nothing happened. What I'm hoping is that she was well taken care of, and there will be no negative effects."

"Me too. Now for the rest of the family."

"What do you mean by 'the rest of the family'?"

Tom stopped on the sidewalk, and Addie turned to face him. "I see a really good family—not just you three, but the overall extended family. I saw Erick and Jack's parents the other day. I may be wrong, but I think feelings and walls are keeping it from being the family it could be. Part of me thinks you know that deep in your heart."

Addie stared down at the sidewalk as people made their way around them on either side. She opened, then closed her mouth, shook her head, then ambled towards home.

Several minutes later, she paused. "I think you're right. I know you're right."

"Can I ask you a very personal question?"

"I'm not sure."

"Don't answer anything you don't want to."

"Okay," Addie tentatively replied.

"Did you know how Jack felt about you in high school and college?"

Addie continued to walk and to stare ahead, pondering the question in silence for several moments before answering, "Yes."

"Do you know why he left the country after you and Erick got married?"

"I do."

Tom continued, "You said Erick has been different this past year since Jack's been back?"

"Um— that seems like the right timing when I've tried to understand it."

"Do you think the change in him is connected to Jack's arrival?" asked Tom.

"I don't know. I think some of it, but it seems worse lately."

"I won't ask if he has any reason for having those feelings."

Addie stared down at the sidewalk as it seemed to move under their feet. "Thank you."

They stopped in front of Addie's doorway. Tom stared at her nonjudgmentally. "I can tell this is difficult, but I do think you're going to need to tell the detectives where you were on that Sunday, and you may need to get into the dynamics of you, Erick and Jack—especially if you believe Jack's innocent and you want to help clear him."

Suddenly, Erick opened the door and came out, taking Addie's arm to gently pull her aside. "I'm sorry, Addie. I'm still feeling emotional and adjusting to everything that's been going on. Do you mind if I have a minute to apologize to Father Tom?"

Addie kissed Erick on the cheek and said goodbye to Tom as she went into the house to be with Elizabeth.

Erick turned to Tom with a half-smile. "I owe you an apology too. I guess I'm letting my feelings get ahead of me and not paying attention to the people I'm with. I know you're only trying to help. I just think there are things you know nothing about."

"I'm sure—and I'm sorry for stepping over the line. I care about you and Addie and Elizabeth. Traumatic situations like this can create a lot of tension for couples."

"How did you happen to be talking with Addie, anyway?"

"I think she was walking off your conversation, and we just happened to bump into each other."

"Where was she headed?"

Tom hesitated.

"Something you're not supposed to tell me?"

"No, no. I think she wanted to see Jack before he was transferred—but he was already gone." Tom could see the reaction to this information in Erick's eyes. "We just ended up talking with Detective Brooks. Addie recognized the photo of Jimi on the wall."

"Jimi? The Jimi Johnson who was with that woman they arrested? Where would she know him from?"

"She doesn't know him, but she believes he was at your home."

"During the attack?"

Tom shook his head. "No. She believes he's the guy that came over to check out your wallpapering job for Elizabeth's room."

Erick jerked his head. "What? He was in our apartment before that day? Is she sure it's the same guy? I have his number somewhere, and we can check."

"That might be very helpful to the investigation."

Erick said, "You seem to be very involved with the police on this. Are you thinking of changing careers?"

"No, no, no. I'm a married man—to the Church," responded Tom with a big smile. "Just trying to help. Like I said, I care about you guys a lot."

"I know. You said that this Johnson was trying to get their baby some medical treatments?"

Tom replied, "It's a cancer-related thing, and the alternative treatments in Mexico are very expensive. I think that's why they were desperate to get involved with this."

"How old did you say the baby is?"

"Just over a month, just like Elizabeth."

"Huh." Erick stared out at the neighborhood in front of his home. "So, Jack's already been moved?"

"I guess so. I don't know what time, but right now, he is sitting in a real prison. It doesn't feel right to me, somehow."

"I guess that depends on your perspective."

"Well, we did notice that the photo of the BMW driving down your back alley here may be suspect."

Erick's forehead furrowed. "What does that mean, 'suspect'?"

"Jack contends that he drove home and has proof of being in a car accident. That fender now has a little dent that wasn't visible in the photo. I know the car had his plate number, but it's one of those things that doesn't seem to fit in this case."

"Things?"

"Just a few things the police need to clear up. They may be of no consequence to the case, but they are loose ends to tie up." Tom sighed. "Erick, how have your folks reacted to all of this?"

"My parents? Why are you asking about them?"

"Sorry, I just assumed they were probably upset."

"Yeah, they are, but I told them that everything's okay now."

Tom gawked at him, wide-eyed. "Okay now? Their son's in jail. I'd think they'd be going out of their minds with worry!"

"I haven't told them that part yet. I try not to upset them. I didn't really say much about what happened. They don't need to know until things are sorted out. You know how older people worry about anything and everything."

Tom nodded. "I do. I hope you only have good news to tell them in the end."

"Me too," replied Erick. "Me too."

Chapter 45

After teaching a few morning classes, Tom heard the phone ringing just as he opened the rectory door. "Hello!"

There was no sound initially before he heard a voice. "Father Tom?"

"Let me check. Yup, it's me."

"Very funny. Detective Brooks here. I thought you might like to know a few updates as a trade for anything you pick up."

"What did you find out?"

"We checked out Jack's story. He was in an accident at nine-thirty-five on the morning of the assault—in Connecticut. The woman took a photo with her phone of her front bumper and his back bumper, and you can see the same dent that exists today. The photo is time-stamped, and you can see his plate. Funny thing about his plate, there is a red registration sticker that reads SEP 06."

"Why's that funny?"

"Cause the one in our photo of Jack's car is green and reads MAY 07. Same car and plate, but not the same car or plate—you know what I mean?"

"I know what you mean, but what do you think it means? Do you think someone is trying to frame Jack?"

"Could be. We also found that girl, Katie, who claimed to be Elizabeth's mother for the adoption scam. She was hard to find, but she gave us the whole story in return for no charges being filed. They made contact with her a few weeks before the actual kidnapping. She appeared young, clean, and healthy, but she was clearly homeless and in need of money. She said that Mariana approached her and made some casual conversation after giving her a twenty-dollar bill. Mariana asked Katie if she might be willing to help a young couple who couldn't have a baby adopt one. Katie was skeptical, but Mariana convinced her this was not a scam or illegal, only that it would help both the baby and the couple. Mariana told Katie the baby was hers but didn't want her daughter to ever find out that her mother was an ex-convict and a druggie at one point. She wanted her to believe her mom was just a young girl who wasn't ready to be a mother but loved her enough to see she had a good home and loving parents.

"Katie said she was still skeptical until Mariana brought Katie over to the car, and someone held up the baby in the window. Mariana showed Katie the signed certificate from the hospital and said she could make $2,000 to just do a good thing. Katie agreed to take the baby to Visitation House and claim it was hers—telling them that she didn't believe in abortion and realized she couldn't give the baby what she needed. Visitation House gave her credit for trying to do the best thing for her child and told her they had a really nice couple in mind and could help with the birth certificate and adoption."

Tom said, "Another witness to Mariana being involved. Was that it?"

"Almost. While she only worked with Mariana, she said it was a man that was holding the baby. She didn't pay much attention to his face, but she thinks he was a thin man—and black. We showed her a picture of Jimi, and she wasn't sure but said it could be him."

"Are you going to pick him up again?"

"That's the plan, but there's only one problem—he's no longer in that abandoned building. He's gone."

"Left the city? Ran?"

"He's still got Marie, but no money for treatment, so I'm thinking he might still be in Boston—I hope."

"Do you want me to try to talk to Mariana?" queried Tom.

"We need to do anything we can to convince them to come clean—and I'm not afraid to use any priest available to do the trick."

Detective Brooks called ahead to Framingham to get an exception approval for Tom to visit Mariana.

Mariana grinned at Tom when she entered the visiting room. "Father Tom, I didn't expect to see you out here."

"It's really not far, and I didn't know how much company you've been getting. I hope this is okay?"

"I have a feeling I should be seeing a priest every day now. I think time is short for this girl."

"Are there no more treatments?"

"Not in this country. No. There is nothing more for me."

Tom sat up. "Mariana, are these treatments in Mexico something that could help *you*?"

The look in Mariana's eyes changed considerably as the reality of her situation was brought to the surface. "I don't know. Some people have been lucky, but it ain't free, and I ain't rich." After a pause, she said, "And I don't think they're going to let me walk out of here. The only thing I want is for Marie to be okay. Can you help me with that?"

"You are a selfless mom who loves her baby girl. I can imagine you must be feeling pretty worried about her. Where is she now?"

Mariana hesitated to respond. "She's being taken care of, but that won't give her what she needs right now."

"Is she with Jimi?"

Mariana didn't respond.

"Do you know where Jimi is right now?"

No response.

"Mariana, don't you think the best chance Marie has is if you both are completely honest and work with the police?"

She looked up, clearly disbelieving.

"You love your daughter, and you love Jimi, right?"

She nodded.

"And you'd do anything for them, right?"

She nodded again.

"What if there were another way to get Marie the treatments and be honest about what happened, maybe even bargain for a deal that would help them both?"

She thought for several moments. "What way?"

"I don't know right now, but if there were, what would you do?"

She shook her head. "I need to make sure she is safe and healthy. I don't know of any alternatives. I just don't."

"Don't give up. The right thing is always the right thing to do."

"Not if my daughter is sacrificed in the process."

Chapter 46

Tom returned from his trip to Framingham MCI, feeling somewhat disheartened. If Mariana was going to offer no more than she had, Jimi was out of sight, and Jack was claiming no responsibility but was openly hiding something or protecting someone, how would there be any final resolution to this case? How would the truth come out?

He knew where he had to go for the answer—always the same place.

He walked over to the church to sit and listen, to be with the One who loved him most. When he walked into the church, lit only by a few candles and the setting sun, he saw the silhouette of a man sitting half-way towards the altar. He genuflected at the back and then slowly made his way down the aisle until he recognized Erick Comghan.

"Erick, don't let me disturb you. I just wanted to make sure everything was okay."

Erick continued to stare forward. "Wouldn't that be nice someday if everything was okay? I came over to talk to you about something, but you weren't home, so I thought I would come in to sit and think a bit."

"No better place for that, and available any time of day or night—and no charge either." Tom sat next to Erick in the wooden pew. "I came over for the same reason."

"I thought you had everything figured out," said Erick in a facetious and humorous tone.

"Oh, I'll let you be the first one to know when that happens."

Erick was still staring at the altar. "I've been thinking. Despite some things I'd like to have been different, I've been very lucky in life—my business provides me more money than I'll ever spend. Besides wanting to have a family, what good have I really done in life for anyone else?"

"You've always been generous here with donations and your time."

Erick shook his head. "That was to look good. What real difference have I made in anyone's life? I certainly have more opportunities than most, but I hoard them and just think I need more. I never seem satisfied with the success I have or the money I make. All around me, I see homeless people, who are dying for all I know, while my money sits doing nothing but earning more money. Even you would say that a good Catholic has more responsibility than that—wouldn't you?"

Tom smiled at Erick. "Even I might say that, yes. What are you thinking of?"

"I was thinking about what the possibility of losing Elizabeth felt like. It was a gut-wrenching eternity. I can't imagine losing a baby. Can you?"

"No."

"I know this may sound crazy, but I've been thinking about that little girl."

Tom was fairly sure he knew who Erick meant, but to be on the safe side, he made him say it. "What little girl?"

"The little girl who needs the treatment. She shouldn't be punished for her parents. They wanted to use that money for her and not themselves. It's been on my mind. How could they risk everything for someone else?"

"They love her."

"Would I do that? Would I sacrifice my own self for someone else, for a baby?"

"It's a question you can only answer when it happens. Courage is doing what you know is right, regardless of personal consequences. It's real love."

"I don't know if I have that in me. I don't know if I was born with it and lost it or never had it." He wiped his hand across his cheek. "There's no risk of doing what I'm thinking of, but it might be a start."

Tom turned to Erick. "What are you thinking?"

"I'd like to pay for that baby's treatment. Forty thousand, or whatever it is, could save her life, and to me, it only means holding off on a new car for a few years. Does that make any sense?"

Tom smiled. "That would be a true and beautiful gift. Right now, I feel very proud to call you my friend. I'm very impressed by this."

"I haven't talked to Addie yet, but I think she'll be okay with it. I haven't talked to her about her feelings toward Mariana after her confession, but I can't imagine her taking it out on that baby girl. I feel a little more at peace with this decision now."

Tom nodded and gazed up at the crucifix over the altar.

Erick turned to him and asked, "What are you thinking about? I can always tell when those wheels are spinning."

Tom replied, "It's nothing I can ask you to do, especially under the circumstances, but I was wondering if there were a way to try to save Marie's mother, Mariana. I visited her, and she let on that these treatments might be effective for her, even though she's resigned to it being terminal."

"Oh, man. I don't know."

"As I said, I'm not asking you. I was just trying to think about any other resources that might be able to help give her a chance. She loves that baby, and Marie deserves to be with her mom."

Erick's eyes drifted downward. "Because it's her very own flesh and blood."

"Exactly. Family's everything. That's why I struggled with believing your brother could be guilty because he's family. Have you talked to him since your visit the other day?"

"What am I, my brother's keeper?"

Tom stood up and smiled. "Yes. If Jack did this awful thing, it's a sin that can shatter bonds between family members, but we can help him to find the path back to rebuilding the relationship and mending the pain caused— hopefully helping him back to redemption and God. Family looks out for each other's well-being. It's easy when they're good to us and love us, not so easy when they don't—but that's what real love is. That's what unconditional self-giving love is, and that is always the answer."

Erick rose quickly to his feet. "Thanks for the sermon, Father." He walked down the aisle, leaving Tom standing in the center of the church alone.

Tom knew he had pushed too hard when he wasn't invited to do so. That was against his nature and normal approach. He knelt to ask God for guidance on the best way to help this family out.

Chapter 47

Monday night and Tuesday were quiet. Tom stuck to his routine, caught up on work, visited some homebound parishioners, taught classes, and met with an engaged couple about marriage. Things almost seemed normal again, except for those nagging loose ends of the case. When he had a break, he changed into his sweats to run off some of his pent-up energy and to clear his mind. He made his way down Massachusetts Avenue to the bridge and ran several miles along the Charles River before making the return trip. He stopped at a platform near the bridge and leaned over to catch his breath to let the sweat drip off his brow. The physical activity felt good as he watched a series of college crew teams rowing by.

He started thinking about Jack sitting in jail, Jack's parents not even knowing he was there, and his brother believing he belonged there. If that car in the photo wasn't Jack's, then someone went out of their way to make it look like it was. What was Jack covering up that didn't allow him to explain his whereabouts? Why did he drive home on Sunday and then come right back, and where was he on the night Angelo was attacked? He had denied any involvement in the break-ins, physical assaults, or kidnapping, yet he wouldn't provide any evidence of where he was. On the way back home, he passed the café where he had sat and talked with Addie's sister, Rachel. Through the window's reflection, he noticed someone who looked like her, and as he got closer, he saw that it actually was Rachel sitting alone with a cup of tea. She glanced up at the window and half-smiled as she waved him in.

"Rachel, I didn't know you were in town. How've you been?"

"Come, sit with me."

Tom sat down and waved to the waitress for a coffee. "How're you doing? I'm so glad I saw you."

"I feel like you are exactly the person I need to talk to."

"I'm all ears, but why am I the person you need to talk to?"

"You still do confessions, right?"

"I do, but not usually in a coffee shop."

"I guess you've got to get with the times. This is where all the young folks hang out these days. You should set up shop here a few days a week. I'm sure you'd be busy."

Tom smiled, "You know, you might have something there. I've got to seriously think about that. Did you really want to make a confession?"

"Of sorts. I can't stand what's going on any longer."

"What is it? Is this about Jack?"

"Of course. Why do you think I'm still in Boston? Jack's in jail and shouldn't be. He's just trying to be a gentleman and protect me."

The waitress brought over Tom's coffee. He added some cream and sugar and started stirring. "Why would you need protection?"

"Well, I know this is a new era, but this is still awkward. He, um—Jack's trying to protect my reputation, my 'honor and dignity,' as he puts it. I think that's part of it, but deep down, I think he can't bear to have Addie know. He hasn't told me that, but I know how he still feels, and it breaks my heart to know how true that is."

Tom took a sip of his coffee. "You were made with honor and dignity, and I'm glad Jack knows that. Look, I'm not going to judge anyone. You can feel free to talk openly with me."

Rachel stirred her tea absentmindedly. "Hum. There aren't many people you can really do that with. I can trust you?"

"You can trust me."

"Okay. I need to talk to someone. I think you know how I feel about Jack. Maybe not how deeply I feel, but I think you have a sense of it. Without his obsession with my sister, I think I would happily be Mrs. Jack Comghan right now. It's the only life I've ever really wanted."

"That must be extremely difficult for you. He leaves for, what, six years, comes back, and he still feels the way he does?"

Rachel gazed into her cup. "More than you know, Father. More than you know. I think it's gotten worse. I've been patient, even understanding, but this year was especially tough to endure. Maybe I'd even like my sister, but it's hard. It hasn't led to the healthiest thoughts at times."

"I was very much in love with a girl whom I lost, so I understand your pain and frustration."

"Really? Huh. So, Jack's in jail, and I know he didn't do it. He couldn't have done it."

Tom looked up with intense interest. "What do you mean?"

"I was with him."

Tom stared at Rachel, his eyes wide with disbelief. "Rachel, you said you'd do anything for Jack. Would that anything included lying for him?"

"I think it would—but I'm not lying about this."

"What do you mean you were with him?"

"At the baptism, I saw Jack and Addie talking. It wasn't just chit-chat. I've been wondering if something's been going on with them since Jack came back home. Well, I've been more than wondering, and I even talked to Erick about it at one point. He wasn't too happy either."

"I can see that."

"Jack wouldn't talk to me at Addie's afterward, outside of small talk. I felt desperate that this was my last chance. I went over to his hotel on Sunday morning to talk to him, but they said he had left. I walked for quite a bit before finally gaining the courage to call him later that morning. The timing wasn't great because he had just been in an accident on the road. He called me back and asked me what I wanted." Rachel's eyes flooded with tears. "I, um, I told him that I, um, that I wanted to live my life, and I believed it was meant to be with him. I told him I loved him, but I needed to move on if he believed he could never love me back. I said, ah, I didn't want to be one of those women obsessed with a man who detested her." Rachel wiped her eyes.

"That must have taken a lot of courage."

"Maybe. I was out of patience to wait any longer, but I didn't want to sound like I was desperate. I just wanted him to know how I felt and that I was ready to move on—I wasn't, but I wanted him to believe I was."

"What did he say?"

"He said that Addie had told him that she wanted to move on without him, for him to move on without her. She wanted him to live his life and not give it up for her. I tried not to be jealous, and I didn't want to lash out at him—well, part of me did, but most of me wanted to hold him. I had dreamed of holding him for so many years; it hurt. It was the solitude that left me empty. I know I'm not a kid, but I had a hard time dating anyone seriously when my heart was completely with him. I've never been with a man and only wanted to be with him."

Tom scratched his head, anticipating where they were going. "Did he respond to you?"

"He was quiet. I told him that I knew his feelings for Addie, but if he was waiting for her, he would be giving up his life for something that couldn't be, something that wasn't real in a relationship sense. I told him that I knew this because I'd been doing the same thing with him—having the relationship in my head and not really with him. I may feel it in my heart, but it wasn't real; it wasn't love without the other person being there fully with you."

"I knew you were a wise young lady."

Rachel smiled at the acknowledgment. "Hey, the words surprised me. I said I'd like to try to see if I could give him what he was looking for from Addie and that he would never get from her. Maybe we could actually begin our lives, to know what love with another person really was, and possibly have a family together—he and I. Jack and Rachel."

"Sounds like a beautiful proposal."

Rachel nodded. "Well, there was a very long silence on the other end of the line. At one point, I thought he'd hung up on me, and I was ready to let loose my tears. Then he said, 'I'd like that. I'd like that a lot. I don't know what I can promise, except that I'll try.' I asked him where he was and if he could come back to Boston. I think he turned right around and headed back because he was here before noon. I know this isn't what you want to hear, but all these years of pent-up emotions seemed to take over, and Jack rebooked the room he just left, and we spent the afternoon there. At one point, he went down to the lobby to pick up my bags that had been sent over."

Tom cleared his throat. "Okay, and you didn't go out at all?"

"Well, we did end up going for some Chinese for a late dinner, but that was it for going out."

"What about Monday?"

"Um." Rachel blushed and let out a long breath. "We were together when we got up, but I could tell something was bothering Jack. He was thinking about something, but he wouldn't share it. I guessed what it was, and we argued before he left to do something."

Tom said, "Actually, he stopped by to see me for a quick talk."

"Well, we got together for dinner at the restaurant and argued again. That is when you came over, and you and I ended up walking to this café to talk."

"So, you don't know where he was that night?"

"Well, after we said goodbye, I still didn't feel we had come to any decision about the future. I knew I needed closure before he returned home, so I went over to his hotel. He was there, and we spent several hours talking and arguing."

Tom sat up, "Jack was with you starting when?"

"I don't know. It was probably eight o'clock until nine-thirty or ten. Why?"

"Huh. Just curious."

"Jack didn't want me to say anything about Sunday afternoon to anyone. I think he believed more evidence would eventually come out, and he'd be released. Then no one would have to know that we were together on Sunday. By 'no one', I mean my sister. I feel more embarrassed and ashamed by that than if everyone knew."

"So, what are you going to do?"

"I'm going to tell the police that he couldn't have done it because he was with me. I went to see him, and he's clearly stressed and anxious. No innocent man should go through being held in prison. It pains me that everyone thinks he could do something like this to his own brother, to his goddaughter, to his family. It's not in his soul to do anything like this."

Tom smiled. "Rachel, I'm glad you are standing up for the truth and someone you know who is innocent. Now, you're going to have to convince them that you are telling the truth."

"You don't believe me?"

"I believe you, but they don't have to believe you until you can prove it. You love him, so you could be trying to save him by providing an alibi. They need rock-solid proof to let Jack go because of all the other evidence."

Rachel finished her tea. "Huh. I guess that makes a lot of sense. I wouldn't have thought of that. Thanks."

They got up, and Tom accompanied Rachel to the station where Mullen took her into an interview room to take her statement.

Brooks stepped out of the detectives' room to see Tom standing by the front desk. "Did you move in?"

"Not yet. I came with Rachel Kerrins. She wanted to give a statement that should clear Jack of at least being at the scene during the attack."

"What? He was with her? How do we know that's actually true?"

Tom smiled. "She's going to have to convince you. I think she's telling the truth, and it could support the questions we have about the car in the photo."

Brooks smirked. "Questions we have?"

"Don't you? The blood, the car, and now this. Something's up."

"Well, something is up. Out of nowhere, Erick Comghan said that he would fund Marie Perez's treatments. He didn't want her to suffer because of this. Shortly afterward, Jimi Johnson turned himself in and took responsibility for the physical assault of Erick and the abduction of Elizabeth for the money. He claims that he didn't want to harm Comghan, only to knock him out. Claims he did it to try to save Marie's life and believed he was putting Elizabeth in a good home. He says he heard the Comghans arguing when he was at the house, and they didn't seem like the best parents."

Tom sat on the desk. "Wow! That's something. Did he say anything about Jack being involved?"

"He said he planted the evidence to throw us off the track."

"What about Mariana?"

"He still claims that she was never inside the apartment and had nothing to do with the crime. He said that she only thought she was helping to provide a better home for the baby and getting a chance to save her daughter. Jimi said she wanted to save Marie more than anything, so it was easy to convince Mariana that the plan was benefiting everyone."

"So you have him in custody. Is he here?"

"Yes, but we aren't letting anyone see him until we have finished all the fact-finding interview questions and validated the timelines and assertions."

"Does this clear Jack?"

"Not yet, but we may be able to let him out of Norfolk. I still have questions about his involvement. I'm going to sit in with Rachel Kerrins to see if she's credible."

"Makes sense. Thanks for the update on Jimi, and good luck bringing this to a conclusion."

"Thanks, but it's never as easy as you would like it to be."

Tom nodded. "I'm getting that idea."

Chapter 48

Tom asked the desk sergeant if he could use the phone for a call. He dialed the number and waited. "Hello."

"Hi, Erick. It's Father Tom. I heard the generous offer you made to help save Marie. It's a great and loving thing to do."

"Money is paper, and her life worth a lot more. Thanks, and sorry for leaving abruptly like that again."

Tom took a deep breath. "Erick, I was out of line. You didn't ask me to preach to you. You were right to let me know that. I have a favor to ask you. Would you have time to meet at the church in an hour or so?"

Erick was silent for a few seconds and then hesitantly replied, "Sure. Anything particular you want to talk about?"

"That's great. I'll tell you when you come over. See you soon, and if I'm not there yet, I'll be right along."

When Tom got back to the church, Erick was already standing outside the side door of the rectory. "Erick, hi. Did you walk over?"

"Yeah, doing pretty good now. No more dizzies or headaches."

"So you'll be ready for some ball soon, I hope. Come on in." As they walked into the kitchen, Tom reached for a couple of glasses. "What can I get you to drink?"

"Do you still have any of that Kilbeggan whiskey I gave you?"

"So, you'd be like'n a wee drop of good stuff, would'ya now?" said Tom in a melodic voice as he retrieved the bottle of rich yellow-golden distilled whiskey from Ireland. "On the rocks?"

Erick nodded as Tom prepared two generous glasses, sat at the kitchen table, and raised his glass. "Well, here's to good news for the Comghan clan to toast."

Erick tapped his glass with Tom's and said, "Good news?"

"Well, you've got your family back, and the two people who tried to take that away have now confessed, and it looks like your brother may be in the clear—I hope," responded Tom as he took a sip.

"They cleared him?"

"Still working on it, but it looks like he has an alibi. It'd be great if he had nothing to do with this, wouldn't it?"

"I'd like to think he didn't do anything wrong."

"How do you think Addie is doing through all this?"

"With Elizabeth back, she's happy, but I think she feels we're still disconnected."

"And Elizabeth is doing fine?"

"Yeah, she's good. Addie just got off a call from the pediatrician's office, and they said she was healthy physically and emotionally. You got very involved with this case, didn't you?"

"You're a good friend to me, and I care about you guys—a lot, actually."

"Well, I'm touched," said Erick as he clinked his glass with Tom's.

"And I really want you to get back on that court so that I can whup your butt too!"

Erick laughed. "Like that's going to happen. Look, I don't know where I am on things with my own family. Everything seems unsettled."

"You have a really good family. We need trust to keep the bonds close, or suspicion and hurt can take over all too easily."

"Are you talking about Addie, me, and Liz?"

"Your whole family, including your parents. I think you have something special."

"How would you know? You just met Jack, and you've never met my parents."

Tom rubbed his chin. "Actually—"

"What? When could you have met them?"

"On Sunday, Angelo and I drove down to the family farm you've talked about. Your mom and dad were gracious enough to invite us to dinner, and we had a nice visit. I'll have to say that I was a bit jealous. You have a slice of heaven there. It's a beautiful spot. I can see why you talk so fondly about it."

Erick sat back, holding his glass on the table. "I don't know what to think. I can't believe you just dropped in on my parents like that. I don't have time these days to visit much."

"I should've told you. It was a spur-of-the-moment thing. I wanted some context to the family dynamics, something I had no business barging into— but it was only because I cared about you."

Erick twirled his drink in his hand as he watched the ice cubes spin. "I feel a little funny about this. So, how were they doing?"

"They seemed good. I think they miss the family being together."

"Well, we aren't kids anymore, and they kind of put that campfire out a long time ago."

"One thing I've found out with people is that things are usually different from what we think. We make assumptions about what the other person thinks or feels, and we end up having the relationship in our head instead of checking in to know the truth. We can't really know how the other person feels without asking."

Erick shook his head in dejection. "My mother always took Jack's side, overprotecting him, doting on him. I felt I was more like my father, but what he did at that championship game really hurt. He gave Jack what should have been mine. He praised him when Jack took the easy way out. He always pushed me more and then was disappointed, ashamed of me if I didn't meet his expectations. All my life, I've tried to prove my worth to him, but I don't think he ever recognized it. No matter what I accomplished, it was never good enough. I'd never be good enough. Why would I want to keep putting myself through that crap? I just needed to start my own family and not make the same mistake."

"That couldn't feel too good. But your new family wasn't coming so easily when Addie had trouble getting pregnant, right?"

"It put a lot of stress on us—or maybe I did? I'm not sure how ready Addie was, but I wanted a family. I needed a family. When years started going by with no luck, I felt like it would never happen. I don't think you can understand. It left me feeling desperately lonely and bitter."

"I could sometimes tell when you talked about it."

"That obvious, huh?"

"Yep."

"I felt like it disappointed my parents too. No grandchildren. Guy can't even make a baby."

"Do you really think they were feeling that way?"

"I don't know. It's just a feeling I was having. Then Jack came back from England, and Addie seemed different to me. She started traveling more for her legal business. She just seemed different—distracted. You know that Jack was in love with her when we were in school, don't you?"

Tom didn't respond.

"I don't think it stopped. But then she became pregnant. I can't tell you how happy I felt. I almost couldn't wait for the nine months. Addie still seemed tentative about it. I kept telling myself it was just the change in hormones or the anticipation, but I could tell something wasn't right."

"When did you begin to feel suspicious?"

Erick quickly lifted his gaze from his drink to look curiously into Tom's eyes. "What are you asking?"

"When did you first wonder about Elizabeth?"

"What are you asking me?"

Tom set his glass on the table and folded his hands together. "This was the child you were longing for. I think you loved your family growing up, and you missed what it meant to you. Then it was finally becoming a reality. Something must have made you check up on Addie's business trips."

"What makes you think I was checking up on her?"

"I don't think you would hit Angelo in the head with a metal box if it didn't contain something important, would you?"

"What? Where do you come up with this stuff? With all due respect, Father, I think this playing detective has gone to your head."

"The assailant that night ran out the front door and jumped into a cab that was later tracked down. The cab driver identified that person as Jack from a photo."

"I don't know why Jack would break in to take that box, but why would you then blame this on me?"

"Seems like Jack was occupied that night and couldn't have done it. It also seems like his photo probably looks a lot like yours. Could you have snuck out of the hospital to retrieve that box?"

Erick moved uncomfortably in his chair as he gulped his glass. "Even if that were true, how would you have any idea what was in that box?"

"I apologize for this, but Angelo and I broke into your apartment the night before to see if there were any clues at the scene that we had missed the day before. Angelo has special skills and found your metal box. Two items seemed interesting—a listing of places Addie had stayed and a DNA paternity test from Boston GenTech something or other. Why would you need to track Addie and order a paternity test unless you were suspicious?"

"Father Tom. This is getting really uncomfortable. Why are you getting into any of this stuff?"

"I get that this is uncomfortable, and I should be hugely apologetic here, but I think you may be destroying your family for no reason except for suspicion. I like you way too much not to fight for you."

"No reason?! How can you say that?!"

"Well, you tested to see confirmation that you were Elizabeth's dad, and it came back positive. Why wouldn't you be happy unless it was not your DNA you submitted for the test?"

Erick ran his hand through his hair and stroked the back of his neck as he tried to think of a response. The anger flared in his eyes. "You want to know why I was suspicious? Because I know Addie met with Jack on some of those trips! Because I know she was different and that Jack still loved her! We can't have a baby, and then Jack strolls back into the picture, and all of a sudden, things change?"

Tom leaned back in his chair and crossed his arms. "After I got off the phone with you, I called Jack and asked him if you had visited him over the past few months. He said you came out unexpectedly and were unusually friendly—'almost brotherly' was the term he used. He was happy that it seemed like you finally wanted to mend the relationship, move on from the feelings of the past. I asked him if there was anything unusual that went on. He didn't think there was, but he did say you asked to borrow his car at one point to run an errand. He also said that you wanted to take some swab samples from his cheeks to do a family genealogy present for your mom and dad. Jack did think that was an unusual thing for you to want to do but was just glad that you were even thinking of those kinds of family things."

Erick sat, shaking his head, his lips pursed as he listened.

Tom continued, "I visited Dr. Levin, Elizabeth's obstetrician, and he said it was unusual, but he accepted the swab samples of your mouth when you said they were your own. He was glad that the test came back positive."

Erick glared at him. "Nothing you said removes Jack's guilt, his betrayal of me."

"Like I said, sometimes we make assumptions about a friend or family member's feelings, intent, or actions without making sure they're true. When we don't have trust, we approach our relationships with suspicion to protect ourselves. It's not uncommon to imagine some of the worst scenarios to make sure we are protected from them."

"So?"

"Did you know that fraternal twins have different DNA, but identical twins basically share the same DNA?"

"Of course."

"One fertilized egg splits but shares the same DNA. Your fingerprints will be different, but not your DNA, for the most part."

"So, what's your point?"

'If you submitted Jack's DNA for the paternity test and it came back positive, that didn't mean that you *weren't* the father. I'm hoping that's good news."

Erick shook his head. "I don't know where you are going with this. Everyone knows that identical twins share the same DNA, but they have tests now that can distinguish between identical twins. I read all about it, so I think your theory is off the mark."

"I asked Dr. Levin about that. He mentioned that capability, but he also said that they don't run that level of testing for this type of DNA work."

Erick sat open-mouthed, stunned, frozen.

"I also asked Dr. Levin about those red dots on Elizabeth's feet and how her blood could have been at the crime scene if she had no cuts or injuries during the attack. He said the only thing he could think of could be a series of small blood draws using a butterfly needle—something Angelo also found in the metal box."

Tom could see that Erick's mind was racing as he stood up and checked around the kitchen. "My God, what have I done?"

"Erick. Erick. Look at me."

Panting with choked breaths, Erick met his gaze, his eyes wide with terror.

"Erick, listen. Calm down. I think you've been in pain for a long time, and you truly believed Jack presented a real threat to the only thing that mattered to you—your family. I think you believed Jack was having an affair with Addie and that this was his baby, and it seemed like everything had been taken away from you by the very person you felt took away the affection and recognition you craved as a child."

Erick rubbed his forehead with the palm of his hand. "Oh, my gosh," he said as tears flowed. "I don't believe this. What did I do?"

In shock, Erick stiffened, his face contorted with confusion. Fear and anger gave way to guilt and shame.

Tom stood up and put both hands on Erick's shoulders, staring him in the eyes. "Erick, remember when I asked if you could ever forgive Jack and try to mend the relationship that was gifted to you?"

Still panting, Erick nodded.

"That opportunity isn't lost. There's nothing that can't be overcome by love and forgiveness, no matter how bad it looks or what we've done."

Erick squeezed his eyelids tight, clearly in physical pain. Tom gave him time to calm down. There were beads of sweat coming from his brow that he wiped off with his hand. "What do I do?"

"We should go to the station and tell the whole story to Brooks and Mullen and then go from there. I know you may feel like all is lost right now—your business, your family, your marriage, and your daughter— but I don't believe that for a second. It may take a while, but complete honesty is the best way forward."

"I don't know. I can't think. Maybe you can come with me?"

Chapter 49

On the way to the station, Tom welcomed the cool night air as he steadied Erick, who was dazed and flushed.

"I don't think I can do this."

Tom put his hand on Erick's back. "Let's just walk for a bit."

"If we share the same DNA, they could still have been together, and Elizabeth might still be Jack's."

"That call from Dr. Levin to Addie was actually me. I called from the doctor's office and pleaded with Addie to come clean on those same questions. I think you need to hear those answers right from her. No more guessing or projecting. No more suspicion or indictments. Everything on the table."

Erick shook his head. "No! No. I can't do that. I can't tell you how terrifying that sounds to me. How can I protect myself? "

"You can start with trust. Not trusting just anyone, but starting with your family. If you assume the worst, you'll see the worst possibilities and filter out what may be the truth. If you start with trust, you might begin to see from a different perspective. You might see the actual intent. You might even be surprised by how they actually feel about you."

Erick replied, "What if I already know how they feel about me?"

"Ah, what if you're wrong? You might even feel certain and process all the information to prove you're right, but that heavy dose of confirmation bias doesn't let you see the reality. What if it kept you from even asking that person if your feelings were accurate?"

"It sounds safer to just stick with your instincts."

"I think that answer feels safer, but it makes you put up walls to protect yourself. It keeps you from having the relationship you could have—from being happy. It also keeps you from sharing all of you with someone because you're too afraid of being rejected. It can keep you from living life and experiencing true love."

Erick ran his hands through his hair and sucked in a breath. He remained quiet as they walked the remaining half-mile to the station. When they stood in front of the entrance, he let out a big sigh and shivered. "I guess what you're trying to tell me nicely is that the real prison isn't in there but out here—self-imposed as my own judge and jury."

Tom patted Erick on the back. "Something like that."

They entered the front doors together and approached the front desk. Tom nodded to Sergeant Doherty, as Erick said, "I'm here to see Detective Brooks if he's available."

Doherty picked up the phone, and a few seconds later, Brooks started down the hallway. "What's on your mind, gentlemen?" Brooks glanced curiously at Tom and then at Erick.

Erick placed his palms down on the desk and replied, "There are some things you need to know—for everyone's sake."

Brooks escorted Erick down the hall to one of the interview rooms. "Mr. Comghan, do you want Father Tom to wait in another room?"

Erick turned toward Tom, who gave him a friendly look back, then turned back to Brooks. "Actually, no. I want him to hear this as well."

Tom sat next to Erick.

Brooks pulled out a notebook and took a seat across from them. Brooks said, "Okay. What do you want to tell me? Is there a piece of evidence we need to be aware of that hasn't come out yet?"

"All of it," replied Erick.

"All of it? What do you mean by, 'All of it'?"

"No one you have in custody is guilty."

"What? What possible evidence could you have to prove that? Two of them have confessed. People don't do that when they're innocent."

Erick leaned forward. "When they love someone enough, they do. I think I might be just beginning to believe that's possible."

Brooks leaned back in his chair and dropped his pen on the table. "I'm really confused. Can we start from the beginning and help me out here?"

Tom nodded encouragingly toward Erick.

"I'm not proud of any of this, and I'm deeply sorry for what I've done. I've been suspicious of my brother's feelings for my wife for many years. When he came back to the States, those suspicions escalated to the point where I checked on her business trips. Some of them coincided with my brother's trips. Tom knows that Addie and I have been trying desperately to have a family but couldn't become pregnant. Having a son or daughter meant the world to me, but when Addie suddenly became pregnant during the time of these trips, I'm ashamed to say that I became suspicious—so much so that I ordered a paternity test to find out if my brother was the real father. When the test came back positive, I was devasted and overwhelmed with anger. I'm sorry to get into that, but it has a bearing on everything else."

Brooks nodded. "I have nowhere to go. Don't feel rushed because the context is important." He paused, formulated his phrasing. "So you believed that Elizabeth wasn't your daughter. When was that exactly?"

Erick sighed again. "Just after her birth. I didn't know what to do. I didn't want to confront Addie, but the thought of having a child that I knew – or at least thought I knew – wasn't mine gnawed at me and seemed like too much to bear."

"So, what then?"

"I wrestled with my anger and my building resentment against both of them during the next few weeks. I thought that the only chance I'd have to stay married and maybe have that family was to take Jack's baby out of the picture. I knew Addie was struggling with being a mother because of her career. If Liz could be placed with a really good family, then I wouldn't be hurting her, and she could get more love than I could give her. I started thinking about how that could happen, and just the challenge of that seemed to lift me out of a sinking depression, something I have wrestled with from time to time in my life."

"Are you saying that this entire thing was your idea, your plan?"

"I'm ashamed. I honestly am. I don't think I was thinking straight at all. I had met Mariana Perez and Jimi Johnson in the hospital when she had her baby. I had sat for hours in the waiting room with Jimi listening to him tell me about his and Mariana's life, including her struggle with cancer before and during her pregnancy. They both had such a difficult road, and I felt ridiculous for thinking that I had it tough with my family. We're talking abuse, abandonment, poverty—you name it, but here they were with joy and love in their hearts. I was most moved when Jimi told me that Mariana's condition was terminal, and the baby might possibly be affected by cancer—with the only hope being an expensive treatment in Mexico. I left there feeling awful for them but still buried in my worries. I was having a baby, finally having the family I've been desperately dreaming of, and I didn't feel happy. I only felt suspicious and insecure."

Tom asked, "Is this when you decided to get the paternity test?"

"Yeah, but I needed DNA from Jack, so I drove out to visit him, something I've never done as an adult. He was surprised but appeared happy that I'd come to see him. I think he thought this might be the opening to mending our relationship, but I was only there to confirm its end. We talked and reminisced. He showed me around his business and home. I told him I wanted to mend and reconnect with him and the family.

I told him I was thinking of a present for Mom and Pop—one of those genealogy things where they use your DNA to trace your heritage. He thought it was a great idea, and I told him that I just needed to take a swab sample from the inside of his cheek and mail it off for analysis. He seemed fine with that. At one point, I asked to borrow his car for a quick errand, telling him I wanted to test out his BMW. He insisted on coming with me to the hardware store, but I was able to separate long enough to make a copy of his car key."

Brooks nodded. "You were really thinking this out, weren't you?"

"I'm a businessman. Strategy, planning, and considering all the details always make the difference between success and failure. Before I left, I grabbed some gravel from his driveway and then asked him if he would be the godfather to Elizabeth. He was so excited and said he was honored I had asked. When the DNA results came through, I was devastated. My suspicions suddenly turned into a hard reality with objective proof." Tears streamed down Erick's cheeks. "I didn't know until today that my assumptions were wrong." Erick sucked in a sharp breath and exhaled.

"Shortly after that, there was a benefit dinner held by the New England Small Business Association. Jack always attends these, but only for the early cocktails, then he leaves before dinner. When this benefit for MS came up in Rhode Island, it wasn't unusual that we wouldn't connect, which we didn't. I sat with a couple, Sam and Becky Larson, and began talking about Elizabeth. That's when they told me about their own struggle to have a family. As we talked, everything seemed to fall into place. They were a perfect and deserving couple. Jimi and Mariana desperately needed help to save Marie. And I needed a solution to my problem."

"But they said that they talked to Jack at that dinner, not you."

"When we said goodbye at the dinner, I took their card. I called them later, and I told them my name was Jacob. I immediately started checking around Rhode Island for possible adoption agencies that could help connect Elizabeth with the Larsons. I did some reading about so-called 'baby-brokers' that entice young pregnant girls to sell their babies for a chance at a better life with an offer of more money than they could earn and a way to solve their problem of trying to take care of an unwanted baby. Visitation House seemed perfect. It was a Catholic agency that helped young women during and after pregnancy with support and resources. They'd find a good home for a baby a young mother couldn't care for."

Tom said, "They do great work."

Brooks asked, "Where did Perez and Johnson fit into this master plan?"

"The way the plan came together seemed like a sign that this was the right thing to do, as long as Elizabeth was safe and ended up in a good, loving home. I never wanted any harm to come to her or anyone else. At the hospital, I told Jimi that I might be able to help a little, and he let me know how to get in contact with him. No phone or address, but someone through whom I could pass the word. I met with him first and said that I'd thought about Marie a lot and wanted to pay for the treatments. The look on his face was priceless, but I had my price for the offer. He listened to the plan and said there was no way he could be involved. I convinced him that he wouldn't be committing any crime."

"What? No crime?"

"If I let him hit me, that's not assault. If I ask them to help place my baby in the hands of a loving couple, there's no kidnapping. He has my permission. Whoever the girl is that poses as the mother would be falsifying the birth certificate, but for a good cause, and she'd get the money that she needed too. He hesitated for a long time and then declined. My plan was dead until he contacted me days later. Apparently, Mariana panicked at the idea that Marie would die of the disease when there was a potential cure. Money was the only obstacle in the way, and she begged Jimi to find a solution. Forty thousand dollars was not something he could get in the best of times, and this opportunity seemed like the only option. The real catch for Jimi was that he had to agree to take the fall if he was caught—Plan B. I would still pay for the treatments."

Brooks said, "I wouldn't feel good about taking that kind of advantage of the situation."

"I just needed a buffer to protect my family and reputation. Mariana started scouring Providence for potential girls who seemed healthy but were in a desperate situation. Couples aren't going to want to take a baby from a woman who looks like a drug addict. I checked out Visitation House and started thinking about a plan."

"A plan that included framing your brother?"

"Just enough to punish him for what I believed he did to me and Addie— or with Addie."

"Did you intend for him to go to jail for years?"

"No. I don't know. I wanted him to feel what I was feeling, suffer like I was suffering. In my book, he was guilty of no small crime and deserved some punishment. I guess I just wanted to see that he got it."

"So, what happened?"

"I had Jimi come to the house as a contractor so that he could get a sense of the layout. We practiced each step over and over at his place. As we got closer, I started drawing safe amounts of blood from Liz's foot with a butterfly needle. I learned and practiced. I didn't want to hurt her. On the day of the baptism, I made sure I was late."

Tom said, "That's right. You told Addie that you had to run an errand, and you'd be right along."

"I did. I was using the time to—"

"Plant the evidence in Jack's car."

"Right. A trace of blood in the back seat. A matching pink bootie under the seat. Traces of gravel in the trunk. Nothing he'd notice, but certainly something the police would find. At the baptism, I was able to place a small amount of blood on his jacket sleeve and a receipt in his pocket while he was busy holding the baby. When I saw Jack and Addie talking after the baptism service, I only became more convinced that this was the right thing to do. After the party, Addie had to get packed to leave on a trip, which gave me time to set things up. I had ordered 30,000 in gold coins. I told Addie it was an investment, but it was a clean way to pay off Jimi without money suspiciously coming out of my account. As far as the police would be concerned, it would be stolen money from the scene of the crime."

Brooks nodded. "That's pretty clever. And you had asked Father Tom to come over precisely at three o'clock to find you unconscious and call in the crime?"

"That was the plan." Erick turned to Tom. "Sorry for using you like that."

"I'm used to being a pawn in the game of life," said Tom with a wry smile.

"I had Jimi rent the same model car as Jack's and had a fake plate made up in case there were any witnesses. I knew there was a camera in the alley but didn't know if you'd figure that out. I let him into the apartment just before two o'clock, and we planted some of Elizabeth's blood on the front door and the rug under the spot I would fall after being hit."

Brooks said, "You took a big chance with your own life to pull this off."

"I know, but it was worth it to me, and I studied where and how to take a blow that was the least risky. I had Jimi whack me in the arm—I wasn't holding Elizabeth but posed as if she were in my arms and then crouched over like I was protecting her. Jimi was tentative in taking a whack to my head. He really didn't want to hurt me and held back on the first one, just grazing me."

"Huh, that explains the doctor's report. He said there were three blows, one to the arm, a lighter one to the head, and then the harder one that left you unconscious. So, you were never holding Elizabeth during the staged attack?"

"No. I wouldn't do that. We just put some blood on the rug where she would have landed during a fall."

Tom said, "That explains the fragments of red brick under your body. You said that you never saw him coming, so there was no way that could have happened if this was a real surprise attack from behind."

"Yeah, I didn't know that. Jimi took the money in a yellow canvas bag and met Mariana at the door with Elizabeth to leave the city, but only after being seen bumping into Jack at his hotel."

Brooks said, "And a bright yellow bag would be easy for even police to notice."

"Right."

"If Jack was leaving for Connecticut that morning, how did you know he'd come back to the hotel that afternoon to be seen with Jimi in the lobby?"

"I didn't know if he would, but I met up with Rachel in the morning and had a long talk about her and Jack. I convinced her to take the chance and call him back instead of letting both of their lives go by without love, without living it. She called him on the road, and he agreed to come back. That was when I told Jimi to go over to the hotel to catch Jack when he came down to get Rachel's bags from the lobby. I had told Rachel that I'd have them sent over and figured the timing to have Jimi pick them up. He was to hide the yellow bag from the camera and expose it when he bumped into Jack. I was hoping this might look like Jack handed it off to Jimi. After that, Mariana, Marie, and Elizabeth were off to Providence to meet up with Katie O'Donnell. Jimi would take the train down separately to avoid being seen with the baby. Mariana would be less suspicious transporting the babies if anyone stopped her. After seeing the Larsons at Visitation House, Jimi would take Marie, the money from the Larsons, and the gold coins to Mexico, and Mariana would hide out at their abandoned building apartment. I think you know the rest."

Brooks sat stunned. "That's unbelievable. Didn't you know that Jack would have an alibi?"

"I didn't think he would want to admit he was with Rachel to Addie, so I took that chance."

"You took a lot of chances. I can't believe this story. You do know that you committed several crimes? Whether or not you think you did, you put the baby's life in danger, and you involved two other people in this fraud and consciously imprisoned an innocent man."

Erick replied, "I know. I could say that Jimi will stick with his confession, and I will deny the entire story I just told you, but I don't want to do that. I want the truth out. I was scared to death coming over here and destroying myself and my family, but now I feel a load off my shoulders getting it all out in the open. Whatever happens to me, I want to help out Marie and Mariana. I want to pay for them both to get those treatments. I'm willing to put this entire story in writing if we can find a way not to involve Jimi or Mariana in the charges. This is my fault, and they did this thinking it was a good thing for both Marie and Elizabeth. I'll take whatever punishment comes my way if you can promise me that."

Tom's eyes filled with hopeful tears when he heard these words coming from Erick and put his arm around his shoulder. "We'll get to a better place, Erick. You're doing the right thing here, and I admire your courage."

Erick laughed to himself. "All I ever wanted was to be admired by a father. I guess you're the best I can expect, and it will have to do."

Brooks put Erick in a holding room for the night. Tom said that he would tell Addie that Erick was helping with the case tonight, and he would explain everything to her in the morning.

Tom left the station and breathed in the crisp evening air. He felt awful about Erick's story but strangely hopeful that this was an opening to a better place for Erick in his marriage and with his family. He didn't know that for sure, but his sudden feeling of hope was strong.

Chapter 50

After morning Mass, Tom felt more than nervous about seeing Addie and relaying Erick's revelations from the night before. How could the man she married, Elizabeth's father, and the brother of Jack, plan such a thing? She didn't marry a callous criminal or a cruel person. How could he possibly be responsible for all the events of the past many days, for the suffering and anxiety, innocent people being held in prison, and taking away their daughter?

When Addie opened the door with a welcoming but curious smile, he felt nauseous at the pit of his stomach.

"Good morning, Addie." Tom stepped into the apartment foyer. Everything was back in its place with no evidence that there had ever been a crime there.

"Thanks for coming over, Father Tom. I hear you've been keeping yourself busy lately."

"Just a little." He handed her a small, gift-wrapped box. "That's for Elizabeth's baptism. With everything going on, I wasn't able to give it to you earlier."

Addie's throat seemed to tighten as she replied, "Thanks. The real gift is that we have her back safely."

Tom pointed to the living room couch and asked Addie if they could sit. She checked the time with curious nervousness. "Sure. Is everything okay?"

As they took seats across from each other, Tom said a short prayer in his head for wisdom in sharing the truth about the situation. His hesitation only seemed to increase the worried anticipation that was creeping into Addie's expression. "What if I told you some awful news that could actually be the start of something really good?"

Addie moved forward in her seat. "Awful? What awful news? Is Erick okay?"

"Yes, Erick's okay. First of all, we found out last night that Jack is completely innocent of any of the charges. He never had anything to do with what happened here or to Elizabeth."

A smile of relief flooded Addie's face. "Oh, thank God! I knew he couldn't have done any of it. I knew in my heart he was innocent. So, why would you say that news would be awful?"

Tom squinted a bit. "Addie, try not to react initially and hear me through. You said that you were trying to help Erick, Jack, and his parents get back to a better place as a family, right?"

"More than anything. Why?"

"After all this time, why haven't you given up on that?"

"Because I know there's something important there being lost due to past hurts. It seems like such a shame not to push through them, even if it's painful."

Tom nodded. "What if I told you that hurt had grown to be an all-encompassing suspicion and resentment?"

"I know it has. Erick seems to be getting worse rather than better—especially since Elizabeth was born. I thought it would be the opposite. I don't understand what's been going on."

"Let me ask you something. You know how Jack feels about you, right?"

Addie lowered her head and nodded.

"How do you feel about him?"

She quickly glanced up with concern for Tom's intent. "I used to like him a lot, but I fell in love with Erick, the man I still love. I love Jack like a brother now, not in any other way. Why are you asking?"

"Do you think Erick knows how Jack still feels about you?"

"Oh, it's come up many times. Yes, he knows, and it bothers him to no end."

"Does Erick know how you feel about him?"

"He should know I love him. I'm married to him."

"Yeah, but have you looked him in the eye and let him know it? Have you told him how you feel about Jack? You just convinced me a second ago."

Addie shifted in her seat and turned towards Tom. She was an attractive woman, and Tom could tell why Erick might be jealous of other men being interested in her, especially Jack. "Why do I have to convince him?"

"Because he needs it. Strong people on the outside are often very vulnerable on the inside. I think Erick has a deep need for affirmation and a sense that he was valued from childhood. It may be very unfair, but he probably looks to fill that need to validate his self-worth in his relationships, to let him know he isn't nothing in people's eyes."

"Erick? He's always been the leader, the strong one, the confident one in any relationship. Way more than Jack. Why would he need constant reassurance?"

"First, I think he lost his sense of trust with his parents that he was loved unconditionally. He feels he deserved the affection and attention that Jack got, that he was of equal value. I think it wounded him greatly and drove him to achieve, to succeed, to present a self-assured and confident man, to win the girl. The good thing is that he won the girl that he also loves deeply."

"I would like to believe he does. I did believe it, but I don't see it in his eyes anymore. It's almost as if he doesn't trust me."

"I think that's the keyword. Trust is the foundation of any healthy relationship. Without it, you can never feel completely comfortable to be yourself, to completely let down your guard, and to risk being rejected. When we're wounded inside, we look to protect. We can be and are suspicious of everyone's motives and feelings. It's something that only grows if you start to have the relationship more in your head than actually with that other person."

Addie stared more intensely at Tom. "Why are you telling me this now?"

"Well, I talked with Erick. He let his suspicions get out of control to the point he believed you and Jack might be having an affair since his return."

Addie laughed in disbelief. "What? An affair?"

"That's why I pushed you on the phone yesterday to tell me where you went on those specific trips. Erick was convinced you were getting together with Jack."

"I did a few times, but that was to talk about business and how to have a closer family. I needed to start with Jack and then his parents."

"I know that, but for a man with trust issues who knows his brother still loves his wife, a rendezvous on Long Island would feel highly suspicious. I know this may be hard to see, but this is much more about Erick's insecurity than you. I'd even say it was all about it. It seemed too coincidental that after years of not being able to conceive, you were able to get pregnant when Jack came back."

"He really thinks we slept together?"

Tom smiled slightly. "I don't think it was sleeping he was worried about. Try to see this from the vantage point of someone who loves you and doesn't want to lose you. From a husband that was looking so forward to having a family with you."

"I'll try. He told you all this?"

"He told me that he had to know if Elizabeth was really his daughter, too, so he had a paternity test done with Jack's DNA."

"A paternity test! How did he get Jack's DNA? He could have just asked me!"

"I don't think it's the kind of question you want to ask a spouse. Well, then the test came back positive."

"What?! That's not possible," said Addie as she stood up and seemed confused. "How could it be positive? Wait, they're identical twins, so it would have to be 'positive'."

"Erick assumed they would run a more complex analysis that would be able to tell them apart, so he thought it meant his suspicions were confirmed. If you were him and it came back positive, and you were suspicious of a brother that you knew loved your wife— and you knew your brother and wife had been together on 'business trips' and you had been having trouble conceiving for several years prior, how would you feel?"

"Honestly, I'd be upset. I'd be worried, but I would ask."

"What if you were so devastated to think your dream was gone? Why would you ask if you thought you had objective proof? Why would you trust your spouse to be honest when they'd been lying to you for a year now and had betrayed the only trust you had left in your life?"

Addie sat back down, shaking her head but not responding.

"What if all that happened when you felt wounded inside, and you didn't think you could raise a baby you knew wasn't yours—and you didn't think your spouse was ready for?"

Addie turned sharply to Tom, "What are you saying? What are you telling me?"

"I think this medical evidence told Erick that all his fears were true, and his dreams and hopes for his life with you were lost unless he took desperate measures."

Addie was shaking her head. "What desperate measures? Are you saying he knew about what happened?"

"I said awful. Everything that happened was planned by Erick. He wanted to punish Jack while putting Elizabeth in the hands of loving parents and helping another baby survive cancer."

"Oh, my gosh. Oh, my gosh. No!" Addie stood up and started pacing as she put her hand to her chest, panting. "Father Tom, did he tell you all this? Is this all true?"

"He couldn't articulate the why, but he did voluntarily go to the police last night and told the whole truth. He wants to drop all the lies and suspicions getting in the way of his relationships. Just so you are aware, Erick has offered this confession on one condition."

"Condition? What condition?"

"That no charges are made against Jimi Johnson or Mariana Perez. He wants to pay for alternative cancer treatments for both Marie and Mariana in Mexico. These are very expensive treatments that they can't afford, and the only reason they agreed to get involved with Erick's plan in the first place. Jimi saw you arguing, and they thought neither of you wanted Elizabeth and that they were helping to get her to good, loving parents and saving their baby, Marie, in the process."

Addie stood, stunned. "I need to see him. I need to talk to him."

Tom put his hand on Addie's shoulder and gazed into her eyes with compassion. "I think that's a good idea. I didn't tell him of our conversation about your meetings with Jack. I thought that should come from you. It may seem unlikely right now, but in every fiber of my being, I believe that Erick, his parents, Jack, and you can all get to a much better place. I think there is a real opportunity here for compassion, forgiveness, understanding, trust, and love that couldn't have happened before. I hope you can find a way to take advantage of it, despite what has happened."

Chapter 51

Addie put Elizabeth in her stroller, and the three of them headed to the station. Addie was quiet during the walk, and Tom didn't push any conversation. As they reached Harrison Avenue and passed Rosie's Place, Tom noticed Mavis sitting on the steps, conversing with a few other women. She smiled broadly in recognition and, without hesitation, bellowed out, "Father Tom! How are you doin' today? Did you hear the good news for Mariana? I just heard it myself. Some rich guy's going to pay for her and her little one to get treatments. There's hope after all! Of course, we both know where that comes from. That man must've come from heaven!"

"Mavis, I'm sure he did," said Tom with a big smile.

"It's a good day today, Father, a good day!"

Tom thought he saw a glimmer of a smile on Addie's face as she remained silent.

Addie hesitated outside of the front entrance of the police quarters. "I don't know what to expect. I don't know what to do."

Tom could tell that Addie was still in shock over the news and hadn't fully processed how this was possible. "Addie, do you want to go in?"

"I don't know. I'm just not sure of anything right now."

"Addie, you just got hit over the head with a sledgehammer. There's no way you could make sense of it involving the man you have known for all these years. When you married Erick, you both committed to staying together in good times and in bad. This is one of those bad times to test that commitment, to show the love that wants the absolute best for the other when they most need it."

"I know that, but no one said anything about something like this," said Addie. "You looked like you were going to say more?"

"Just that when we marry, we know we will fall. We know we will fail the other person in some way. Maybe we held back giving all of ourselves to the other? Maybe we didn't give them the benefit of the doubt? Maybe we put ourselves first. We are human, and we will fall—and sometimes badly. It is then that we most need friendship, love, and forgiveness. As hard as it is, when we are angriest is sometimes when the other person needs the most

231

understanding. The hopeful thing here—and this is something I strongly believe is possible for you and Erick—is you could end up in a better place than you were before. If you focus on loving your best friend and you let God be active in this process, I really think you'll be stronger, closer, and more in love."

Addie's face tightened as her tears began to flow. "Do you actually believe that's possible?"

"I do. I have a strong feeling about it, too. When God created the universe, he made a perfect paradise for man and woman, but they turned their backs on him, they didn't trust him, and they fell. The good thing for us is that Jesus redeemed us, and God not only restores that offer to us, God also makes it even better. That 'even better' is what I think you and Erick have an opportunity to have."

Addie let Tom hold her as she continued to cry. "I feel a little hope if you believe that's possible."

"I really do, but I also think it won't all go smoothly and will take some work and commitment to get over those hard bumps and build trust, not only between the two of you but for Erick to allow himself to trust in general because of his childhood issues." Tom backed off as Addie nodded. He put his hand to her cheek. "I've counseled a lot of people and have found that when broken trust is addressed by a couple, they can actually have a stronger relationship and a deeper level of trust from working through it. They've seen the worst and survived it." When she seemed more under control, Tom asked, "Do you feel ready?"

Addie nodded, and he held the door as they made their way into the lobby and approached the front desk. "I'm here to see my husband, Erick Comghan."

Tom nodded to the morning desk sergeant as he picked up the phone to inform Detective Brooks. Brooks came out into the hallway and waived them to the detectives' room. "Mrs. Comghan, I assume you understand that your husband has confessed to the—the—whatever it is?"

Addie nodded. "Father Tom told me everything. Will I be allowed to see him?"

Brooks pensively sat back. "Do you think it's wise to bring the baby in with you?"

Addie turned to Tom, but Tom remained impassive. It was up to Addie.

Addie nodded. "I understand your concern, but I'd like to have her with me. I'd like Father Tom to be there as well."

"It's highly unusual after something like this—well, I haven't run into anything exactly like this before, but to let a baby into a room with the person alleged to have put her in harm's way wouldn't be the wisest thing to do."

"I don't believe Erick would ever harm Elizabeth, and Father Tom will be there."

Brooks took a deep breath and played with the pack of cigarettes on the desk. "You are her mother, but we'll have an officer ready at the door if anything happens. He's being brought to the visitor's room right now. I just wanted you to know that I'm happy Elizabeth's safe. I don't know what will happen to your husband. Even though no crimes for the assault, theft, or kidnapping will be charged, there are still several crimes of fraud, false imprisonment and testimony, and misuse of police time to be addressed."

"How serious are those charges? Are you saying he could go to jail?"

"He definitely could, but it will depend on the final charges and the judge."

When Addie walked into the visitor's room, an officer stood next to Erick, who was seated at a table in the middle of an empty room. Erick looked up, his eyes red from crying with dark, puffy circles around each, showing his lack of sleep. His sorrowful, fearful gaze penetrated Addie's concerned expression. He asked the officer if he could stand, and as he slowly got up, Addie approached him and hugged him tightly with one arm as she held Elizabeth with the other. With that hug and kiss on the cheek, the world seemed to change for Erick.

"I am so sorry," he said. "I don't know what to say; I'm just so sorry for everything I've put you and her through." He sobbed as he held his family. "Would you trust me to hold her?"

Addie glanced at Tom and then the officer, both watchful and remaining at a distance. "Of course, you can. She's your daughter—she *is* your daughter." Addie slowly held out Elizabeth as Erick took her gently as if he were handling a precious gem. He closed his eyes and took her cheek to his and breathed in her scent before kissing her on her soft, light auburn hair. He held her tight as if he'd never let her go again.

Tears streamed down Erick's cheeks until the baby cooed and made everyone in the room smile.

Finally, Erick asked Tom to take Elizabeth as he and Addie sat down holding hands across the table. "Addie, I want to say so much and can't seem to find the words that could explain anything I did. I just hope you can forgive me someday, even if it seems impossible right now. I know I have no right to ask anything, but I need to know I haven't lost you and Elizabeth forever."

Addie gazed into Erick's tear-filled eyes, and she took a deep breath. "Erick, I haven't stopped loving you. I don't know how to absorb all I've been told. I still don't believe it, but seeing you here does bring a dose of reality. I love you, but I'm confused about why you couldn't trust me and how you could do this. I don't know if you even love me."

"Of course, I love you! Maybe I loved you too much to see straight. All I can tell you is this has to do with issues I have to work through and has nothing to do with not loving you. I just need to learn to get out of my own way, to love you the way you deserve and not through my distorted needs. I'm sorry for ever doubting you. You mean everything to me and, until last evening, I didn't believe Elizabeth was my daughter. I want to be the husband you deserve and the father she will need."

A tear rolled from Addie's eye as she watched Elizabeth happily resting in Tom's arms.

"No fair using her."

She smiled but knew the reality of Erick's words.

Erick clenched her hands even tighter with that sign of hope.

Addie continued, "I promised to be by your side, no matter what. When I married you, I never imagined this, but that was a promise of love that I will not break. But I have to tell you something."

"Anything. You can tell me anything," said Erick.

"Besides wanting to belt you a few times right now, I want you to know that I love only you. I don't love Jack. He is family. I only visited him for three reasons. He's my brother. He was good enough to help connect me with some really important clients for my job. And—"

"And?"

"And I met him to talk about you."

"Me?"

"I told him I was very much in love with you and always would be. I told him I wanted to find a way to mend the hurts in the family between you and him and with your parents. He told me how empty his life has been without the brother he used to have. He didn't understand what had happened, but it was his largest regret in life."

"He said that? I thought losing you was his largest regret in life."

"I might have thought so too, but that's not what he feels."

"Why did you meet him in Sag Harbor?"

"When you were starting to act more distant and, I guess, suspicious, I wanted to get away to the happiest place I could remember—where we had our honeymoon. Jack came over to have lunch with me, and we talked about you. I wanted to see if the hotel we stayed at was still as nice as I remembered before I booked it for our anniversary in July."

Erick sat back and closed his eyes. "I can't believe how unfair I've been to you. How could I ever doubt you when all you've done was to love me?"

"Don't make me out to be a saint. Father Tom here knows better. I have things to be sorry for too. I haven't always given myself completely to you. I've been selfish and over-focused on my career, to the point where I didn't even know if I wanted this precious girl over here. I thought that mending all these family hurts might help us, might help me. I missed your family, and I think distancing yourself has hurt you as well. When I left for my trip after the baptism, I stopped by your parents' house to talk to them about ways to tear down this wall between everyone. Now, with Elizabeth in the picture, it has made the pain of separation even greater."

"You saw my folks?"

"I did. I've called them regularly over the years to let them know how you're doing. They love you, Erick. You're still their baby. That never changes for a parent."

"I'm having a hard time believing that, but that may be one of the things I need to work on—right, Father Tom? What do you think?"

Tom replied, "I think you're standing at what may be the biggest crossroad decision of your lives. You may have to do some hard and uncomfortable work to get to an open and trusting relationship, but I know it'll be the best decision each of you will ever make for yourselves and this little one. You've already made the commitment; now it's just a matter of following through on it, supporting each other, and listening in a life-giving way. The Erick and Addie I know have a great loving marriage in front of them."

A tap on the door preceded Detective Brooks walking in. "I think that might be time for today. There are official statements to take and other prisoners to let out."

Erick and Addie stood up and held each other close and said, "I love you."

Tom asked Brooks if it was okay if he picked Jack up from the Norfolk Prison, and he saw no issues with it. After walking Addie and Elizabeth home, he drove his car west to Norfolk. Jack didn't know who was picking him up, only that he had a ride back to Boston. When he saw Tom standing by his car waiting, he stopped short, but going back inside wasn't an option, so he tentatively restarted his steps. "I'll take your ride, but no sermons on forgiveness today."

Tom opened the door. "I promise to only talk about what you want to talk about."

"Okay. So, why did you come?"

"Just thought it might be a long walk for you." Tom smiled as he closed the door for Jack, got into the driver's side, and then pointed towards the prison entrance. "That could not have been fun for you."

Jack closed his eyes, his facial muscles tightening. "Fun! I've been living a nightmare. Do you know what it's like to believe you might be sentenced for years in a place where you have to worry every day about being beaten, knifed, or raped?" Jack turned toward Tom with deep fear in his eyes. "Do you know what it's like to think about actually killing yourself to avoid that hell?"

Tom laid his hand on Jack's shoulder. "Jack, no, I don't know what that's like. A nightmare sounds like the right description. I was focused more on your being proven innocent and being free."

"Is there anything worse than it being your brother who put you there, on purpose? He might as well have tried to kill me, and for what? What could I have done to deserve such vindictiveness?"

Tom could feel Jack's fury and knew he needed time to let it out. Tom pulled the car down a road that led to an open area along the Charles River. There were no houses or buildings in sight, only the slow movement of the river banked by trees that hung peacefully alongside. Jack didn't question why they had stopped as they watched the occasional leaf floating down on the surface. At one point, a pair of finches landed on the hood of Tom's car and cackled before flying off.

Jack's breathing slowed, and he broke the silence. "You want to tell me something, don't you?"

"Well—I can't imagine what you must be feeling. It's almost unthinkable for him to get to that point where he wanted you to feel his pain."

"For him to get to that point? To feel his pain?"

"Yeah. Do you honestly believe your own brother could lose his perspective on what he was doing if he wasn't in a lot of pain? If something hadn't pushed him over the edge?"

"What are you talking about? What did I ever do to him to deserve being set up and going to jail?"

"Often, it isn't anything we did, but the perception that we did something due to distorted thinking, insecurities, and loss of trust."

Jack shook his head. "Loss of trust, in me? I never gave up on my brother. I only wanted to be close again, to break through that wall of his."

"I believe you. The reason my gut thought that you couldn't be guilty was seeing how much you loved your brother. That's why something like this hurts even more—because you care."

"I'm getting totally confused. You think I love my brother, care about him, but he believes I betrayed him or did something to hurt him?"

"Jack, you told me that you loved Addie and may still have strong feelings for her."

Jack nodded.

"And you know that your brother could obviously see that, right?"

He slowly nodded again.

"Clearly, he let his jealousy and suspicions get out of hand. He checked on Addie's trips and believed you two met several times."

"Not for anything like that! Addie wouldn't do that. He should know that."

"I agree. But you know that they were trying for years to get pregnant and start a family with no success. Then, you come home, and Addie started traveling more."

"That was for her business."

"And suddenly she becomes pregnant. Can you see how the question might at least come up?"

"No. This is Addie. I'm his brother, for Pete's sake!"

"That's what healthy thinking would look like, but Erick couldn't rest without knowing that Elizabeth was his daughter and not yours."

"Why didn't he just ask Addie?"

"Not a question you ever want to ask your wife. Instead, he did a paternity test, and it came back positive."

Jack turned toward Tom. "Then he should have known Elizabeth was his?"

"He used your DNA sample to do the test."

"What? Where did he—you mean he used those swab samples I gave him for that genealogy thing he wanted to do for Mom and Pop?"

"Yup."

"But—" said Jack as he thought for a second. "Of course, it was positive.

We're identical twins."

"Easy for you to say. You're a doctor, but he wasn't aware that they didn't do the level of analysis that would be able to distinguish between you two, so you could see how devastating those results were. He thought there was no question that Elizabeth was yours. She was a living reminder of your and Addie's betrayal, and he felt he couldn't live with that reminder his entire life. He couldn't be the father that she needed, and he was angry at you."

Jack opened the door, stepped out of the car, and walked to the river's edge. He watched it as it gently flowed.

After a few moments, Tom got out and walked to the spot next to him, a gentle breeze rippling against his face.

Jack finally said, "Why?"

"Why, what?"

"Why did it get this mixed up? Why was he so suspicious of me to begin with?"

"I don't know. I think the wounds started a long time ago and had nothing to do with anything you did. I think you loved your brother, and I think you still do. I think that relationship has been a loss in your life, and you've tried to be a good brother your entire life. You never know how insecurities developed as a kid will impact adult relationships."

"Insecure? Erick was always the leader, the strong one, the one with all the confidence. He always knew what he wanted and how to get it."

"That may be true, but that's the Erick he let you see on the outside. Inside, he saw you get the attention, the affection, and the protection from your mom. His sense of self-worth was damaged. He felt he didn't get the love he deserved. That made him need recognition and attention more to prove to himself that he wasn't worthless."

"This sounds so opposite of Erick. I can't see this being him."

"Your father was harder on him than you, wasn't he?"

"I think so, but that's because he knew he could do more."

"He knew you could do more, too. Why did your father want you to take that last shot in the Championship game? The biggest thing that had ever happened to you or Erick?"

"I don't know."

"Why did you pass the ball to Erick and give him the winning shot and all the glory?"

"Because he was the better shooter, and the team needed that basket. I knew he was upset, and he had a right to be. It was the right play. I'd think that would let him know how much I cared about him."

"Sure. But what happened? Who got the recognition, not only in the papers but from your father? The recognition and blessings that he felt like he deserved, at least in part, all went to you."

Jack picked up a twig, tossed it onto the river, and watched it float downstream. "I knew he was angry. Things were different between us after that—but not that bad."

"So then there was Addie. You both loved her."

"But he got her."

"Sure. He married her and wanted to have his own family, but then it looked like that was all lost. Lost in humiliation, betrayal, and deceit. He lost everything that meant something to him—at least, in his mind. You took his place, his recognition, his wife, and his family. You had his parents' love and admiration. Jealousy becomes envy, and he couldn't bear to see the brother that deceived him take everything away."

Jack rubbed his hands down his face. He half-laughed. "Funny. I thought Erick had everything. He won that game. He had all the traits I wished I had. He was successful in his business, and he had Addie and was starting a family. I was alone, thinking about the life I missed while he was jealous of me? Huh. How's that possible?"

"Jack, do you still love your brother?"

"A few seconds ago, I think I would have said that I didn't know."

"And now?"

"Yeah. I sat terrified in that cell. I only thought about things from my perspective. When I found out what Erick did, I was so angry, hurt, and confused. I don't think I could have gotten out of myself, my anger, to see anything from his perspective. Now, I actually feel sorry for him." He stared into space for a moment, then turned back to Tom. "So, what happens, now?"

Tom patted Jack on the back. "That all depends on what you want, deep down."

Jack gazed up at the blue sky with a handful of wispy clouds slowly passing by. "What do I want—really want? A few weeks ago, I could have answered that one easily. I would want to have my relationship back with my brother. I'd want our family back together before it's too late. I'd love to find someone who loves me and have my own family to share with Erick and Addie. That's what I would have said at the baptism if you asked me."

"What do you want now?"

Jack laughed, "Now that I'm out of prison? Maybe the same things. Maybe the same things after all."

Chapter 52

Jack asked Tom to come with him to help explain to his parents what had happened over the past few weeks. When they returned, Jack phoned ahead to Detective Brooks about visiting Erick with his parents.

At the station, Erick sat in the visiting room as Tom watched from the viewing room. When the door opened, Erick glanced up to see his twin brother in the doorway, his face contorting with conflicting emotions.

Jack stood for several moments, staring at Erick through somber eyes until a familiar smile made its way to one side of his mouth. "You didn't really think you could get rid of your brother that easily, did you? I guess you don't know the first thing about how twins work."

Erick shifted in his seat, unsure of himself.

Jack approached Erick and put his hands on his shoulders. "Brother, I still love you. That has never changed for me, not even now."

"How can you say that? How can you say that you still love me after what I did to you? I tried to destroy your life."

"Oh, I was angry and pretty pissed at you. And, mind you, I will certainly repay you somehow but not with hate or revenge. I know you thought I broke your trust. I don't know what I would've done if I were you. Probably not what you came up with, but I would've been devastated. What I care about right now is you. We're brothers, and that's what brothers do—no matter what."

Erick's shoulders slumped as he began to cry. Jack stepped in and hugged his brother. Erick reached around and pulled Jack closer as he shook and sobbed. "I don't deserve your support. I can't believe I didn't trust my own brother enough to know you couldn't – you wouldn't do those things."

"Hey, do you know why I went to London, leaving behind the family that meant everything to me?"

Erick stepped back and shook his head.

"Because I wanted you to be happy. I wanted you and Addie to have the marriage you deserved and the family you always dreamed of. I didn't want to be in the way."

"I never knew that. I thought you just wanted to get out on your own or that you might be jealous."

"I can't say that I wasn't a little jealous, but you two were meant for each other. When I came back, I still wondered how I felt about Addie, but I could tell she was so in love with you that the answer didn't matter. I cared about her too much to not want her to be with the man she loved, not to have the marriage and family she wanted. I only met with her to help with some contacts for her business, to be her brother, and to talk about you."

"Talk about me?"

"Yes, you. She knew the walls you were putting up with the family were only getting taller and creating more distance. She wanted to figure out how to bring everyone closer together. You can trust her more than anyone. She loves you enough to want you to have your family back."

"Have my family back? I've just done something unforgivable. I've disgraced the family and will probably be going to jail. Are you honestly saying that you could forgive me for what I did to you?"

"I'll only forgive you on three conditions."

"Conditional love?"

"No, just conditional forgiveness."

"Okay."

"Wise man. First, if you're the one to be lucky enough to have Addie and Elizabeth, you have to swear on your own life that you'll do everything it takes to be the best husband and father you can be. And I mean the best!"

Erick nodded.

"I need to hear it."

"I promise, on my life, and yours, that I'll do everything it takes to be the husband and father Addie and Elizabeth deserve—everything. What's the second condition in this hostage situation?"

"These get tougher as we go along. You have to agree to go to as many counseling sessions with Father Tom as it takes to get healthy—and that includes sessions with me."

Erick gave half a smile. "That last bit seems a bit excessive, but, okay, I will agree to commit myself to that. What's the third?"

Jack stared directly at Erick as his eyes narrowed. "This one may take time and work, but you have to be open to forgiving someone else."

"I don't understand. Forgive who?"

Jack got up, opened the door, and there stood their mother and father.

Erick's head dropped in shame. More embarrassed than happy, he sat, staring up at his father as his father stared down at him in the piercing silence, neither knowing how to begin.

As the silence grew in awkwardness, Becca broke in. "For heaven's sake." She pushed past Zak and approached her son with open arms until her hands were around his face. He was now the vulnerable one, the one that needed compassion and protection. "My Erick. I missed you so."

Erick reached out and wrapped his arms around his mother.

When they separated, Zak was by his side. "Son, you might be in a pickle, but we're here for you, 100 percent." Erick reached out to shake his father's hand, but Zak pulled him up and gave him a firm hug. "My boy. Erick, you are always my son."

Erick's voice cracked. "Do you know what's going on?"

"Father Tom and Jack filled us in on all the excitement from the past weeks."

"Excitement? I'm so ashamed of everything I've done—for years."

Zak reached out to grab his son's hand. "Some shame is healthy, but let's focus on where we go from here."

"How can you ever forgive me? I haven't been a son to be proud of for so long."

"Erick, your mother and I have always tried to be the best parents we could be. That was always out of love, but that doesn't mean we always gave you what you needed. I'm going to ask you if you can forgive us for any of the pain you may have felt as a child when we failed to give you what you needed. You were always the strong and confident one, so we may have thought you didn't need as much affirmation. I know I always pushed you harder because I wanted to challenge you to be the best person you could be."

"I know that, Pop."

"But I may not have always realized what you were feeling. I may have thought I was doing the right thing for you out of love, but I don't think I always gave you what you needed deep inside." As Erick began to sob, his father teared up too. "I was trying to teach you to do things for the right reason and not to seek personal recognition before the good of the team. I'm not saying that what I wanted to teach you was wrong—"

Erick stared at his father.

"But, I didn't recognize I was creating a void inside of you that desperately needed that recognition, that affirmation that you meant everything to me."

Erick tightened his grip on his father's hands.

Tears ran down Zak's face. "I don't expect you to believe me or to even forgive me right now, but I'd like to spend the time with you to build that trust again. I want you to know how much I love you and how much I've missed my boy."

They stood and embraced.

Brooks entered the room to end the visit, and they said their goodbyes. The last one to leave was Zak. At the door, he turned to Erick and said, "That was a great shot, son. I'm proud of you."

Erick stood visibly stunned at the visit and the unexpected reception from Addie, Jack, and his parents. Where shame and disgrace had filled him only minutes ago, now there was hope.

Chapter 53

Erick Comghan agreed not to go to trial and received a one-year sentence, including six months suspended with community service. Brooks helped to have him placed in a minimum-security prison in Danbury to allow for his family to visit often. This location was close enough for Tom to do weekly counseling sessions for a year with Erick and each member of the family.

In the spring of 2007, Tom and Angelo were invited to the Comghan's farm to celebrate the first anniversary of Elizabeth's baptism. As they arrived, the late afternoon golden sunshine brushed the fields and the front porch where Zak sat, watching his sons playing basketball with the old hoop against the barn. Tom stepped up on the porch, "Mr. Comghan, I imagine that isn't a sight you expected to see again."

Zak greeted Tom and Angelo as they sat with him to watch the competitive match.

"This allows me to watch Erick's moves from another vantage point, so I can use it when I play him!" said Tom with a laugh.

"Father Tom, Angelo, I'm glad you came. I don't think I'd be watching this if it weren't for both of you. You're like angels from heaven."

Angelo sat down with Tom and Zak. "I think we'll eat more than angels would. Speaking of Heaven— it's good to be back in this beautiful spot of yours."

Addie stepped onto the porch and gave Tom an endearing and grateful smile. "I'm so glad you could make it to this baptism party." She hugged him and whispered, "Thank you. I can't believe where we've come in a year and how much work Erick has done to get to a better place. None of this would have been possible without you. We can never repay what you did. Thank you again."

Tom stepped back. "I think there was plenty of love and work done by everyone in the family. That made the difference."

A shout followed by a laugh from Jack turned their attention. The game heated up. Rachel stepped onto the porch with the others to cheer them on as the score seesawed back and forth with alternating great shots. With one point to go for the win, Jack had the ball and dribbled hard left and then to the corner, where he faked the shot and then surprisingly fired the ball to Erick to take the winning shot.

Erick chuckled. "You're not supposed to pass it to me when we're playing against each other." He went up to shoot and then rifled a pass back to Jack, who took a long shot and swished it through the net for the win. "I told you, you should have taken that shot to win the championship."

Jack howled in laughter. "Sure, you did!" He put his arm around Erick as they walked toward the porch, breathing heavily from the back and forth game.

Zak shook Jack's winning hand and turned to Erick. "Great pass."

Jack exclaimed, "What about my shot? I won the game!"

Everyone laughed while Addie and Rachel brought out a tray of iced teas for the thirsty players and spectators. Tom smiled at Addie as she handed him the cool glass.

Erick came over and put his arm around Addie's waist. "Hey, that's my wife you're flirting with, Father."

Tom nodded. "A lucky Irishman you are, Mr. Comghan, to have a wife as fine as she."

Erick pulled her a bit closer. "I know that now; I really do."

Jack's arm around Rachel, he smiled at his brother, the picture of a contented man.

Becca stepped onto the porch and rang the small dinner bell next to the porch door. "Now that we're all here, dinner is on!"

Everyone entered the dining room to see the long table ready for a plentiful farm-style dinner of roasted lamb, bread, and farm vegetables. Before they started, Zak got up to give a toast. "To my wife, whom I love with all my heart, thank you for this feast. To my sons—"

Erick stood up. "Pop."

Zak turned to Erick.

"Pop, would it be okay if I gave the toast today?"

Zak put his hand on Erick's shoulder and nodded to give him the floor.

"Thanks, Pop." He peered around the table at each person and then hesitated as he collected himself. "If anyone had told me a year ago that I could feel what I'm feeling right now for each one of you, I would have said they were crazy. If they had said to me that I'd betray my family, my brother, end up in the hospital, then in jail, and that would be the best year of my life, I would have said they were more than crazy!"

Everyone chuckled.

"Angelo, I'm truly sorry for the bop on the head. The good thing is we both have hard heads."

Angelo smirked.

"Father Tom, you are the best pain in the tush that I could ever call my dear friend. Your persistence, counsel, wisdom, and willingness to show love when others would've held back is a debt this entire family owes you."

Tom smiled and nodded as everyone else applauded.

"To Mom and Pop. How many kids don't know what a gift their parents are to them before it's too late? I certainly squandered too many years, not knowing how much you loved me and how much I hurt you. I was so self-focused that my sense of what you were giving me was smothered by my belief in what I was owed, on my terms. Now, with new respect and love for you, I only hope I can make up those lost years."

Zak said, "You already have, son. You already have."

Erick raised his glass to Jack with a slight tremble in his voice. "To my brother, Jack, my friend through thick and thin. More than a friend in every way—and good looking too."

This made Jack smile as the rest chuckled.

"I don't know if I can ever say I'm sorry enough times for not celebrating you, your triumphs, your talents, and your gift to me as a brother. I thought I had the right to be ahead of you, to be recognized above you, to be better than you. I could never be better than the greatest man I know. I put you through hell to pay for my sins and shortcomings, and you came back with forgiveness and love. You believed in what we could have instead of carrying resentment and revenge in your heart as I did for so long. Now I only feel love and admiration for the man I'm proud to have as my favorite brother."

Jack got up, shook his brother's hand, and then gave him a heartfelt embrace. "It's about time."

Finally, Erick turned to Addie, holding Elizabeth. "I literally gave away the most precious gifts in my life. It pains me more than any of you could even know to believe that I could do that—" Erick's voice cracked as he choked up. "But I'm now blessed to share my life and love with my wife and daughter. I have learned that trust is essential to any loving relationship." He took Addie's hand. "I hope you can trust me to love you with everything I have."

Addie got up, hugged Erick, and gave him a long kiss. Erick took

Elizabeth in his arms, kissed her on the cheek, and held her close before turning to everyone at the table. "I'm finding out that life is a journey, and that journey means everything when it is shared with a loving family like this one. Elizabeth is the hope of the next generation of Comghans, and I want her to grow up understanding how very precious this family is—and how precious she is to us."

The End

About the Author

Jim Sano grew up in an Irish/Italian family in Massachusetts. Jim is a husband, father, lifelong Catholic and has worked as a teacher, consultant, and businessman. He has degrees from Boston College and Bentley University and is currently attending Franciscan University for a master's degree in Catechetics and Evangelization. He has also attended certificate programs at The Theological Institute for the New Evangelization at St. John's Seminary and the Apologetics Academy. Jim is a member of the Catholic Writers Guild and has enjoyed growing in his faith and now sharing it through writing novels. *The Father's Son* and *Gus Busbi* were his first two novels. *Stolen Blessing* is his third.

Jim resides in Medfield, Massachusetts, with his wife, Joanne, and has two daughters, Emily and Megan.

Published by Full Quiver Publishing
PO Box 244
Pakenham, ON K0A2X0
Canada
www.fullquiverpublishing.com